The Boy Orator

Other Books by Tracy Daugherty

What Falls Away

Desire Provoked

The Woman in the Oil Field

The Boy Orator

A NOVEL BY TRACY DAUGHERTY

SOUTHERN METHODIST
UNIVERSITY PRESS
Dallas

Requests for permission to reproduce material from this work should be sent to:
    Rights and Permissions
    Southern Methodist University Press
    PO Box 750415
    Dallas, Texas 75275-0415

Jacket art: Jerry Bywaters, *Autumn Cotton Fields*, courtesy of Richard P. Bywaters

Jacket and text design: Tom Dawson Graphic Design

LIBRARY OF CONGRESS CATALOGING-IN-PUBLICATION DATA

Daugherty, Tracy.
    The boy orator : a novel / by Tracy Daugherty. — 1st ed.
        p.   cm.
    ISBN 0-87074-433-X
    I. Title.
    PS3554.A85B69   1999
    813'.54—dc21   98-38959

Printed in the United States of America on acid-free paper

10 9 8 7 6 5 4 3 2 1

For my mother and father
and for my sister Debra,
with love

I am deeply indebted to House Speaker Glen D. Johnson and to Larry Warden, Chief Clerk-Administrator of the Oklahoma House of Representatives, for their time and generosity. Thanks also to Joe Ray Blough for his exhaustive search through House records. The folks at the Oklahoma Historical Society, Division of Library Resources, were extremely helpful in expediting my research, as were several articles in their publication, *The Chronicles of Oklahoma*. For background information I have also drawn upon James R. Green's *Grass-Roots Socialism*, Garin Burbank's *When Farmers Voted Red*, James R. Scales's and Danney Goble's *Oklahoma Politics: A History*, Sally M. Miller's *From Prairie to Prison: The Life of Social Activist Kate Richards O'Hare*, *The Selected Writings and Speeches of Kate Richards O'Hare* edited by Philip S. Foner and Sally M. Miller, and *An Oklahoma I Had Never Seen Before*, edited by Davis D. Joyce.

J. C. Daugherty opened doors at the state capitol that I could not have opened on my own. Gene and JoAnne Daugherty and Fern Stone reintroduced me to the Oklahoma countryside. Edwin and Anita Low shared with me their memories of the cotton fields.

Oregon State University granted me a sabbatical leave to begin this novel; Molly Brown provided a computer at a crucial time. Brandon Brown, Elizabeth Campbell, Jennifer C Cornell, Richard and Kristina Daniels, Ehud Havazelet, Ted Leeson, George Manner, Marjorie Sandor, and Marshall Terry offered encouragement and advice. Grace Low had to live with my distractedness during much of the early writing; Jake the cat kept my lap warm as I typed.

To Kathryn M. Lang, who stuck with me, and who provided shrewd editorial suggestions when I needed them most, and to Keith Gregory, Freddie Jane Goff, and Michelle Vardeman at SMU Press, I am most thankful.

A portion of this novel appeared in *Southwest Review*. I am grateful to Elizabeth Mills and Willard Spiegelman for their support, and for their permission to reprint.

Finally, my greatest debt is to my grandfather, Tracy, who lived the life behind this book.

The Boy Orator

Politics is the art of extracting money
from the rich and votes from the poor on the pretext
of protecting each from the other.

OSCAR AMERINGER

We spoiled the best territory in the world to make a state.

WILL ROGERS

PROLOGUE

Wichita County, Texas, August 1898

Their first night out, Andrew and Annie Mae camped on the south side of the Red River near a tributary called Prairie Dog Fork. The river was high from recent rains; driftwood splintered on rocks and tore at thorny brambles on the banks: loud, scratching noises that kept their infant, Harry, awake and crying. The ferry captain told them he'd try to cross at dawn, but if the water rose while they slept, they might have to wait a couple of days until the stream calmed. He was a Civil War veteran, name of Parker, he said. He wouldn't stop staring at Annie Mae.

"He's making me nervous," she told Andrew just after dusk, dropping a handful of dry twigs near the spot, in a clearing ringed by bluestem and saddle-high switchgrass, he'd picked to pitch their tent. He smiled at her, stopped and rubbed her shoulders. "You're radiant," he said. He told her she still had the glow of pregnancy in her cheeks. Her skin was as bright as moonlight on the river.

"You hush this sentimental nonsense, now, and build us a fire. I don't know how you talked me into this, anyway." She brushed the blowing auburn hair from her face and wiped her hands on her thin yellow dress.

Andrew grinned. The whiskers on his jaw, dark brown, seemed to scurry toward the hollows of his cheeks. "Would you rather have stayed in Bonham and faced that dust storm? I hear the sky was so full of sand, out west, gophers popped out of big fat holes in the air."

"I've chewed on my share of dust storms," Annie Mae said, twisting her hair in a bun around a scrub oak twig and staking it up off her neck, which was misted by a fine sprinkling of sweat. Her back ached—she'd pinched a nerve during labor, she feared, but these days Andrew couldn't hear her complaints, no matter how often she raised them. For him, all their troubles would cease across the river.

"We'll do good, Annie," he repeated for her now, wrapping her hands in his rough, meaty palms. "More than that. We'll prosper. It's wide open in the Territory."

Annie Mae laughed. "I wouldn't trust Lee's word on that any more'n I could hurl a stone across this water."

When she'd married him, Andrew's sentimental streak had pleased her: feelings of any sort were hard to tug out of most of the men she knew, taciturn farmers and ranchers. But now that Harry was here, Andrew's faith in new places and ideas—as though happy endings were foreordained—seemed reckless, even dangerous, to her. Their boy needed solid footing, not the constant uprooting that accompanied a life of dreams.

"Don't fret," Andrew told her. "Your new life'll be a garden of blessings."

"I'm here, aren't I?" But really, what choice did she have? He'd made up his mind. She loved him. And she knew he couldn't return to the world he'd had. For seven years now, he'd strung barbed wire for wealthy ranchers south of Bonham, Texas. His brother, Lee, thirty, six years older than Andrew, had fled Bonham eighteen months before for the Indian Territory. It had a reputation for liberal divorce laws, he'd told them: its residency requirement was only ninety days; a man could sue his wife with a public notice instead of a personal subpoena.

Lee had married young—a bitter Baptist girl—and from the first he'd looked for an easy way out. He wrote Andrew regularly from the Territory, praising it as a "wide open place where a man can find— and stand—his ground. Lehigh, especially, is an ideal divorce resort. Warm climate, lots of attorneys, plenty of folks willing to hire out cheap as character witnesses." His letters always ended with the warning, "Don't tell anyone where I am." This troubled Andrew, but after his boy was born, joining his brother appealed to him. His family's politics gave him a mighty distaste for the men who employed him, Annie Mae knew; besides, he didn't earn enough to feed an extra mouth.

Andrew's father, Michael Roy Shaughnessy, a tenant farmer scraping by near Bonham, had been for a dozen years or more an ardent Populist, a follower of a Dallas newspaper publisher named Harry Tracy. When he was courting Annie Mae, Andrew talked often about this fellow Tracy, with unshakable conviction. The man's editorials in the *Southern Mercury* blamed capitalism for ruining farmers, who depended on the time frame of the seasons, not on the speed of investment, Andrew said. To please him, Annie Mae had tried to read the old *Mercury* articles (Andrew still saved them, yellowing now, in a box), but never understood them.

Relishing his boyhood memories, Andrew told Annie Mae how every night at the supper table Michael Roy would open up the paper and read to his sons. "Tracy favors paying farmers for what they actually produce, heedless of the market's fickle needs," Michael Roy explained, his normally reedy voice bolstered by pride. "The gold standard's an 'absolute wrong,' he says here, 'threatening the stability of modern civilization.'"

Andrew absorbed his father's pride, and his anger at bankers and lawyers. In May, when Annie Mae had given birth after a long and arduous labor, Andrew named his son Harry Tracy.

Now she sat by the fire, cradling their boy in a faded gingham blanket. As soon as she and the baby had been strong enough to travel,

Andrew had thrown their clothes in an old buckboard and driven them north, toward opportunity and dignity in the Indian Territory.

What choice? she thought again. What else could I have done?

Parker approached from out of the dark, his face slick and ruddy in the popping light of the flames. He smelled of the earth—of *worms* in the earth, Annie Mae thought. Muddy, reeking of cheap, killing alcohol, licking long, tobacco-blackened teeth. Quickly, she tucked the wet breast Harry had been suckling back inside her dress. The baby began to make low, liquid noises in his throat, as if muttering to himself.

"Storm's a-comin'," Parker said, sniffing the air. "Might be you'll have to stay on here a tad longer'n you figured." He grinned.

"Yes," Annie Mae said quietly.

Andrew emerged from the tent in a fresh cotton shirt and a clean pair of denim britches. He was tall and fair, with a graceful stride. Parker stiffened and glanced away from Annie Mae. He cleared his throat. "Y'all come up the Wichita?" he asked.

"Followed the north fork of the *Little* Wichita," Andrew said, folding his soiled clothes.

"Fellow told me once the old-time Spanish explorers called the Wichita 'Rio del Fierro—River of Iron.'" He laughed—a nervous bark. "I've always liked that, always liked that." His hands fluttered around the pockets of his dirty khaki pants. "Didn't pass through Whiskeytaw Falls by any chance, did you? I sure could use me some Red Draw. It'd just about make my miserable week if you's to let on you had a bottle or two nestled inside your wagon there."

"Sorry."

"Well. Beer and 'mater juice." He shook his doughy head. "Sure would hit the spot this evening, eh partner?"

Andrew didn't answer. He'd raised his ears to the wind. A brackishness weighted the breeze; thunder murmured in the east. Cottonwood blossoms, soggy white medallions, drifted across the river's choppy current.

"It's a-brewin', all right. Big one. Hit about midnight, I expect."

Harry gushed a stream of high-pitched gibberish. He plucked at his mother's black buttons.

"That baby of your'n. Sure is a noisy little feller, ain't he, ma'am?"

"Yes," said Annie Mae. "He's going to be a talker."

"Keeps you wide-eyed most the time, I s'pose." He wiped his nose, his mouth. "I stay wakeful, myself, most nights, wishing for company."

Annie Mae went rigid, and wouldn't look at the man. Harry squirmed in her arms.

"All right. Well then, I hope you folks have a pleasant eve," Parker said, and moved away, out of the circle of light.

Andrew watered the horses, an old Arab and a roan he'd bought with the last of his wages, then rubbed them down with hay. He currycombed their coats, mixed for them a couple of quarts of sweet feed, corn, linseed meal. Annie Mae couldn't watch him for long. She blamed him for Parker, she realized, turning her face toward the water—for bringing her to the edge of the world, whose rocky rim was paced by such grimy, god-awful men.

Later, in the darkness of the tent, she wouldn't answer Andrew's quiet "Good night." She heard him sit up. "Annie?"

"Hush and go to sleep."

"Things'll get better, I promise."

"How do you know?"

"Because you're with me."

"Don't start." Durn his sentimentality, she thought.

"I mean it, honey."

Though she knew better, she never could fight his sweet optimism, and he knew it. Tears came to her eyes, but she couldn't help smiling. "Hush."

"Annie—"

"Go to sleep, I say."

Harry *did* keep her awake, howling at the curtain of rain lashing their tent. In a short lull in the downpour, she picked her baby up and carried him outside, into a wave of throbbing thunder, shielding his head with the blanket. Andrew needed his rest; if they made it across tomorrow, he'd have long, hard hours guiding the horses. She stood on the riverbank, ankle-deep in grama grass, and gave her baby a breast. Lightning prickled above her; in the brief flash she saw Parker straddling a rock, not ten feet away. She jumped. Harry's lips slipped her nipple, and he started to bawl. Parker, sour and soaked, smiled at her broadly. She stumbled back to the tent.

All night she shivered, cold and scared, listening to switchgrass buzz in gusting breezes. She imagined zippers sounded like this, a hundred of them opening in unison. Andrew had sworn to buy her fancy leggings, or gaiters, with the new metal hasps, once they got settled. She'd read about zippers, sitting in a soda fountain in downtown Bonham one day, flipping through a magazine—the writer had called them "wondrous," guaranteed they'd revolutionize women's clothing. A few years back, the zipper had been a curiosity at the Chicago World's Fair, but it had its believers, and Annie Mae was eager to see a dress fastened with one. Andrew had promised her this, and much more, in their new life.

Now, she was less confident than ever about their decision to move. What kind of men rushed into unmapped territory? Men like Lee, fleeing family trouble, men like Andrew, nursing foolish dreams. And Parker. He was just the first, she thought, imagining whole towns swarming with soggy drunks, scrambling to snatch a glimpse of any young woman. Parker was her future.

She prayed for the strength her family had always found in challenging times. As usual, in moments of stress, the face of her late Aunt Jenny fashioned itself in her mind. "Buck up, Annie," her aunt used to tell her, "you come from hardy stock." The old woman would always tuck her in at night, when Annie Mae was a girl, and tell her stories of their ancestors who'd emigrated from Belfast, surviving scurvy and smallpox on a leaky cargo boat. They had fought in the Revolutionary War, leaving buckets of blood and an arm or two in the chilly fields of New England; had moved to Texas on the promise of cheap farmland, the same promise her husband was following now.

And her? What promise was she following? None, she had to admit, beyond the desire to keep her family together, beyond the dim conviction that, somehow, she'd find strategies to shield her boy from men like Parker, from drunkenness and irresponsibility, from sudden, silly dreams.

In the morning, the water was three feet deeper, Andrew estimated, than it had been the evening before. Waves swirled. Tree limbs, fallen in the night, and small, broken bushes vanished swiftly into angry brown whirlpools. Parker stood casually by his raft, a ragtag of two-by-fours snugged together with dark, wet ropes. Annie Mae ignored him. "I'm not about to get on that ferry with my baby," she told Andrew.

"Honey, I agree the water's a little squirrelly, but it might get worse in the next day or so. This may be our best chance."

"No." Holding Harry, she backed away from the raft and bumped one of the horses. Harry reached out to touch the moist, warm flank, and laughed.

Andrew watched his wife, scratching his head. Parker asked him, "You want I should tie her arms and legs and th'ow her on board?"

Andrew glanced at him sharply. "No!"

Disappointed, the old man skulked away.

Annie Mae sat on the bank, hugging her baby in the blanket, for two whole days until the river receded enough to pass. Each night, she fed Harry in the moonlit darkness, sticking close to the tent, keeping watch for the grizzled vet. She didn't see him, but she always felt him near, crouched among the rocks. During the day, he grinned at her—not a leering grin, Annie Mae realized now. She'd been observing him carefully. He smiled the same way at Andrew. The man was simply lonely, hungry for human contact, *any* contact. He no longer scared Annie Mae, but she saw in him the end result of crazy dreams. A man heads for the edge of the world, seeking pleasure and fortune, she thought, and winds up a parched old ghost. She saw in him Andrew's brother, Lee. She saw a possible future for her husband. For these reasons, she didn't like being near him. Harry kicked and blubbered whenever he came close, as if warning the man to stay away from his mother, and Annie Mae was grateful for her son's frightful noise.

Finally, she agreed to cross the river, not because the water seemed significantly safer to her, but because she couldn't abide the ferry captain any longer—the reminder, in his dusty, sad dishevelment, of false expectations. Better to move on and know your own troubles firsthand, rather than pace the banks anticipating them.

"Promise me," she told Andrew, "wherever we settle, you'll keep men like him away from us."

"I promise."

She shook her head, crying.

"I do, honey."

"You can't. He'll be everywhere. Who else travels where we're going, except lost old souls like him?" She tightened her grip on her baby.

"Now, Annie—"

"Promise me Harry won't be a slave to the land all his life."

"Of course not. That's why we're moving. Harry'll get whatever he wants."

"Promise me you won't drag him into politics."

"Honey—"

"Promise me."

He looked at her, then slid his gaze toward the water. "Now's the time," he said softly. "It won't get calmer than this. Not for a while."

"Andrew—"

"We're leaving. Get your stuff, now."

He guided the team onto the raft. The wagon's wooden wheels rumbled like echoes in a tunnel on the smooth, floating planks. Annie Mae, lanced with pain in the lower part of her back, stepped aboard with Harry, and the ferry captain shoved off with a long oak pole. "Don't know why you want to go," Parker muttered to Andrew, watching Annie Mae. "It's nothing but savage country, up north."

Precisely, she thought.

Andrew only nodded. The ferry dipped slightly at the edge of a rowdy whirlpool—Annie Mae, tipped upward, saw clouds like rags plugging scattershot holes in the sky—then straightened out, heading for a line of tender elms on the opposite shore. Andrew reached for her hand. She grasped it, reluctantly at first, then gratefully as the raft's rocking increased. Clinging tightly to each other, they slipped into the Indian Territory, Harry yammering, all the while, at cottonwood, bluestem, mistletoe.

PART ONE

Cotton County, 1910

1

Later this evening, Harry knew, he'd celebrate his twelfth birthday with his father, just the two of them, in the restaurant of the Palmer Hotel, where all the waiters wore bow ties and jackets, and all the windows, spread before the wide, dusty streets, showed knots of huddled strangers who'd come to trade their goods—Comanches hawking jewelry and skins, cotton farmers stacking hoes on wooden walks in front of the millinery shop and the pharmacy. Harry's father would tell him to order anything he wanted from the menu: steak and Irish potatoes, chicken and dumplings, hot apple pie. He'd claim, as he always did on these trips, he was proud of his son, and maybe as a treat back in the room he'd offer Harry a sip of warm choc beer. The bottle, Andrew's "after-dinner blessing," was stuffed in the leather grip they shared that didn't shut all the way. But before any meals Harry had to give his speech.

Anadarko, Oklahoma, a townsite of two thousand folks or so, was hot and humid this early May afternoon. The tradesmen rubbed their eyes with dirty plaid bandannas. It wasn't likely they'd stop to hear a serious talk, Andrew had warned Harry. They'd want to get their business done and go home.

Besides the market, Harry had to compete with the comet. Any hour now Earth would pass through its tail. The experts Andrew had seen quoted in the papers didn't know if this would harm the atmosphere. Two years ago they'd detected toxic gas in Comet Morehouse; this new visitor, speeding much closer to the planet, might trigger influenza outbreaks. On the other hand, comet tails were exceedingly thin: a change in the wind, nothing more.

A young man in a green tweed suit set a cardboard box in the street next to a sweaty team of horses near the makeshift platform Harry and Andrew planned to use. He wiped his face with a long yellow kerchief. His companion, a small Indian woman in a white dress, helped him open the box. From its depths he pulled a rubber mask. "Don't let the first decade of the twentieth century be your last!" he shouted above the din of sales, the tool prices, the buggy rattles, and whip-cracks. "Protect yourself from Heaven's hellish messenger! I hold in my hand here a one-hundred-percent authentic breathing mask—guaranteed to help you survive Halley's Comet! Six bits for the breath of life, step on up, that's it sir, step right ahead!"

Andrew grumbled then said to Harry, "Come on now, before he draws all the crowd." He lifted his lanky boy onto the platform, a series of chicken crates stacked and wired together, fashioned this morning by an industrious cattle auctioneer. On a street-pole behind the crates, Harry's thin face, sketched in pencil, beamed from a poster:

17 May 1910
Come Hear Harry Shaughnessy
THE BOY ORATOR
Main Street, Anadarko (Weather Permitting)
Endorsed by the Farm Labor Progressive League
GOOD LOUD SPEAKER

He wasn't the only "baby" orator in the state; Andrew had stolen that idea. The Baptists every politician hoped to reach—a powerful bloc of voters—literally believed the Bible's promise that "a little child shall lead them." At rallies, brush arbor revivals, even in the halls of the state capitol, parents and party bosses taught any kid with volume a patriotic nugget or two, urged him onto stages, and hailed him as a prophet of Oklahoma's coming economic miracle.

Harry, though—Harry was the genuine article. Andrew had recognized his talent instantly when, in a school Christmas pageant, at the age of six, he'd overcome his stage fright long enough to blurt, "Welcome ladies and gentlemen, and bless us all on this holy night of our Lord." The cadence and timbre of his voice were steady as oak, strong enough to fill the auditorium. Afterwards the other fathers told Andrew, "Sounds like you've got a young firebrand there" or "Dress him up, take him on the road."

Andrew saved for months, scoring a timely timber sale to the mines, to buy his boy a nice cotton suit, dark blue. He bought pomade for Harry's curly red hair, taught him to stand up straight and slap color into his flat, freckled cheeks right before each speech. At seven, with his daddy's eager help, Harry began learning the Socialist gospel. Late most afternoons, they'd practice together in the windy barn behind their house near East Cache Creek. The Cache, just north of the Red River in Cotton County, was a muddy burble, and a former Kiowa homestead (before white settlers drove the Indians out "long ahead of us," Andrew's neighbors had told him when he'd moved there years ago).

Harry was tall and awkward for his age; his arms poked like kindling from the sleeves of his wrinkled suit. Andrew would stand him on a hay bale, prompt him from the shadows, while barn cats scurried through the horse stalls, and a horned owl aired its wings, creaky and expansive, in the broad walnut rafters. "American farmers are stragglers of rooted armies—," Harry would begin.

"*Routed* armies," Andrew corrected, "scattered by the money men."

"—routed armies, always hoping that somewhere in this great land of ours, there's a piece of dirt for them."

The way his voice thickened in recitation, the way his face flushed dark crimson the first few times they worked on a speech, reminded Andrew of his own father, gentle Michael Roy, resting now seven years in the ground, the hard Texas ground he'd plowed until the strain of loving it, and paying all its costs, burst his heart.

"And who do the money men serve?" Andrew would shout at his boy, eyes salty with tears, thinking, Father, listen, your dream hasn't died.

"The forces of greed!" Harry yelled back.

For you, Father. Listen. "Greed?"

"The smasher." Sunlight burst through slats in the barn. Harry's face flushed with excitement and a swelling desire to please: Father, watch me, listen, for you. "The smasher of souls!"

"Louder!"

"Of souls!"

"What?"

Harry planted his feet, shaking with energy, love (Andrew saw it in the lurching tilt of the boy's whole body), fear of letting his father down. He closed his eyes. *"Souls!"*

THIS AFTERNOON IN ANADARKO, Andrew felt anxious for the first time in weeks. The crowd was tired, overheated, close to fury over bad deals, inflated prices. These were just the poor wretches Harry could aid if they were willing to listen but Andrew feared they weren't. Farmers weren't the only ones tending to business. Men in ties—bankers, lawyers, owners of the farmers' rocky lands—strolled among saddles, plows, and furs, counting the county's wealth, their kingdom's gold. Klansmen, Andrew thought, spitting into the dirt. Most of these bastards were night-riders. They wouldn't welcome Harry's message.

Three or four fellows approached the platform. They didn't look friendly. Andrew preferred camp meetings in the country, addressing honest, hardworking folks with their simple hand-stitched clothes and coal-oil lamps, to these market-day affairs. In the country, people hungered for the word; they'd come to a rally dragging water in big tin buckets, hauling firewood and bedding. Fiddlers played reels and boisterous jigs, tunes the farmers' ancestors danced to in Ireland or Scotland, generations ago. For the oratory, the stirring advice, crowds straggled in for miles, slatternly, weary, but full of vinegar. Here, in county seats like Anadarko, where most people ate three full squares a day, sympathy for the poor was hard to scare up. Andrew had said as much to the Socialist League, who sponsored Harry's trips, but the party was after converts, it didn't matter where. Andrew didn't trust anyone in the electric light towns.

"The standard beginning," he whispered to his son. Harry cleared his throat, straightened his black string tie. "Live to see the coming century!" called the breathing mask man. "Don't let this evil apparition rob you of your dearest years!" Down the street a strained buyer argued the cost of a scythe: "You thieving son of a bitch, I'm not blind. Who do you think you're talking to?" Harry said softly, "The rent you pay your landlord—what is it now, twenty-five dollars a bale?—would buy a lot of biscuits for your wife."

One of the men who'd faced the platform stepped forward, removed his hat, and said, "What's that, son?" His teeth were brown and his skin, beneath his whiskers, was a dark, mottled red, relieved here and there by hooklike scars.

"I said"—Harry raised his voice, gestured crisply at the crowd— "your landlord's wife wears silks and gets to ride in an automobile, while *your* wife walks!" His words rained like straw on the bent shoulders of all the men, or so Andrew imagined, startling them lightly at first, then itching, working down beneath their shirts and into their skin. They turned, two at a time, three at a time, to see the source of this storm, and were shocked to find a skinny kid.

"While your sons and daughters labor in the fields, the children of the men who own you bask in the finest educational facilities this country has to offer," Harry went on. "*You've* paid for these schools but can your family get near them?"

Farmers flocked together as Harry spoke; the men in suits had vanished. The fellows Andrew had noticed before—the unfriendly ones—stood by the platform and glowered.

The mask salesman had lost his audience. He shook his rubber headgear. "You won't even *have* any fields, don't you understand me? All will be destroyed. This wayward star is a divine plague from the Lord. Rescue yourselves!"

For a couple more minutes Harry, the salesman, the tradesmen competed—

"Two dollars a yard—"

"—angered the Lord Almighty—"

"—no farther than this town's steel vaults to discover the cause of your woes—"

"Two dollars my ass!"

—but Harry soon held sway. He paced the platform, shaking his fists. Sweat spread along his sleeves, his dark red hair sprang forth. With every other breath he swallowed a darting mosquito, but he'd learned to do this without choking or even pausing in his speech. "Gangs of parasites infest the towns of this county, and they fatten their hides at your expense, my friends, your expense! You do the work of the world yet nothing but crumbs come your way!"

Andrew stood behind his boy watching the streets. He'd taught Harry well, those days in the barn, whispering, "Louder. Okay, softer now, make them strain to hear you." The listeners were rapt, but a bad pulse beat in this town—Andrew could feel it. He noticed keen eyes studying him like a sum, the harsh scrutiny of older, meaner men: solid citizens with much to lose and no intention of doing so. At the camp meetings, Harry spoke mostly to friends, liquored up and happy. These were impatient strangers at the end of an aching day. The event was not well-timed (he'd *told* the league!). He waited. Then it came.

"Lousy Reds," said the man with the scars. He turned to size up the crowd. Waved his hat. "Rotten Reds!" he yelled. His voice seemed to die in the air. For a second, Harry lost the rhythm of his speech, became aware of his circumstances, conscious of his movements, and in that second he saw the mask salesman slap the Indian woman. She'd tried to lift the box, lost her grip and spilled the masks in the dust. The salesman whacked her head, stamped her feet with his boots. Harry looked away and saw in the sky a massive thunderhead, angry, cumulus plumes, yellow and green. A moment ago the land was still. Now, without warning, wind sucked dust from the road, shading the sky brick-red, ripping handbills and his very own posters from their nails, filling his nose with a dry rain-smell and stinging his skin ice-cold. The comet, he thought, it's here. He imagined bank roofs sailing off into fields, crushing empty wagons, dollars snowing into pockets, horses somersaulting over the town. He looked around. He wanted one of those masks. He wanted his birthday dinner; it might be his last.

The swift change in air pressure roused the mob even more. Men blinked grit from their eyes. Andrew felt the blood-rush rise. The scarred man hit the platform with his hat, raising a head-shaped ball of dust. "These Reds want women to vote!" he barked. "They want to give niggers your land!"

The crowd shook. Andrew, unthinking, shoved Harry aside. The boy nearly tripped off the platform. "You don't *have* any land, that's the point!" Andrew shouted. The wind seemed to flatten all sound, like a heavy iron lid clamped on the town. "*You're* the niggers here!" As soon as he said this he regretted it. Men swarmed the front of the platform. "It's the devil's work they do!" someone yelled. "Drag them down from there. This is a Christian town, with good Christian morals!"

20

Andrew grabbed Harry, smoothed the small, padded shoulders of his coat. "God," he whispered—a signal for a different kind of speech. Harry lifted his right arm, magically stilling the crowd. "I pray for the Kingdom on Earth," he said, his voice trembling with conviction. As he spoke, he kept an eye on the salesman, who was dragging the woman and the box down the street, past the bakery, the Good Luck Café, the Palmer Hotel. Horses reared in the stiffening breeze. "While men are underpaid, women overworked, and children underfed, the Kingdom of Heaven will never appear in Oklahoma. Socialism can remove these unhealthy conditions. Socialism can relieve you of your animal existence. Brothers, I pray we see Socialism *in our time!*"

The clouds were frothing now. Harry's tie whipped his face. The listeners, stunned by this boy's endless breath, the great power rising from his belly like a pipe organ, shivered.

"Okay, that's it, let's get," said Andrew, tugging Harry from the platform, down a gas-lighted alley smelling of orange rinds and coffee, rose perfume, piss, and the sweet cedar wood of nearby buildings. The crowd still hadn't moved. Harry choked on dust, wondered if the comet had poisoned him already. "Anadarko," Andrew said, nearly breathless. "Fellow told me once it's Caddo for 'People of the Bee.'" He wheezed. "Good place to get stung, all right. When we get back to the hotel, I want you to put your suit in the bag right away—"

"Aren't we staying for dinner?" Harry asked, torn between his terror of the sky and his hunger for ice cream and cobbler.

"No, I think we better get on back to your mother tonight."

"But you promised—"

"Harry, hush up and do as I say now. We got a long ride ahead of us." Andrew was always amazed at how quickly Harry slipped from the wise little adult who'd paced the stage into a nagging kid again. An only child, he was used to attention; Andrew was usually glad to give it—an extra helping of mashed potatoes and gravy at supper, one last game of checkers just before bed—but not when Harry acted stubborn like this against good advice. How many times had Andrew told his son, believing it, "You have to straighten up. The eyes of the world'll be on you."

"I don't care," Harry would reply, angling to stay up later than usual, or to wriggle out of his chores.

"You *will*."

"Won't!" the boy used to shout—but lately, Harry hadn't protested quite so much, even when he was grumpy and exhausted, Andrew had noticed, grateful for this new sign of maturity.

A fat raindrop hit the ground like a bullet. "Hurry up, son. Maybe we can beat the storm."

Back in their room Andrew pulled a wool sock from under the mattress, reached in and emptied the league's money. All there, still. Good. He'd settle up downstairs and they'd be on their way. Harry stuffed his coat and tie into the bag, around the smooth, hot bottle of beer.

By the time they left the lobby it was just after five. Lights were snuffing out in the stores, flaring up in noisy coffee shops and inns. The sky had a midnight pallor. "You don't suppose there's something to that comet nonsense, do you?" Andrew said.

Harry didn't hear. He was pouting. His father seemed to hate this town but he didn't see what was so bad about it. The crowd had turned a little sour but this wasn't the first time he'd faced a restless group. The women wore bright dresses and the food smelled good. Three years ago, when President Roosevelt signed Oklahoma into statehood, Andrew brought the family here for a fireworks celebration. Harry still remembered the egg-yolk bursts among the stars, the dying-flower smell of the gunpowder as it drifted past the cemetery they'd found with a marvelous view. He liked this place. He wanted sparklers for his birthday.

Andrew led him down back streets toward the smithy's barn where, this morning, they'd boarded their wagon and team. As they rounded a corner by a small barbershop they were blocked by five big men. "Oh shit," Andrew whispered. Their arm hair, Harry saw, was as thick and matted as the sleeves of wool sweaters. They all wore overalls and veils on their heads—bandannas or soiled-looking pillowcases with needled edges. One man hid his features behind a dark green rubber mask. "Well well well," he said, his voice as muffled and watery as a frog's.

"Wait now, gents, we don't want any trouble," Andrew said, setting down the leather grip, raising his calloused hands.

"Then what'd you come here for, talking your devil talk, huh? Damn Reds." The man lifted the bottom of his mask to spit. Harry saw hooked scars beneath his stubble.

"Say, boy." A man in a pillowcase stung Harry's ear with a hard, muddy finger. His spooky eye-holes were the size of silver dollars. "You suck niggers' dicks? I'll bet you suck niggers' dicks, am I right?"

"Please. The boy doesn't know anything," Andrew said. His voice shook. "I write his speeches. Honest. He doesn't understand a word of them. Whatever you're going to do, leave him out of it."

A second hooded man knelt to inspect Harry's face. He smelled of onions, sweat, wet animal hair. "Your pappy doesn't think you're too smart, now does he? Are you a Red, boy? Do you know what that means?"

"Yessir."

"Yes, you know what it means? Or yes, you are one?"

Harry steeled himself. "I believe in the noble tenets of Socialism, sir."

Andrew shut his eyes.

"Tenets!" The man in the mask laughed with a low rumble like rolling marbles. "Well now, he sounds pretty smart to me." He turned to Andrew. "Shaughnessy. That a mick name?"

"Sounds mick to me, Billy," one of his buddies answered.

"Damn it, I've told you, don't identify me." He tightened his rubber disguise. "So, not only are you Reds, you're goddam Irish Catholics. You want to take our land *and* Romanize our schools, that it? Enslave our kids to the Pope?"

"No," Andrew said. "We want what you want. Honest, we're just like you."

"Listen, mick, we got a nice town here. Folks work hard, go to *Protestant* churches, earn what they have. We don't need country scum coming 'round telling us how to live. So you go on back to your nasty women and your niggers, you hear?"

"Lucky for him we're fresh out of hot tar, eh Billy?" The man cracked Andrew's nose with the flat of his palm. Andrew wobbled and fell to the ground. The group swarmed on him, kicking. Blood bloomed in a swell of dirt.

Harry hollered. He looked around for help, pounded one of the men. Someone grabbed him from behind and tossed him into a woodpile. A loose ax bit his side. Squatty logs, fat as little bulldogs, tumbled all around him. He tasted dirt and blood, the smoky tinge of oak.

THE NEXT THING HE knew, rain was hammering his face and his feet were cold. He picked himself out of the rickety stack of wood, ripped his shirt on a splinter. The ax had left a big gash in his side just above his right hip. He'd landed at an angle so the wound wasn't worse. The rain pasted his hair to his face, washed blood down his thighs. Shivering, he stumbled toward his father who lay face up in a thin crater of mud. Andrew's eyes and lips were swollen, purple-green. He groaned when Harry touched his shoulder.

"I'll get a doctor," Harry croaked. In the rain, bubbles formed on his lips. He remembered a pharmacy on Main Street. No one was around.

Andrew raised a bloody arm. "No," he hissed. He tried to speak without moving his mouth. "Don't trust . . . the bastards here. I'll be . . . fine, with rest. Did they take our money?"

Harry turned and found the half-open bag. He looked inside. The clothes were soaked. "I think everything's here," he said.

"Good. Are you hurt?" Andrew tried to sit up, groaned again, sank deeper into shallow streams of muddy yellow rain.

"Not bad."

"Thank God. If you can get me . . . to the hotel, check us in, same room. Rest. Rest the night . . ."

Twenty minutes later Harry had managed to pull his father to his feet. They traveled stiffly. In the lobby of the Palmer Hotel, Harry snapped at the startled clerk in his most effective tones, "No, we don't need a doctor. Just our room. Now!"

The clerk, a pasty man with a mole near the top of his head, persisted. "I think I should inform the manager there's a serious injury on the premises."

"Please," Andrew said. He dripped blood and water on the desk. "Listen to the boy. There's an extra buck in it for you. I'll be fine. You won't be liable for anything, I swear. Harry, give him the money."

Harry opened the bag and did as he was told. As he helped his father up the stairs he glanced into the restaurant. Waiters with trays shot from the kitchen in their crisp red jackets, trailing feathers of pleasant smoke. There'd be no "blessing" tonight; no birthday, even.

The bedsprings squealed when Andrew flopped onto the sheets. Harry lit a white candle on the night table. Gingerly, he washed his father's face with a cool, wet rag. His own cut he cleaned without soap. He wrapped one of Andrew's suspenders around his waist to stop the bleeding.

Andrew motioned Harry to his side. "In the morning . . . you'll have to drive the wagon. Do you think you can do that?"

"Yessir." Harry smeared tears from his eyes. He'd never seen his father so helpless. The sight of Andrew battered changed the world. The ground, the air around him, no longer seemed a sure bet.

"Son, it's important . . . you know why this happened."

"I know why it happened," Harry said. "Because we're right."

"Yes. Those men are scared." Andrew sighed so heavily it seemed his features would alter forever. "Make a good family, make a good life. There's no higher calling for a man—my own daddy used to tell me that. When you talk to people like you do, Harry, you're . . . doing that. Trying to make life good. Some people don't understand. They want to—" He rolled over in pain.

"It's all right, Dad," Harry said, gripping his father's hand. "I know. You don't have to say any more. Rest now."

Soon Andrew was snoring, threatening the candle flame with his breath. Wax peppered the floor. Harry's stomach growled. He unrolled the sock with the money inside. The hard, dark coins were warm as sunny pebbles in his palm. Maybe not steak, but a slice or two of bacon? Creamed corn, a mashed potato? No, his father would notice if even a little was gone. "That's not our jack!" he'd say. "It belongs to the league. You don't spend a dime without my permission, you hear me?"

Harry wondered what his father would say if he admitted to him, "Dad, I'm tired of making speeches." The trips weren't fun if he and Andrew couldn't eat a nice meal or do something special. Once, in Guthrie, they'd watched a traveling circus. A woman in a silver gown wrapped herself like a pretzel around a barrel of water; later, she stayed for Harry's talk. He liked his time onstage, the warm cedar smells of the platforms he paced, the crack of his shoe heels on the shiny new wood. He loved using his voice like a rope pulling people toward him, the red flags in the trees waving like pairs of pudgy hands applauding, but everything else—the long wagon rides, the meetings with league officials—wore him out.

It wasn't true his father wrote his speeches. Harry found his own right words. He'd read the great Oscar Ameringer, the father of their movement ("Socialism grows when every other crop fails"). Heard the chicken-eating preachers at brush arbor revivals. From them all he'd learned to plant ideas, like burrs, in people's minds. He knew what worked. If only he could talk from his porch, never leave. He craved his mother's biscuits, the warm flour smell of her apron as she rocked him in her arms.

He walked to the dresser mirror to adjust the strap around his wound. In the near-dark he almost tripped on the open leather bag. He heard the choc beer slosh. His belly murmured again. A sip or two would surely ease his pain . . . he could throw the bottle away, say it rolled into the alley and smashed when the men attacked them. His dad would never know. He reached inside the grip.

Last summer Andrew had taken him to the Wichita foothills west of Lawton to watch a man he called an "old family friend" mix a batch of corn liquor. "Don't ever tell your mother," Andrew warned him as they groped through stickery woods. They saw a hand-painted sign in a clearing: "All Nations Welcome But 'Carrie.'" His father grinned. "It's not far now."

"Who's 'Carrie'?" Harry asked.

"Carry Nation. Saloon-buster." He stopped to shake the sweat off his face. "Like your ma, she doesn't approve of this sort of thing." They walked a little farther, past post oak and gnarly mistletoe groves, until they heard hushed and serious voices. "I'm a friend!" his father shouted and raised his arms. Harry did the same. Immediately, they were surrounded by shotgun-toting men in dirty blue overalls. A big bearded fellow spat tobacco onto a pine stump. "It's all right," he said. "It's Andrew and his boy." The men lowered their guns.

All day Harry watched them brew. His father's friend, Zeke Cash, said, "Now, the Anti-Saloon League and the Christian Temperance Union'll tell you this stuff's a sin but don't you believe it. The Bible says, 'Wine maketh glad the heart of man.' Psalms 104. Look it up." He poured sweet mash from a barrel into a still-pot, added oak chips for flavor. Meanwhile, his buddies, swatting off horseflies, dug sacks of unground corn out of cone-shaped manure piles, to see if they were ready to mush with sugar and water. One of the men, standing guard beneath the mistletoe, played lonesome love songs on a mouth harp.

"How much of this Ruckus Juice you want, Andrew?" Zeke said.

"Couple of bottles."

"Two bottles of Panther Sweat comin' up."

He ran off the first batch of bran, threw the slop on leafy ground by a pair of strutting chickens. The birds pecked at the bristling foam, dithered in half-circles, then fell down drunk. Zeke offered Harry a sip; he stalled. His father said, "I'll tell you a secret, son. When you were teething as a baby, screaming all night and keeping us awake, the only thing that'd soothe you was a bit of Zeke's Bust Head. Your ma didn't like it, but I told her to rub a spoonful on your gums each night and you settled right down, like a sweet, lazy lamb. That's the only time she ever let the stuff in the house."

"All right," Harry said, doubtful. He raised the wooden cup, rolled his head back slowly, gagged. A huge, raw hand had reached into his throat and stolen the breath from his lungs. He hacked and gasped while all the men laughed. Later, he tasted the murky choc from the bottom of the mash barrel, liked it better than the whiskey. Since then his father had always tossed a "blessing" in the bag when they went on trips. He didn't let Harry have much; a quick shot if his speech was particularly good.

Now, while his father slept in the dim room, Harry chugged the beer. "Happy birthday," he said to his face in the mirror. He heard piano music from lighted rooms across the street below. Restless, stirred by the choc, and a little dizzy already, he cracked the door, tip-toed down the hall and slipped downstairs to the lobby. The desk clerk stared at him. Harry balanced the bottle with both tingling hands behind his back. He still wore his torn, bloody shirt.

"Everything all right?" the clerk said. The black mole quivered on his forehead.

Harry nearly dropped the bottle. The clerk squinted, tried to peer around the boy to see what he was hiding. Harry realized he'd stuffed the money sock into his pants when he was thinking of ordering dinner. He walked to the desk, set the bottle by his feet so the clerk couldn't see it, pulled out the sock, and spilled a mound of coins. He'd think of something later to tell his father. "Here." He arranged the change in a circle. "Just go about your business, okay?"

The clerk grinned. "Big guy, eh? I know who you are. I've seen the posters." This sounded like an accusation. He swept the coins into his coat and turned away.

On the street Harry hid in the shadows of a newspaper office across the way from a raucous café. He leaned against a hitching post, nursing the choc. A few men passed, talking, smoking. They didn't see him there in the dark. He watched their swinging arms as they walked, ready to run if he spotted the thick hair he'd glimpsed on the gang who'd hurt him. He smelled pepper-beef from the place across the street, heard women's laughter, deep and lively as his mother's. He shivered.

The storm had left as quickly as it rose. The air was warmer than before but his shirt was damp. The street was rutted with puddles. Someone strummed a banjo in the kitchen. His stomach gurgled. He took a step into the street, dodged back when two men passed. What if his attackers were in the café? He couldn't risk it. And there was still a problem with the money. His father would see he was short already.

A ruddy dog with spots on its back yipped at his feet. "Get!" Harry hissed. A strolling couple looked over and saw him. "Get away from here. Leave me alone." The dog was playful, insistent on sniffing the choc, surprised at its own frequent farts.

Voices accompanied the banjo now. Harry went soft in the knees. "Well well," someone said. Harry jittered, startling the dog. It farted loudly, a sound like clattering brass, then scampered off down the street, dark then light, dark then light, as it passed through shadows then under sidewalk lamps.

"Take it easy, friend." A figure approached from the alley. "You're pretty skittish for a Communist. I thought all you fellows were fearless, out in front, fighting the people's war." The breathing mask man, weaving with drink, still in his green tweed suit, stained now under the sleeves. His yellow kerchief dangled from a hip pocket next to a curly rubber string.

Harry hadn't thought about the comet since the beating. He looked up now. Clouds flat as planks, stars like nails, nearly hidden, holding them all together.

"I'm not a Communist," he murmured. Beer ambushed his head, pinching, pinching.

"Could've fooled me." The man rolled a cigarette. A sliver of brown hair bobbed on his chin just below his lower lip, a woolly wood chip. "You know how many of these I sold today?" He pulled a mask from his pocket, spilling his kerchief onto the ground. "Five. Yesterday, in Shawnee? *Fifty*-five." He lit the fag, flicked the match into the street. A brief flare. A comet-tail. "You and your Communist talk, stirring folks up. You ruined it for me, kid." He staggered and belched.

Harry set his bottle down. He staggered too. "Maybe tomorrow—"

"Hell, tomorrow'll be too late. Halley's will have come and gone. Have to find another scam. Where's your old man?"

"Asleep."

The salesman laughed, nudged the empty bottle with his boot. "You and me, we got something in common. The thrill of the pitch. Afterwards you can't settle down, right? Others hit the sack, your blood's still racing." He fingered the loose threads of Harry's shirt. "What happened, you bust a longhorn? Boy, you *do* have energy."

Harry didn't answer.

"Well, I say us drummers, we gotta stick together."

"I'm not a drummer, either."

"Sure you are." The man swirled his cigarette like a stubby yellow sparkler over his head. "You're selling the biggest idea of all. Promise of a better life. And it's about as useful as the crap *I* push. You're pretty good, though, I gotta say. What was that line?—'I pray we see the Kingdom on Earth.' Pretty good, kid, pretty good. How old are you?"

"Twelve. Today."

"Well now, happy birthday."

"Thank you."

The man offered his hand. "Bob Cochran."

"Harry," Harry said.

"Harry, you stick with this business, you'll be a damn fine drummer someday. Got the spark, that's a fact. I only wish you'd take it somewhere else." He'd smoked his cigarette quickly. He ground it out in a knothole on the hitching post then rolled himself another.

Harry looked at the mask, stuck now back in Bob Cochran's pocket, glanced nervously at the sky. Behind him, in the doorway of the newspaper office, a cricket rattled. "Where's your friend?" Harry asked.

"Who?"

"That lady with you."

"Sue-Sue?" Bob Cochran smiled a mean-looking smile, the closest smile to a frown Harry had ever seen. "Waiting for me back in the room. That's how I get *my* energy out."

"You hit her," Harry said.

Bob Cochran frowned his smile. "She's Kiowa," he answered, as if that explained everything. He noticed Harry eyeing the mask. "You want that? Think it's going to save you? _____ Harry's hands; the rubber was cool and crav. _____ save you, kid." He bent level with Harry's face. _____ his breath. "The coming century, it's going to be a _____ that? Electric lights are just the beginning. People a. _____ drink—believe it—*travel* with speed. There'll be sh. _____ .ie machines doing all our work. Buildings tall as stars. And y won't see a whit of it. Know why?" He stroked his wood-chip beard.

Harry, weary, hungry, befuddled by his daddy's beer, said, "The comet?"

"Ha!" Bob Cochran sailed his second fag at the farty little dog, who'd returned and was crouching in the street as if waiting for him to leave. "'Cause you're stuck in Shithole, Oklahoma, that's why." He rose unsteadily, angled off down the walk. "Nice talking to you, Harry," he called from the dark.

Harry sank to the ground, picked up the choc bottle and smashed the rubber mask with it, scaring then drawing the curious dog. Here, sitting in the dirt of Anadarko, hearing music fade in the place across the street and knowing he was too late to get any supper; here, on the night he was twelve, while his beaten father slept, he determined his story would begin. The speed Bob Cochran had mentioned, the chrome machines and the buildings, Harry Tracy Shaughnessy would bring them here, *right here*, to Oklahoma. Why not? Fired by the beer, and the thrill of the pitch, he decided the century would deny him nothing.

When he rose he noticed Bob Cochran's yellow kerchief, crumpled like a tiny paper parasol in a puddle. He picked it up, squeezed it almost dry, and wrapped it around his wrist.

The clerk was nodding off on a stool behind the hotel desk when Harry returned to the lobby. He crept back up the stairs, tripping twice, found his father still lost to the world. His face, in poor, reflected light from the window, had turned the color of split-pea

The candle had long since guttered out. Labored snores. Harry stood, holding the money sock and the kerchief, watching the street below. The little dog did an agitated dance. It seemed he was looking for Harry. A wagon passed, drawn by a single white horse. A tuckered-out farmer, leaving market day late. Harry looked up to see if he could see the coming century, or maybe just the comet, its fantail wide as a peacock's, sowing sparks like seeds above the bank's peaked roof. Clouds packed the sky; he couldn't see very straight after all the beer he'd drunk. When his gaze dropped again he saw in the street Bob Cochran and Sue-Sue, her dark skin bold against the paleness of her dress. She was—in Harry's blurry sight—the most beautiful woman he'd ever stopped to watch. They danced (she stiffly, with swollen, trampled feet) to music he couldn't hear—music from the future, perhaps—in front of the café window, silhouetted, ghostly, by a faint electric light.

2

The day Harry carted his father back from Anadarko, Annie Mae hurried them both into her kitchen. "That's quite enough of politics," she said, seating her men in rough wooden chairs. "From now on you'll stay home where you're needed and wanted."

Andrew wasn't one for doctors; she knew this from their earliest days here in the Territory. She fired up her kerosene stove, boiled burn-weed tea for his chills, then pole beans to mix with honey and butter for a poultice. She ground ivy in a mortar, added sugar, soot, spider webs, and water to stop Harry's bleeding.

Andrew winced while she sponged him clean. "I'm sorry. Sit still and I'll try not to hurt," she whispered, as she'd done every night when he'd first found work in these parts, a dozen years ago. Each dawn, in early spring, she remembered, he'd be out, biting into trees with his hand briar saw, slicing the ridged bark as if cutting hard bread; then, using a steam-powered skidder cable rented from a neighbor, he'd drag the logs, with their sweet meat exposed, out of the mud. Some evenings he'd straggle home from the woods slashed across his back from a snapped choker chain, flying out of the crazy steam contraption, and Annie Mae would stand over him in the dim lamplight of her kitchen, spreading butter on the bumps of his swollen skin.

She did this now, recollecting those early days, humming random tunes to soothe him as she worked. "Is it okay if I touch you here?" she asked him, "or here?" brushing purple patches on his shoulders, back, and arms. He groaned and shook. She whispered, "Shhh, shhh. Just stay still."

After feeding Harry a bowl of hot beef stew, and insisting he swallow some tea, she tucked him into bed.

"Ma?"

"What is it, honey?" She kissed his forehead.

"I'm not really tired." But his eyes were fluttering even as he spoke. "Can I have my marbles?"

"Tomorrow, Harry. You'll play with them tomorrow."

"I just want to hold them."

She smiled. He was her *boy* still, not a politician in those wild, drunk towns, as Andrew insisted he'd become. On the floor, she found the little bag of cat's eyes and placed it in his palm. His fingers twitched, but before they could close, he was out.

For hours, Annie Mae kept the poultice pressed to Andrew's flesh, massaged him gently with her mixtures of sugar and leaves: Choctaw cures she'd learned shortly after arriving in the Territory.

She shivered, recalling those grinding first days. When they'd first got to Lehigh, Andrew's brother, Lee, who'd promised to find them a place to live, was gone. His wife, June, had the law after him—he'd never actually divorced her, he'd simply disappeared. Posters showed up on every wall in town, describing Lee's beefy build, his thin brown hair, declaring his wife and kids destitute. Finally, June found herself a fine new man, printed her own divorce notice in the paper, and that was that. To this day, no one had heard from Lee.

Annie Mae and Andrew had missed the first Oklahoma land-rush by a good nine years, but cheap lots were still available for families willing to work them; Andrew claimed sixteen grubby acres (at just over a dollar apiece—money he borrowed from the bank) west of East Cache Creek. Within a month, he'd met and befriended officials from the Osage Coal Company over near Krebs and the Rock Island outfit out of Alderson. They wanted the red oak on his land. Immediately, he began supplying them and helping them build their mines.

How did we ever get through it? Annie Mae thought, feeling again her loneliness at home and the depth of Andrew's exhaustion. How do we get through it now?

Each week, he hauled the timber over amber hills, vales punched flat into the land, in the wagon he'd brought from Texas. Sometimes its wheels sliced through thickets of fleshy brown mushrooms, he told Annie Mae, and the whole forest filled with a scent as dark and honeyed as boiling sugar.

The fellows he supplied with logs, the mining operators, were "ruthless capitalists," he said, like the landowners his father railed against in Bonham, but they treated Andrew well as long as he kept the lumber coming. He had a child to feed, so he took their money without much thought.

Meanwhile, Annie Mae had stocked her shelves with flour and cornmeal she'd bought off the backs of traveling salesmen, set up a sewing machine, hung in her kitchen a large calendar mailed out each year by the Citizens National Bank of Oklahoma City. On it she marked the dates of Harry's first haircut, his first coherent phrases. By the kitchen door she stacked magazines she'd bought in Walters, a town of eight hundred, two dusty miles down the road—the *Farmer-Stockman*, *Capper's Weekly*, *Comfort*. The family used them in the outhouse, fifty yards away down a narrow, bushy trail.

She felt leaden with memory now as she washed her husband's face, delicately, as though his injury were a threat to her, too. Life could crumble in a heartbeat. Harry moaned in his sleep. She went to check on him. He'd rolled on his side, twisting the sheet around his legs. The marbles had slipped to the floor; one by one she picked them up.

She kissed Harry's cheek, drew the sheet to his chin. One day, when he was still an infant, she remembered, she was hanging clothes on a line when she heard a rustling behind her. She turned and saw a small Indian woman standing by the side of her house. Annie Mae was so startled she dropped her clothespins. Harry slept in a basket nearby.

"I came to see you," said the woman. She didn't move.

"Yes?" Annie Mae stood still too.

"I thought you might be lonely."

The woman's name was Mahalie. She was Choctaw, married to a white farmer from whom she'd learned her English. In the next few weeks, as Annie Mae got to know her, Mahalie said most of her sisters married whites because they were gentler and richer than Choctaw men. "In most places, I'm told, a white man who marries one of us is immediately cast out of his circle," she told Annie Mae. "Around here, there's not much trouble over that—people don't see each other often, anyway. We're too busy and our homes are far apart."

Annie Mae understood, then, that Mahalie felt lonely, too. She brought around other Indian women—Choctaws, Creeks—some of whom she hadn't known long herself. "So you'll never want for company," she said, clearly happy to be fashioning a new group of friends. They cooked together, tended each other's babies. Annie Mae hung a fat iron pot from an oak tripod in her yard; around it the dark women gathered, hushed, watching her stir soupy beans. Now and then, one of them would pull a waxy square of lard from beneath her dusty shawl and toss it into the pot, making the beans hiss like snakes. The women nodded solemnly at the progress they were making with the food.

Harry was the first white child some of them had ever seen. They touched his face, kissed him, passed him around. Annie Mae was eager to learn their tongues, but "hegee" was the only word she ever acquired—Creek for tobacco. The women wanted to speak only English, the "language of the future," they said.

They *did* introduce her to burn-weed, scurvy grass, mayapple and other medicines to ease the chronic ache in her back, to break Harry's fevers, keep him regular and free of worms. They soaked wagon chains in buckets of rainwater to make an iron tonic for the babies.

Annie Mae commented once on the robustness of all the Indian kids she saw.

"Yes," Mahalie said. "The weak ones die right away."

HARRY RECOVERED QUICKLY UNDER Annie Mae's stern daily care, with only a minor scar to remind him of the Anadarko incident. When his strength returned, he followed her through the house as she arranged pear blossoms in a fine bouquet on the table, fed premature chicks in a pen in a corner, or drew water for the washtub. Always, for him, she was a commanding, comforting spirit. He loved her hay-thick auburn hair, the whisper of her floor-length dress when she moved from room to room.

Andrew's maladies lingered. He wouldn't leave his bed or talk much. He drifted. Annie Mae sat by him, quietly crying, washing him, holding his hands.

Harry had to handle the chores. Besides selling timber to coal interests, his father earned a living farming, repairing neighbors' wagons. Harry had always helped around the place. In late spring, as temperatures warmed, Andrew asked him to watch the alfalfa field behind the barn, to look for the first violet blossoms on the stalks, which meant they were ready to cut. He'd help his father bundle the stuff and sell it, as silage or hay, to feed the county's sheep.

He watched the potatoes, too, for early signs of blight. The dark green leaves of Andrew's Pink Eyes and Lumpers crumpled like paper if the fungus had infected their stems. Harry loved it when the spuds turned out healthy (usually they did) and his mother roasted them over a mild fire in a pot full of buttermilk.

From constant horse traffic, the farmyard was pitted, worn down in certain places to skull-white limestone beneath the topsoil. Sometimes, when he was running around the yard, pulling burdock from the tangled tails of the horses or keeping an eye on the crops, he'd find a tiny crinoid or a brachiopod shell—a slender stone daisy—in a chewed-up patch of dirt. His father identified them for him, told him these were petrified creatures from an ancient age, when all this land was sea.

This spring, Andrew had encouraged Harry's public speaking more than his farmwork; despite his hours in the sun, Harry had failed to take in the finer points of cultivation. Now, with his father laid up, he over- or under-fertilized the fields, damaging crops. He fed the chickens too much—he *tried* to be sparing!—making them sluggish and lazy.

Andrew was already angry at him for shortchanging the league, chugging the choc—when it came right down to it, he couldn't lie to his dad—and dragging the dog home. It had followed the wagon out of Anadarko that morning. Andrew slept fitfully all the way back; Harry stopped the horses three or four times, stood in the loose spring seat, yelled, "Shoo!" but the dog's tail leaped as if Harry's shouts were a promise of food. He gave up, hoisted the poor creature into his lap, and named it Halley. "Sit now, Halley, be a good boy." Halley farted with pleasure.

Andrew was too weak to punish Harry, but his scowls let the boy know he wasn't happy about the money, the new pet, the beer, or his work. Annie Mae frowned on Halley, too—she called him "filthy, a burden, a pest." So Harry spent most of his time outdoors with the dog and the swaybacked mule, Patrick Nagle. The real Patrick Nagle was an Oklahoma Democrat-turned-Socialist, an active member of the Friends of Irish Freedom, and a hero of Andrew's, who tended to name his animals (and his son) after people he admired. The mule had hauled timber for years until its back gave out. Now Harry helped it enjoy a pleasant retirement. He patted and talked to it while Halley yipped around the spiked stakes of the old loblolly fence.

At first Harry was happy to be off the road, home with his ma. His chores exhausted him, but the long sunny weekends lightened his mood. He loved the smell of grass, the cool of the mud, the long corridors of afternoon sky where thunderheads swirled like buttery curdles of cream. In the fields upwind, dry cereal oats spilled, crackling, through steel bins in the county's grain elevators, settling into troughs. From there, men would shovel them onto the MK & T when it next came through on the rails. The elevators were stark white, splashed with colorful words: Poag Grain Inc., Equity Coop Exchange, General Mills. Harry squinted into the sun, watched the letters dance in fly-riddled ripples of heat. The elevators' spires rose like the massive columns of cathedrals he'd seen in picture books, shading cows and rows of brittle wheat.

In the evenings, Harry, Patrick Nagle, and Halley chased fireflies around the mule's narrow, fenced-in pen. Harry crushed the bugs, spread the glow all over Patrick Nagle's musky neck. The animal hummed with warmth, and Harry hugged him close.

On weekdays he rode four miles to school in the county's John Deere wagon, a boxlike contraption with tall, spoked wheels and a canvas roof, drawn by two red mules. He always had makeup homework to do, from the many trips he'd taken, but he was a quick learner. The schoolhouse, a single square room packed with kids of all ages, buzzed with news of the comet the week Harry returned from Anadarko. Eddie McGarrah, a farmer's boy from over near Cookietown, swore that diamonds fell from the sky that night, slicing the ears off his daddy's prize hogs. Randy Olin, from Walters, said his sister had given birth to a bloody mess, cursed by the star, that smoked and fizzed and finally disintegrated in her hands.

"I don't believe it," Harry said. "That comet talk was nonsense."

"You calling me a fibber?" Olin pushed him into McGarrah, who shoved him back at Olin.

"You bet I am, both of you," Harry said. "Filthy liars." The boys scuffled, knocking over desks, until the teacher, a stout woman with red, blocky arms, separated them.

"Look at him—always up on stage," Olin said. "I'm just as good as you, Shaughnessy, any day of the week."

Harry's side began to ache. When he reached for his books he felt his skin burn. He untucked his shirt, examined his scar. It hadn't split, but in the fight he'd bruised himself again. That day the ride home in the school wagon, over spidery tree roots exposed in the road, pained him so much he nearly fainted. His mother was too busy to pay him any mind when he reached the house. She was haggling with the salesman, the man Andrew called the "Jew Peddler," who rode by once a month in his red-painted hack offering sleeve holders and garters, thimbles, pins and ribbons, K. C. Baking Powder, soda, salt, and Cloverine Salve. He wore a flat black hat and a long black shirt that looked too hot to Harry. His beard formed a thick, round pad on his chest. When Harry first saw him, years ago, he laughed, but Andrew shushed him. "That old fellow has more stamina than you and me put together," he said. "He works hard and I wouldn't be surprised if he earns enough money someday to rent him a building or two in Oklahoma City. Then we'll be traveling to *him*."

As his mother counted her coins, Harry washed his tender wound in the kitchen. The chicks in the pen were getting downy and big. Harry cooed to them to take his mind off the soap's subtle sting. He remembered Olin's words, about the stage. Usually Harry kept quiet around his classmates. He sensed their jealousy and tried to fit in, but he couldn't. They mocked him: "Come *speak* to me, Boy Orator." "Oh, open your honey lips." Loneliness pierced his chest. Never, he thought. Never again will I give another speech.

He fed Halley some day-old bread then went to check on his dad.

Andrew was sleeping with the shades pulled. He always slept these days.

Annie Mae ran inside, her arms full, hoping to reach her kitchen shelves before she dropped all the powders, thimbles, creams. She didn't make it. Jars rolled across the wooden floor, frightening the chicks, who fluttered brainlessly against the twisted wire of their pen. Their thrashing excited Halley; he flitted around the table, barking, kicking jars out of Annie Mae's grasp. "Harry! Get this infernal creature out of here!" She'd been short-tempered ever since Andrew came home hurt. Harry stepped carefully around her. "That old Jew," she murmured, gathering her stuff. "I swear, he jacks his prices every month."

She put up her jars. Harry waited until she'd calmed herself, brewing dark tea. "Mama?" he said.

"What is it?"

He looked at the floor. "Is Daddy going to get better?"

"Oh, honey." Annie Mae swept a curl off her forehead. "You know what I think? I think he's saving his strength for—Harry, your shirt's soaked." She lifted the ragged tail, discovered the bruise. "How on earth—?"

He told her about school.

Her face went gray. She knelt beside him. Her long skirt bunched at her knees; he caught a rare glimpse of her ankles, milky in her stockings. "What am I going to do with you? What's all this fighting?"

"I didn't start it."

She patted his cheek. "It's those rough towns your daddy's been taking you to. Lord knows what you've seen."

"It's not that, Mama. No one likes me at school."

"Well, you won't be taking any trips for a while." She primped his shirt. "Maybe if you spend regular time here, you'll make some real friends. Will you try?"

"Yes, ma'am."

"Meanwhile, you have to help me out, okay? With your daddy down, I'm counting on you to stay out of trouble. I need you."

"All right." He smiled. He liked his mother's trust.

That night Andrew sat up for supper. He hadn't spoken in days. He slumped in his chair over steaming porridge, staring at his family with the startled expression he'd had when the Klansmen cornered him. He'd lost weight. Suspenders slipped off his shoulders, brushed the floor, where Halley playfully pawed them. "Honey, would you like some tea?" asked Annie Mae, lifting the cup. She talked to him gently, the way she talked to the chicks in her kitchen.

He smacked his dry lips. Black circles rimmed his eyes. "I need a blessing," he wheezed.

"Of course, Andrew, I pray for you every day. And Father McCartney asked the whole congregation to speak to God on your behalf."

Harry knew what he really meant. After supper, while Annie Mae scraped the dishes, Andrew grabbed Harry's arm and told him to walk into town on Saturday, get in touch with Warren Stargell, a buddy of his in the Socialist League. He knew Zeke Cash. "Tell him to tell Zeke it's an emergency."

The rest of the week Harry swelled with quiet anticipation of his mission. His mother trusted him, his father needed him. He wouldn't let them down, though what he really wanted was for them to agree he needn't do his chores, that he could talk and talk and talk to his dog and his mule.

At school he volunteered for games, trying to make friends. The boys played cops and robbers. Randy Olin was always the sheriff. Harry was his prisoner, in a cardboard box at the edge of the school lot. The box had once held textbooks and Harry could still smell in it fresh paper and ink—small consolation for the humiliation of crouching in the dark while Olin scuffed dirt at him and called him a killer. "You're going to pay for your crimes now, Shaughnessy. What do you have to say for yourself?"

"Nothing." In a Socialist world, would he have to be *everyone's* brother?

"What's that?"

Showy bully. "Put me out of my misery." Harry felt his cheeks burn and wondered if friendship was worth it.

Or they got into rock fights, teams of six or seven squaring off on either side of the school wagon, parked behind the outhouse. The rocks raised welts on the boys' bare arms, wounds they wore with pride. In these more active games Harry enjoyed himself, though he was always the last boy picked for a team. He wished summer vacation were months, not days, away. With a little more time the boys might start to like him.

At home he did his chores distractedly. He walked around the mule pen with Patrick Nagle, imagining ways to approach Warren Stargell. Each dusk, to call him in, his mother tapped the kitchen window with her thimble, a brisk cracking that carried clear across the yard. He kissed the mule good-night, scattered chickens as he ran through orange evening light. Breezes stirred the loose steel bins of the grain elevators; they groaned in the growing dark like old Apache warriors back from the dead, Harry thought, howling in loss and pain. Crows veered above sweet-scented columns of wheat.

Annie Mae lighted the coal-oil lamps, shading green the blond pine wood of the house. Over the stove she heated her curling iron. When it was hot enough to brown a page of newsprint she ran it slowly through her hair. Afterwards she figured the family's finances. The local coal companies were calling for timber to prop up their mines, but Andrew was in no shape to accommodate them. Harry could see she was worried about the bills.

He cleared dishes from the table, opened his books on the oil-cloth mat, and finished figuring the sums his teacher had assigned. Andrew slumped in his chair, nodding at his son: their little secret.

On Saturday morning Annie Mae set out on her weekly visits to the neighbors, to relax and gossip with her friends. She filled a basket with fresh brown bread. "Back this afternoon." She kissed Harry's cheek. "Watch your dad for me."

As soon as she left, Harry packed a turkey sandwich in a knapsack, promised his dad he'd hurry, and headed down the dirt-and-gravel highway to Walters.

Grasshoppers ticked against the cuffs of Harry's long denim pants. A violet sky, peppered with blue and gray clouds.

A shouting man in a Model T nearly ran him off the road. "Damn clanky things," Andrew always said of cars. "I swear, Model T's have shook more hell out of people than all the preachers in the county."

Eight years ago, spring rains and river floods had wiped out most of the roads. Harry didn't remember, but he'd heard his father's stories. The Oklahoma Territory passed a "road tax," requiring residents to spend four days a year grading and raising beds for proper drainage. "'Course, we all squawked like Thanksgiving turkeys running from the ax," Andrew said. "Fellows failed to show for work, the Territory fined 'em five bucks. Finally, they changed the law but we all wound up on the road gangs, anyway, otherwise we'd never have had clear paths into town."

Harry had asked him once, when they'd first started practicing speeches, "If you want to change a law, you squawk like a turkey?"

Andrew laughed so hard he popped a button. Since Anadarko, Harry missed his father's laughter. "No. It's better to *sell* a bunch of turkeys, then pass the jack along to your friendly congressman."

This was Harry's first political lesson. Recalling it now, he ached for his father's health. Maybe the whiskey would help.

Two shirtless young men with shovels cleared packed mud and stones from ruts where the automobile had passed. They nodded hello.

On the edge of town he saw other young men centering poles in a row in the ground, uncoiling rigid wire from giant wooden spools in a field. One of the workers winked at him. "What are you doing?" Harry asked.

"Gonna set some houses ablaze," the man said.

Harry unwrapped his sandwich, sat and watched awhile, recalling Bob Cochran's prediction: "Electric lights are just the beginning."

Shouldn't dawdle, he thought, rousing himself, shaking crumbs from his shirt and rolling up his knapsack. His ma would be back in just a few hours. The men strung wires like webs, crosshatching a section of sky. Harry tried to imagine pulsing light inside the lines waiting to explode in someone's home.

Walters, just west of the Shaughnessy farm, was a little smaller than Anadarko. In its ongoing bid to become the county seat, it called itself the "New Jerusalem," a farmers' paradise in the center of fertile bottomland. Harry had heard his father discuss the governance issue with his friends at political gatherings—he even understood most of what they said—and he was eager to poke around the place on his own.

This wasn't a market day, but Walters stores were blocked by heavy plows, farmers buying tools for next fall's harvest. Men with dark, rich soil on their hands sat talking in wagons or in shadows by the livery stable. Horseflies dived at the split carcass of a quail, shoved against the base of an empty water trough in front of the jail.

A leathery man on a mule strummed a guitar and sang:

> Farmer said to the boll weevil,
> "I see you at my door."
> "Yessir," said the boll weevil,
> "I been here before.
> Gonna get your home, gonna get your home."

On a nearly vacant side street Harry noticed the Jew Peddler's fiery red hack. The right front wheel had cratered, pitching the wagon forward at an abrupt and dangerous angle. Harry approached it cautiously, peering through the canvas curtain in back of the rolling store, inspecting the boxes and jars and paper-wrapped objects for sale. Red, yellow, and purple gleamed in a blade of sunlight through the narrow part in the curtain; he was dazzled by a blurry impression of crystals and soft, waxy edges. He knew these were simply the things his mother always bought—soaps and lotions and candles— but here in the dim wagon they appeared to be strange elixirs from a distant continent. An exotic scent—a mixture of greens and earth and musk—dizzied him. He turned aside to swallow air and ran into a looming black shirt. A huge hat hid the sun. Harry blinked. A fleshy animal rose in front of his face. Then he saw it was just a man's hand. "Hello. My name is Avram," said a low voice.

Reluctantly, Harry shook the hand and introduced himself. He didn't know why, but he was afraid to touch the man. Up close, Avram was younger than Harry would have guessed, probably in his late twenties or thirties, though it was hard to tell beneath the bramble of his thick black beard. Harry's father had told him, many times, not to judge people by their appearances, but no one else hereabouts looked as strange as Avram did, and Harry flinched from him, involuntarily. Besides, though his mother seemed to like the peddler, she always complained about his prices, as though he couldn't be wholly trusted.

"Yes. Young Harry. Your mother's told me all about you," Avram said. "Your speeches. Her sleeplessness when you travel."

Harry's face burned. He felt exposed. He wouldn't look up. "I won't be going anymore," he mumbled.

"Oh? I'm surprised. I thought you were much in demand."

"I don't know." Harry shrugged. "Accident?"

Avram thumped the shattered wheel. He wore a big ruby ring. "A stone in the street. I didn't see it until it was too late. Do you think you could help me move the wagon into that alley, out of the way? I'd appreciate it."

Harry really wanted to go, but no one else was coming by to help.

"It won't take a minute," Avram said.

The man's heavy, hooded eyelids reminded Harry of looks he'd seen on the faces of lizards—a kind of cold and brooding amusement.

Was that the peddler's true manner? Harry fought his fear and revulsion; after all, Avram was what his father would call a "fellow worker." "Okay," he said.

Avram unhooked his mule from the hack, secured it to a post. Then, while Harry pushed from behind, he steered the wagon into a shadow, carrying it on his back where the wheel had disengaged. Afterwards, sweat trickled like dew through the rings of his beard. "Let me see," he said, crawling through the curtain. "Perhaps I have—" He combed through fallen bottles. "Yes." He popped back out and handed Harry a tall, curved flask. "Homemade lemonade," Avram said. "For a job well done. Thank you. It's a little warm, I'm afraid." He grabbed the broken wheel and walked with Harry through town. A woman with a shady parasol, crossing the street, gave them a curious glance.

"Tell me, are you leaving the road because of what happened in Anadarko?" Avram asked.

"My mother told you?"

"Yes."

Harry felt shy again, to be so *revealed* to a stranger, especially one as odd as Avram. "My dad was badly hurt. He may not get well."

"I heard. I'm sorry." Avram studied the boy. "Forgive me, it's none of my business," he said, "but if you let those men silence you, you're doing just what they want, you know? They've won. You realize that?" He grunted, shifted the wheel to his other arm.

Harry blew into the flask. "So?" His voice sank, trapped in the glass.

"So . . . don't you believe in what you say?"

"Of course." He didn't like being challenged this way.

Avram laid a hand on his shoulder, stopped him too roughly in the street. "Then you must keep saying it."

Harry glanced up. The man wasn't tall but the sunlight above and behind him swelled his frame.

"You're right," Harry said. "It's none of your business."

Avram nodded but wouldn't let go. "I know you're afraid. There's reason to be."

"I'm not afraid," Harry said. Who was this man to judge him, this funny-looking man? "They hate me at school. It's getting better—" He caught himself. Now *he* was baring his secrets. He wanted to run away.

"You're special, that's why."

Harry cocked his head.

"Your mother's convinced. I trust her. A smart, solid woman, your mother. A prudent buyer."

"She said that? About me?"

"She says you have a gift."

"Really?" Pleased and embarrassed, he twisted the flask in his hands. They'd arrived at a blacksmith's shop. Avram dropped the wheel. "Here we are," he said. "I hope I haven't overstepped my bounds. Thank you again for your help."

"You're welcome."

"Will you pardon an old man's concerns?"

Harry smiled and looked away. How old *was* he? Who could tell?

"My people," Avram said, scratching his beard, "have been chased and silenced all over the world. But still we persist." He offered his hand again, then disappeared inside the shop, which smelled of ashes and lye, a hot, stabbing odor, and clattered with the chilly *ping*s of hammers.

Avram was probably a decent sort, after all, Harry decided, but still he felt relieved to get away from the peculiar eyes and wiry beard. His distrust of the man shamed him.

As he turned to go, he noticed a poster tacked to the blacksmith's door. Kate O'Hare was speaking tomorrow in Waurika. His heart jumped. Kate O'Hare!

Recently, his father had told him about this woman. She'd come from Kansas, the daughter of a farmer who'd lost his savings in the drought of '87. A former machinist, trade unionist, and now a committed Socialist, she was praised as one of the finest speakers of the cause. Harry longed to hear her, to learn her inflections and gestures. He could almost taste the road again, in the sweetness of the lemonade, the dust on his lips from the street.

He stuffed Avram's flask in a back pocket and ran for the barbershop where his dad said he'd find Warren Stargell. His mother said he had a gift!—the thought made him smile (she was so hard to read) but then he felt sorry, running off like this without her okay. All week he'd schemed without her knowing, practicing remarks in Patrick Nagle's pen: "Sir, we need your help on a mission of mercy." "Could I trouble you, sir, with an urgent request?" His mother thought he was doing his chores. His belly hurt when he imagined her face; maybe he should cancel his secret task.

Just then, though, Warren Stargell glimpsed him through the barbershop window. "Well lookee here, if it ain't the Boy Orator," he yelled, stepping into the open doorway. He held a blank brown domino. "How's your pappy, Harry?"

Harry was startled. He'd forgotten the lines he'd perfected. "He needs . . ." He remembered his father's words. "He needs a touch of medicine. From Zeke Cash."

Warren Stargell roared. His belly, big as a coal sack, swayed above his belt. "Good. Sounds like he's getting his dander back up. You tell him no problem. I'm riding to Lawton on Monday. I'll stop by early next week with the cure." He ruffled Harry's hair.

The barber shook a bottle of tonic; it hiccuped. The man in the chair, waiting for a shave, chuckled over something. Dark curls sailed in the air. On the wall, the razor strap, twisting in a breeze from the door, bumped a coppery mirror. Harry felt bad about his mother again, standing here in this world of men. Like the boys at school who mocked his speeches, the brewers in the hills who kidded him when he drank, the men who beat his father, these fellows, trading sly confidences over dominoes, were full of secrets that had nothing to do with home. Since Anadarko, Harry understood that awful laughter and danger often accompanied circles of men. Dark looks. Jokes. He wanted out of here, but Warren Stargell held his arm. "You see where Kate O'Hare's testifying in Waurika?"

"I just saw the poster," Harry said.

"When're *you* gonna speak again? What does Andrew say?"

"My ma doesn't want me to."

"Your ma—hell, we need you, Harry, you're good for business. Who can resist that baby face, eh?" He squeezed Harry's cheeks. "The league's arranging a circuit, three or four of our best speakers, make a little tour next month. What do you say?"

"I don't know."

"All right, we'll work on her when I come out next week. Take care of your pappy, you hear? He's a good man."

"I will." My mother's good too, he thought.

" 'Ataboy."

On the road home, remorseful, Harry passed the electric wires, hooked now to all the poles. He saw in a nice house a warm, orange glow, just visible in the midafternoon sunlight; the silhouette of a woman sweeping a kitchen.

His mother wouldn't let him see Kate O'Hare. "Once and for all, I want you to get this politicking out of your system. It's no business for a little boy. Besides, you've got plenty to do around here." He didn't argue. He still felt guilty about his trip into town, and tried to atone with his chores. In the evenings, though, when all his work was done, he sat on the gate of the mule pen and raised both his arms. "You ask me why I'm a Socialist!" he shouted, choosing one of his father's fervent themes, extemporizing on it, paraphrasing Oscar Ameringer.

Patrick Nagle's ears bobbed. He kicked up dirt. Halley panted, wagged his tail. "I'll tell you, friends. Money-love and the two-party system are the roots of all evil, strangling the uninformed voter. The national banking system is the tree. The trusts are its branches, bearing poisoned fruit. Brothers!" Patrick Nagle raised his head and let out a squeal. "The sunlight of liberty is setting behind mountains of sin!" Halley ran deliriously around the pen, yapping, chasing bugs.

Harry had forgotten his boredom on the road, his classmates' taunts. All he remembered now was the excitement of the crowds. The applause. "Turkey in the Straw," "The Arkansas Traveler"— songs of the fiddlers who sometimes played before he talked. He pictured skinny women dancing—"malnourished," his father had said—stooped farmers shouting affirmation. The combination of music, stews on open fires, the beat of his own rushing words made him dizzy. Giddy with delight. How could he give up so much fun?

Avram, Kate O'Hare, and Warren Stargell had turned him, like a weather vane, in the right direction again.

His impromptu speeches restored Andrew a little, even as they worried Annie Mae. "That's my boy," Andrew mumbled, sitting on the porch. "God, don't he make you want to lay down your life?"

Annie Mae covered his shoulders with a heavy patchwork quilt. "I'm glad you're home," she whispered in his ear.

He patted her hand. For the first time in days his gaze settled on her face. "Yes. It's a nice home, isn't it?"

In spite of everything, she almost answered, aware of her daily chores in each gripping twinge in her back. "It ought to be. We crossed a mighty rough river to get here."

"Only because I made you. I was right, now wasn't I?"

She smiled. "I'll never admit it."

"Things haven't turned out so bad, have they?"

"Not so bad." She kissed his cheek. "How are you feeling?"

"Better this evening," Andrew said. "You? You look tired."

"A bit."

"Take a rest tonight, Annie."

"There's a few more bills to pay before bed." Her back screamed. She stood up straight.

"Annie?"

"It'll pass." Fiercely, she pressed her palms into her hips. Each week, she prayed for the torment to cease—the same misery she'd felt after Harry was born, recurring now month after month. She knew she shouldn't pray selfishly; there were much bigger favors to ask of the Lord, said Father McCartney, than one's own personal comfort. "Catholics are under attack here, daily," he often reminded his congregation, "so it's incumbent upon us to put the community first," and she knew this was true.

In '98, right after she and Andrew had crossed the river, a Baptist preacher stumped the countryside with seven "rescued nuns." The incident proved to Annie Mae how welcome her faith was locally. The women testified to being tortured by evil priests in the convent, forced to learn "devil's words" and curses. The preacher damned Rome's growing influence. A day or two later, an enterprising journalist exposed the "nuns" as Oklahoma City prostitutes, and a mob with lighted torches ran the revivalists into Texas. Still, most folks here were willing to believe the worst of Irish immigrants. They carried a "European virus," according to some of the papers, "harmful to our homegrown way of life." Father McCartney said Catholic merchants frequently changed their names and hid their beliefs so sales wouldn't suffer.

Annie Mae wasn't about to worship in secret. She proudly joined a Catholic temperance league, and was one of the few women who attended town meetings of the Friends of Irish Freedom. Each week she cheered speakers who disdained the British Empire. "Sinn Fein!" she shouted with her fellows, celebrating a hopeful new movement in Belfast. "Rehabilitate Ireland from within!"

She liked her new life, her Indian friends, and the church. She liked sitting with her family in the sanctuary. Her only regret these days was letting Andrew take Harry on the road. Irish politics, an ocean away, was one thing. Local wrangles, seething with high tempers and swift retribution, were a different matter entirely. Just last month, a Socialist organizer had been hanged in Panther Run, south of Walters. She hadn't slept for days after that.

Her men were home now, though, regaining their strength. She kissed Andrew's cheek, adjusted the quilt on his arms. "I'm so happy to see you improving," she said.

He held her hand. "Maybe tomorrow I can ride into town, talk to the fellows from the Osage mines, set up a sale."

"Let's not rush things," she said, but she felt the stress in her back unwind for the first time in weeks. She watched Harry gesture and declaim in the shadows of the mule pen. Usually he was her shy little boy, quiet and polite, she thought, but when it came to politics he'd talk to any waking creature. Durn him, she told herself. Along with his father's ideas, he'd inherited Andrew's sentimental streak. Both her men thought the planet was theirs for the changing. "Harry, time to wash up for bed!"

Later, as she blew out the lamps, raising a drifting, dusky smell in the house, she heard him whisper through his window to the yard, "Good night, brothers! Stay brave!"

A FEW DAYS AFTER Harry's trip into Walters, Warren Stargell showed up with Zeke Cash and a case of corn liquor.

Before Annie Mae could object to anything, Zeke told Harry, "Run get your mama's Bible. Psalms 104—"

"The Good Book says nothing about mash whiskey, Mr. Cash."

"If Jesus was born in Oklahoma, Miz Shaughnessy, his daddy would've been a bootlegger 'stead of a carpenter, and that's a natural fact."

Warren Stargell shook Andrew's hand. "I promised your boy here I'd rescue you."

Annie Mae frowned at Harry. He blushed. She turned to go

inside; Andrew, from his seat on the porch, grasped her arm. "A few drops, honey. For fortitude. I know it'll help."

"You know how I feel about that stuff."

"Honestly—"

"Annie Mae, I hear you want to retire the Boy Orator here," Warren Stargell said. He patted Harry's back. "I'm afraid we can't let you do that. We need him on the circuit, starting next month. School'll be out—"

"Please excuse me," said Annie Mae. She strode into her house, slammed the door behind her. Zeke laughed. Warren Stargell popped the cork on a dark, smoky bottle. "Zeke's best," he said. "Hops, tobacco, fishberries, barley . . ."

Harry ran inside. His mother was feeding the chicks in their pen. "I'm sorry," he murmured.

"You should be." She wouldn't look at him. "I take it you've not only become a whiskey distributor, you've planned your summer as well."

"Mama—"

"Go outside, Harry." Her cheeks had flared a spotty red, the color of late-season raspberries, Harry thought. "I want to be alone now."

Her tears made him shiver. Her kitchen was the warmest room in the house; she'd never let him in it again. He rushed into the yard, toward Patrick Nagle's pen. His father and his friends were shouting with laughter. He heard a cork pop. Yesterday he'd buried Bob Cochran's yellow kerchief and Avram's lemonade flask in a bed of straw just inside the barn; he went to them now as to a treasure, a life of his own apart from his mother and father, the worlds of women and men. Sunbeams filled the holes in the barn's split slats; he inhaled the straw's damp smell, a scent that would always, after this day—as it did to him now—bring a wistful sting of sorrow to his eyes.

The kerchief and the flask, souvenirs of the road, made him ache again for travel. Their textures, much smoother than the ragged hoe he held every day, the splintery spine of the rake, sailed his thoughts to the east, the west, the north, leagues away from the farm, Andrew's injury, Annie Mae's anger.

But his mother's face wouldn't leave him in peace. It followed him now in his mind. He hadn't meant to hurt her. His father had needed him. He'd tried to do his best for them both.

He secured his treasures again in a little hill of hay, then went to find a spring and a chain, in a bin in the back of the barn. He'd make a gopher trap. Yes, that was the thing to do. He remembered Annie Mae complaining about her ravaged garden just this morning: tomato vines shredded, radish plants crushed. If he could catch one of the critters, she might forgive him.

Gonna get you, gonna get you.

For the rest of the day he whittled blunt notches in a pine stake to fit into the lip of a wooden pan. It was always best to set a trap after a good hard rain, Andrew had told him once: gophers dug fresh mounds then, plugging their burrows with dirt to equalize the barometric pressure. Harry wondered how they knew about barometric pressure. Anyway, he couldn't control the weather, but he could follow the rest of his father's advice. The plan was to slide the pan with its spring lid inside the narrow entrance to a gopher's hole; when the animal wriggled in, the lid would close, and you'd pull the whole thing out with the chain.

Town Hall in Walters paid a penny apiece for gopher paws, to encourage the pests' capture.

All afternoon, as he worked in the sweet-smelling barn, cooled by the frequent flapping of the horned owl in the rafters, Harry glanced past the heavy red door to his mother's kitchen window, watching her shadow.

THAT NIGHT ANNIE MAE helped Andrew out of his clothes and tucked him into bed, careful not to bump his swollen leg. His snores reminded her of ice in early spring, thawing on ponds, crackling and heaving, sounds she'd heard the April afternoon he kissed her first, twenty years ago.

She folded his pants over the mahogany quilt rack, and remembered her handsome young beau. On her fifteenth birthday he'd come calling first thing in the morning; he had his daddy's wagon, drawn by a drooling old mare. They'd headed east out of Bonham, toward the honeysuckle groves west of Paris. He'd been courting her for six months then, ever since they'd met, sweating and filthy, in a cotton field at harvest time. He was lanky and tan, with sandy hair and a big, easy smile. From the first, she'd fancied his manner, respectful and kind.

Annie Mae's parents had both died in an influenza epidemic when she was five; she'd been raised by her father's sister, Jenny Dodderer. Jenny, big as a rain barrel, had a pair of boys, always fistfighting and cursing. She only relaxed when Andrew dropped by. "The Shaughnessys are good people," she told Annie Mae when Andrew had first come calling. "Tireless workers, thoughtful neighbors. You be nice to that boy." Jenny gussied up for him in her best cotton dress, and loved to bake him oatmeal cookies.

That morning, when he'd arrived to celebrate Annie Mae's birthday, he'd stood on Jenny's back porch praising her "do" (she'd cut her gray hair short in front of her bedroom mirror). He snatched a handful of cookies. "I swear, I could live on your sweets, ma'am," he said. "Sometimes at night, I dream I'm swimming in your chocolate, a big old backstroke." Jenny blushed.

"You're shameless," Annie Mae told him in the wagon, on their way to the spicy groves. "Flattering an old woman so you can steal her niece." She sat beside him on the rickety buckboard seat, fiercely gripping his arm.

"I can turn around and take you back."

"Don't you dare."

The white and yellow honeysuckle buds, bursting with sugary dew, trembled as Andrew parked the wagon in their midst. He helped her down. Sunlight was beginning to unlock the ice on the ponds. Steam rose through the oaks' fingered leaves. Andrew pulled her close. She could feel her aunt's cookies on his hands, the grit of the crumbs when he smoothed her cheeks. His lips were cold, brushing her skin. "I love you," he whispered once, between a flurry of bird-like kisses, and she knew right then she'd marry this boy, this decent young man, if he asked.

Now, the liquor on his breath burned her nose. The house smelled bitter and scorched, from all the blown-out lamps. She pooled the sheet loosely around the heat of his tender leg, leaned over, touched her fingers to his lips. This impossible man. This life of hers. Well. She was luckier than most women she knew. He was a foolish dreamer, like his father, stubborn and sometimes naive, but he never raised a hand to her. She didn't have to sew or take in laundry for a living, as Jenny did for years. Annie Mae even knew a woman near Temple whose husband had forced her to do the family washing, drawing water from a cold cistern, a day after birthing a set of twins. "God bless you," she whispered to Andrew, though even as she said it, she felt annoyed again at the way he pushed their son. She was just as proud as Andrew of Harry's talents, his ability to carry himself well among adults, but she feared—she knew—he was growing too fast. Buying whiskey for his father!

Tonight, she chained the front door, a precaution she didn't nor-mally take, since the family lived so far from other folks. But Zeke and Warren Stargell had passed out in the barn. Annie Mae was in no mood to entertain a groggy drunk who might wake and take a notion to go poking around in the dark. She remembered the ferry captain, that awful fellow on the river, all those years ago. What was his name? Peters? Parker? She'd known, even then, what the future looked like. She shook her head bitterly. Men like Parker—like Andrew since the beating—everywhere she turned. She checked the chain again.

* * *

SHE MADE THE MEN hotcakes and bacon the next day and the day after that. They seemed in no hurry to leave. At Andrew's request, they borrowed his wagon and fetched the coal boys. For two days they all sat in her yard, Andrew and his friends, Mr. Lechman and Mr. Gibson from the Osage mines, passing bottles, making deals. She didn't understand why men needed whiskey to talk to each other freely.

While the men got drunker and drunker, she and Mahalie soaped shirts, darned socks, dug a rose bed. Mahalie's sudden appearances by the house had always startled Annie Mae—at first, she never knocked or said hello. She waited for someone to come outside and find her. "Why do you do this?" Annie Mae asked her one day. "It scares me when you sneak up on me like that."

"I'm still unsure of white people's ways. You scare me too."

"Mahalie, you're my friend. I'm always glad to see you. Please knock on my door."

From then on, Mahalie pounded hard enough to shake the sugar from the shelves.

Even now, after all their time together, she was usually quiet at the beginnings of their visits, then, in the midst of laundering or cooking, she'd start a story as though Annie Mae had asked her a question. This was how Annie Mae learned of the march Mahalie's people had made from Mississippi, a generation ago, forced by the government to leave their home. Wolves and buzzards tracked their every move, Mahalie's father had told her. There wasn't time to bury anyone who died of exhaustion or hunger. Her grandmother's body had been abandoned by the side of a road, covered loosely with willow limbs.

When she was two her mother died. Following Choctaw custom, her father gave her away to an aunt and uncle. This couple didn't really like children; she'd spent many years living in silence, working like an animal in the fields.

Annie Mae didn't know how to react when Mahalie told her these things. Her friend had great dignity and pride. She might consider sympathy an insult. Annie Mae decided to honor her by sharing her own confidences, and this seemed the proper thing to do. She'd always wanted more children, she admitted now, but she'd miscarried twice since Harry, fueling the pains in her back. Soon she'd be too old to have another chance. "Nowadays I don't even know my own boy. It's not like him to sneak off without telling me."

They watched Harry play with Halley, dangling the yellow kerchief like a bullfighter's cape, urging the dog to charge him. Harry had apologized to her again, and this morning she'd baked him some oatmeal cookies, using her aunt's old recipe. He'd tried to catch a gopher for her. "I set the trap in a tunnel by your garden, and this big old monster tripped the pan just like he was supposed to," he'd told her, breathless, both excited and embarrassed by his morning's adventure. "But then, when I tugged the chain, he started hissing something fierce, and it scared me. I hesitated just a bit, and I'm sorry, but he got away."

"That's okay, son." She'd rubbed his thick red hair. "I appreciate you giving it a shot for me. I really do."

"The world is calling to him," Mahalie told her now. "If you try too much to tie him down, he may leave and not return."

"I know." Annie Mae swallowed hard.

She saw Warren Stargell toss a bottle into the yard. He ambled up the porch steps. Always, a mischievous squint lighted his lazy left eye, shining in the corner like a wicked little tear. It unsettled her.

"Annie Mae, we need to chat," he said. He smelled damp, pickled, ripe.

"Oh?"

"Now listen to me, 'cause I'm only going to say this once." He swayed a little, talked to the shirts at her feet. "I want your boy on the road next month, spreading the truth. Whether you're aware of it or not, he's one of the finest speakers in this great state of ours, a downright progidy—"

"I think you mean prodigy, Mr. Stargell, and I'll thank you to call me Mrs. Shaughnessy. *And* to give me credit for knowing my own son's abilities. Furthermore, I want you *to leave my property and take your brutish friends with you!*" Immediately, she hoped the other men hadn't heard her; after all, two of them were Andrew's business partners.

Warren Stargell tried to tip his hat then apparently realized he wasn't wearing one. "Thanks for your hospitality, ma'am." He walked carefully down the porch steps then turned to face her again. "He wants it," he said.

"Excuse me?"

"Harry. The road. He wants it real bad. You know he does." He smiled. "Zeke, my boy, let's get!" he called across the yard.

"The gall!" said Annie Mae, but Mahalie wasn't there to hear. She'd fled at the first sound of raised voices. Later, she told Annie Mae, "White folks angry always means trouble for people like me."

As she watched her husband stumble with his cane, Annie Mae knew, as firmly as she knew how much the family owed and couldn't pay, her troubles were just beginning.

PART TWO

The Heart of the Planet

3

The mules plodded in the direction of the sun wherever it moved in the sky. Harry had to keep a tight grip on the reins to hold the wagon straight.

Snakeweed and creamy yellow sumac lined the road under scruffy junipers, the kind his mama called "alligator trees" because of their rough gray bark.

His dad was sleeping off his binge on the buckboard seat beside him. Yesterday he'd taken Harry and Annie Mae for a picnic in a bright green meadow near the house. He'd prepared all the food. He picked a bouquet of widow's tears and asked Annie Mae to forgive him for the whiskey. "Anadarko threw me but I'm over it now. I promise," he'd said. "It's time to be a family again."

Annie Mae smiled and seemed to relax but her face fell when Harry mentioned he might get to share a stage with Kate O'Hare. Warren Stargell had told him so. She wouldn't talk at all when Andrew said he and Harry had to rent a couple of mules, leave in the morning for the mines. He'd promised Lechman and Gibson he'd visit a few sites and assess their timber needs.

Earlier, Harry had ridden to school and turned in his final homework assignment, a series of algebraic equations. Randy Olin gave him a hateful glance but he didn't care now. The sun was on his face, he was free for the summer—cotton-picking season was three months away—and he might get to speak again soon. He wasn't going to let anything ruin his pleasant mood.

He'd never been to the mines with his dad. Andrew needed him this time because his leg was still sore and his back was stiff. He couldn't drive the wagon and he wasn't sure he could manage underground in some of the narrow shafts. Before he'd fallen asleep he'd told Harry that, where they were headed today, coal lay so near the surface of the ground, the veins had once been mined by plow. "Lots of Italians working there now. Friendly fellows—and good free thinkers. With the proper push they might even build a union someday."

Harry stopped and watered the mules, ate a dry ham sandwich he'd packed. By nightfall he'd steered the wagon into the hills. Tuckahoe leaves shaped like little spades brushed the wheels, purple pickerelweed trembled on the banks of a shallow, dusky pond. Harry heard a fish jump. Andrew guided him toward an irregular row of tents where the air smelled of sulphur: the evening's first lanterns. Crickets trilled in the ferns.

Andrew leaned on Harry's shoulders, hopped to the ground on his good leg, dragged the cane behind him. "Let's see if they've got some grub," he said, limping toward a large, lighted tent with a sign that said "Supplies." Inside, wooden shelves held dozens of Vaseline jars, bottles of iodoform labeled "Burn Relief." Raw linseed oil filled a barrel by the cash register. A man stood behind it, rolling cigarettes next to a candle. "Looks like they're ready for anything," Andrew said.

"Except supper," Harry mumbled. Behind him, moths tapped the tent's loose flaps.

"Evening, Frank," Andrew said to the man. "Are we too late to grab a can of beans?"

"Mr. Shaughnessy! Pleasure to see you again. Lord, man, what happened to your leg?"

"Got in a little scrape but I'm better now, thanks."

"Wellsir, I don't sell food no more. Since you's here, Osage has built a eat-hall over by the boardinghouse. Serves eggs and grits for company scrip. That's where everyone goes this time of night." He sprinkled tobacco into his palm from a little cloth sack.

"Eggs and grits it is, then," Andrew said.

"This your boy? The little preacher you's telling me about last time?"

"Yes. Harry, this is Frank. Say hello."

"I gotta warn you, Mr. Shaughnessy, the new manager, fellow named Fawkes, he don't abide union talk or nothing of the kind. He's thrown a couple of boys outta camp already. Best watch yourself."

Andrew nodded. "All right. Thank you, Frank."

Harry helped his father back into the wagon, circled the pond, heading north. Dew shivered from drooping pines all around them. Venus pulsed above the tallest limbs. Recent rains had muddied the roads, gouged them with twigs and weeds. Andrew grabbed his leg whenever the wagon lurched. A woman's voice drifted through the trees, carried, it seemed, on panes of light from a yellow window up ahead. Harry stopped the mules.

A sign on a square pine building said "Floor Space—25 Cents A Night." The window they'd seen was set in a low building next to the boardinghouse. Someone had painted "Beaver Trap" on a two-by-four above the door. Harry heard the woman's voice again, weaving through laughter and shouts: a woeful tale of squandered love.

Andrew's cane sank several inches into the ground. He tripped, muddying his pants. Stale sweat and cigarette smoke nearly smothered Harry as soon as he opened the door, along with something else—dust and ash, bitter clay. He couldn't be sure. Faces turned his way, scratchy and dim like the old, sepia-tinted photographs his mother kept of her Irish family. Glimpses of whiskers, flat brown eyes. Bruises and scars, purple burns on bony cheeks. Women danced around the room, dropped into laps, raising dust from the miners' grubby clothes. Perfume and liquor, dizzying, sweet. Kohl stained the singer's cheeks.

Andrew ordered scrambled eggs for Harry and himself, let a buddy buy him a drink. Harry sat on a stool in a corner by a black upright piano, listening to the talk. These were the ruggedest, weariest men he'd ever seen but they certainly knew their politics. They cursed Governor Haskell for stealing state funds; damned the Democrats, who wanted all voters to pass a literacy test—a blatant attempt to exclude most Negroes.

One man wondered aloud in lilting, heavily accented English, "How can the party betray its own ideals?"

His listeners shook their heads. Harry said, "Simple. Standard Oil." He'd heard his father say this dozens of times, usually when they practiced speeches in the barn, or read aloud together from Oscar Ameringer's pamphlets.

The man who had spoken looked at him with one eye closed and a twitching mustache.

"Campaign contributions in exchange for looser drilling regulations." Harry stood and stuffed his hands in his pockets. The singer's voice cracked on a throaty lament. "And that, gentlemen, is just one in a long series of Democratic compromises. The Republicans, of course, have never been a viable alternative."

The men laughed to hear such serious conversation from a boy, but nodded gravely. "I like-a this kid," said the mustached Italian. He slid a bottle of corn whiskey across the table to Harry. He shook his head but happily joined the discussion. The men were lively and smart. He thought it might be good to be a miner.

A short man in a gray suit and bowler hat entered the hall. Quickly, people tried to hide their liquor, under tables or behind the bar. The man saw them but didn't say anything. He walked straight up to Andrew. "How-do. Name's Dugan," he said, planting his feet like a gunfighter in the dime novels Harry sometimes read. "I assume you've heard by now we've got a new manager here. Lester Fawkes. I'm his assistant. You're Andrew Shaughnessy?"

"That I am. How'd you know me?"

"Oh, I know things, Mr. Shaughnessy. For example, I understand you have an arrangement with Mr. Gibson and Mr. Lechman."

"I do."

"Fine. I'm not here to interfere. But I also understand you have a reputation for agitation."

Everyone listened, frowning, tense. A cook brought Harry an egg on a warped tin plate.

"The owners make their deals in clean, comfy rooms," Dugan said. "They don't have to worry about on-site operations. They don't hear the stories. Me—my bloody ears ache, end of the day. Work's disrupted for any reason—any reason whatsoever—Fawkes and I have to answer for it." He spat a brown stream into a cuspidor by the bar. "The Osage mines produce the finest steam coal west of Pennsylvania and I aim to see it stays that way, understand?"

Andrew slipped a protective arm around Harry's shoulders. "I've never hidden my inclinations from your bosses, Mr. Dugan. Whatever my disagreements with them, I can be trusted in business. They know that."

"Good." Dugan smiled. "Glad to hear it. Welcome back, then. Just wanted to introduce myself. You'll find I'm a prince as long as we maintain our production schedule. You have a pleasant evening now." He tipped his hat. Before he left the hall he yelled, "You boys better not be drinking *alcohol* in here!" Harry knew he'd seen the whiskey; so did everyone else. Clearly, Dugan allowed them this little rebellion to head off bigger trouble. Harry was both abashed and impressed by this show of power.

When Dugan had gone, several of the miners slapped Andrew's back or shook his hand. Swedes, Russians, Italians, Lithuanians. The men's clashing accents formed a rousing, dissonant music in the air.

As Andrew was exchanging money for company scrip the singer slipped into his lap. She wore a dress as red as her hair. Lip rouge smeared her dimpled chin, making little X's. "How 'bout a friend tonight?"

"No, thanks," Andrew said.

"What about him?" She poked Harry's chest. He stumbled backwards.

"He's twelve."

The woman stood and pulled Harry toward the peach-scented cleft at the top of her dress. "Twelve's old enough, right?"

"Yes," Harry stammered, not sure what he was agreeing to. The softness and warmth of the woman's skin paralyzed him.

"Finish your supper, Harry," Andrew said. The singer stuck out her tongue, danced toward the bar with a laugh.

They finished eating, unloaded the wagon, fed and secured the mules. In the doorway of the boardinghouse Andrew gave a guard two Osage certificates worth fifty cents. It was dark inside. Harry tripped over half a dozen grumbling men as he groped for vacant floor space. A man lit a cigarette; in the brief flare Harry saw yellowed newspapers on the walls. The place smelled of dirty feet, damp wool. He heard what must have been a rat skittering over gritty boards in a corner. Coughing and snores. Sloshing whiskey.

Andrew stretched out beside him in a narrow nest between saddle bags, boots, and men. He whispered, "I don't think your mother needs to know the kind of conditions—"

"Shhh!" someone said.

"All right, all right!"

Harry lay awake listening to the owls in the hills; they were high-pitched, catlike in their calling, not like the deep, rolling hoots of the

Great Horneds he was used to hearing on the banks of the Red River. An unknown bird *peer-peer-peer*ed in a tree just outside the door, huffed a great wind with its wings, and splashed the surface of the pond.

He recalled the singer's smell, the delicate swell of her breasts against his cheek, but it was Bob Cochran's companion, Sue-Sue, prettier than the singer, he kept seeing: her straight dark hair, her copper skin.

He got cold in the night, woke with sore bones and a crick in his neck. He heard a man praying in a language he didn't understand.

Mist seeped between boards in the walls, through rips in the newspaper strips, when his father whispered it was time to get up. The sun wasn't out. The birds were still. Harry followed Andrew next door to the dining hall. Their boots crunched acorns and frost-rimed pine needles in gravel. True summer was still a week or so away. They ordered eggs again and toast and buttered grits. The place was full of breath-clouds, tobacco smoke.

They loaded the wagon and drove to the Number Nine Mine.

At the shaft house, a square wooden structure no bigger than an outhouse, Andrew shook hands with a man in a long canvas coat. He wore a round metal hat with a little candle stuck in front. "Light me up, Andrew. I'm the gasman this morning." Andrew struck a match and held it to the candle. The man grabbed a kerosene lamp, stepped onto a platform—it reminded Harry of a washtub. Several fellows, including Andrew, tugged greasy ropes; the platform disappeared into the ground.

The gasman had to probe each cavity, Andrew told Harry, check the air circulation, locate leaking gas. "He makes it safe for the rest of us."

The fellows smoked, rubbed their arms for warmth. The sun still wasn't up. Occasionally a bell sounded from below, signaling the men to drop the ropes some more. They talked softly about friends they'd lost in other mines, suffocated by afterdamp or buried in rockslides after misfired windy shots.

An hour later they hauled the gasman up. A flaky black film chalked his cheeks. When he grinned, his teeth were as straight as piano keys. He said, "Safe as a baby's crib down there."

Andrew snatched a measuring stick, his level, and drafting tools from the wagon. He assured the others Harry was a mature, responsible boy who'd do as he was told.

"He don't bother me," one said. "There's younger'n him in some of these drifts."

Another gave Harry a canvas coat, too large, and a hard hat. He struggled to keep his hands and eyes uncovered. Andrew lit the candle on his head. They stood beside two young miners on the platform. It jerked, started to sink. Harry watched the men's muscles as they worked the ropes around him, saw the first sunlight on the hills. Stars began to fade. Then he was traveling through earth.

He couldn't breathe. The smell of creosote and sputtering paraffin torches singed his nostrils. Water trickled over and across the yellow walls around him. The rope pulleys squeaked; the platform rocked against wet stone. The shaft became narrower, darker, black and shimmering green. A wooden pallet appeared, floating in the light of their torches. "Here," Andrew said. One of their companions tugged something Harry couldn't see. A bell rang, hurting his ears, echoing endlessly. The platform stopped with a violent jump. He lost his balance, reached for the walls. His hands slipped on moist brown clods thick with roots. His father gripped his arm.

"Hand me that pickax," Andrew said to one of the men. With the blunt end he tapped each board in the pallet, wedged into rock. Then Andrew thumped the thin oak supports on either side of the tunnel's opening. The wood was wet and soft. "Is this a busy drift?" he asked.

The miners nodded.

"Harry, step on out into the room. I can't get back there with my leg."

Harry left the platform, moving cautiously onto the pallet. His candle flickered. He was standing in a tunnel that spiraled as far as he could see into the earth. He imagined himself a bee in a vast, dank honeycomb.

"Take this ax," Andrew said. "Gently, gently now, tap those boards above your head. What kind of sound do they make?"

"Sort of hollow," Harry said, hoisting the ax. Dust scratched his eyes.

"You sure?"

"Yessir."

"Have to replace 'em," Andrew said. "One more time, Harry, double-check. Listen closely now. Don't let the echo throw you."

He blinked, raised the ax. With his eyes closed he smashed the boards harder than he wanted. A chunk of rotted wood the size of a milk bucket tore from the ceiling with a *crack*, thunked his shoulder, jolting the ax from his hand. It flew past the lip of the pallet. "Jesus!" said one of the miners, leaping back. His arm hit a rope attached to the platform's railing. Harry slipped, lost his hat. His candle went out. Dust and splinters and pebbles showered his head and back. He heard the ax bouncing off rocks in the dark. The platform made a scraping sound; his father yelled. "Whoa, whoa!" the miners screamed. The bell clanged once, twice.

"Harry, Harry you all right?" Andrew said. His voice drifted up from below with a cloud of dirt. The platform had tottered several feet.

"I'm fine. I can't see." He felt the edge of the pallet, empty space beyond. A sudden, rushing dizziness. He coughed, couldn't get air.

"Don't move," Andrew said. The words, echoing, seemed to come from three different places at once. Harry crawled back, away from the edge, rested his aching shoulder against rough, jutting stone. He'd never experienced darkness so complete. It had weight and a shape, big enough to swallow a man. Though the tunnel was warm, his pain made him shiver.

The men rang a series of bell-signals, managed to get the platform level with the pallet again. Andrew pulled Harry to safety. Their dirty grins in the candlelight dissipated anger and fear. "They'll take that ax out of our pay," said one of the miners but he was smiling, relieved that no one was hurt.

"I'm sorry," Harry said. "I didn't mean to—"

"It was about to go anyway, kid. Don't worry. We've all had our share of close shaves down here."

Swaying there on the platform, wheezing in the dark, Harry saw how physical danger could be a kind of intimacy. It could make a stranger a friend. The shared panic and animal joy of survival sparked a deeper recognition of frailty and chance, the sense that together you'd cheated death—or life?—a little. Harry began to understand why men huddled in hills brewing potions—boiling away the ghosts of not-knowing—or sat in barbershops playing games they could win, with a little luck.

His father patted his back. He wondered if he could ever feel this kind of warmth with his mother. Was the threat of bodily harm always crucial for a bond like this?

He spent the rest of the day underground, helping Andrew test and measure timber. By midafternoon the drifts were crawling with men. He heard the clack of gondola cars on rails in twisting tunnels above and below him, the *tik-tik* of hammers on coal, the hiss of kerosene lanterns. The two young miners kidded him. "That tapping you hear—it's the Tommyknockers. Little people of the earth clomping around in their thick wooden shoes, looking for a good game of cards."

The truth was, *they* were the little people of the earth—Harry and his father, the miners. As the platform moved up and down the main shaft Harry caught glimpses of arms and legs, dirty faces peering out of holes. Phantoms digging, squatting, pulling at the heart of the planet. Visible in flickers, then lost again in foul, dry blackness.

Above them all in warm grass, he thought, children batted balls, mothers went to market, unaware of the desperation beneath them, the indignities, the camaraderie, the insect motions that built their communities.

"This new manager?" Andrew asked the miners while Harry hammered an I-beam. "He raise your pay?"

"Naw. Still a pittance per ton."

The other man spat over the edge of the platform into the hot bottomless pit. "Helping you is dead time for us. We won't see a dime today. No scrip if we don't haul coal."

"It's worthless anyway. The company store's raised its prices twice in the last month. Poor Frank over in the supply tent, they're pressuring him to move. Then the company'll take all the supplies we need out of our checks."

Their bitterness snuffed the good feelings from before. They worked glumly, dropping deeper into the hole. Harry lost track of time but the miners knew how long they'd spent even without checking their watches. Toward evening the tunnels cooled off, less a chill of the air than of the spirit. Harry couldn't shake it, even when he emerged into the heat of the shaft house and felt the setting sun on his skin.

He washed off with lye soap and a bucket of water behind the boardinghouse. His shoulder was bruised. He helped his father bathe; Andrew's leg had stiffened up on him.

They walked next door for supper. In the waning light Harry noticed shacks and tents behind the hall he hadn't seen last night. Men scrubbed coal dust from their bodies over boiling pots of water; babies grabbed at their legs, women hung clothes out to dry. A dozen men and a pregnant girl stood in line in front of an outhouse.

Inside the hall the miners were somber, whispering, heads bent. Harry heard something about a "shot in the hole" and "firedamp." He was about to salt his eggs when the door swung open. Four men carried a stretcher into the hall. On it, a filthy young man with a bloody, bandaged leg and his arm in a cast. He was raving drunk. Dried spittle webbed the corners of his mouth. He shouted, "Boys, I'm a lucky son of a bitch!"

The miners all rose and toasted him. Andrew and Harry got the story from a fellow at the bar: an explosion in Number Four, south of here. A new kid, hired by Fawkes, had broken the rules and set up a shot while men were still in the mine. In his haste he hadn't run a gas check; the shot ignited coal dust and firedamp—a mixture of methane and oxygen—sending a wing of flame through the busiest drift. Kit, the guy on the stretcher, was knocked down and slightly burned. No one else was hurt. "Fucking miracle," the fellow told Andrew. "I've seen a blast like that shatter heads."

"Smelled like a field of violets," Kit said, waving a bottle.

"That's the carbon monoxide—white damp. It's thick after a blow," a buddy of his said. "If the impact don't kill you, the air usually will. You *are* a lucky son of a bitch."

"Greenhorn kid," said another man. "Where'd Fawkes find him?"

"Probably an Eye-talian."

"Hey, watch-a you mouth!"

"What the hell does Fawkes know about shot-firing?"

"What the hell does he *care*, long's he gets his tonnage?"

"Shit, this'd never happen if they'd let us hose down the drifts so stray sparks wouldn't catch."

Andrew interrupted them. "Have you asked—?"

The men all laughed. "Oh yeah," said one. "It's not a 'productive use of company funds.'"

"In other words, our lives ain't worth protecting."

"For God's sakes, you're entitled to basic safety. If not, it's a violation—"

"Of what? Company policy?"

"State law."

"Shit, Andrew, the company *is* the state. You know that."

"And it can't move without you. I've told you all before, if you sit down and say we're not working till things change, they've got no choice but to listen. Roberto over there's the only one who was with me, right, Roberto?"

Kit sat up on his stretcher. "Mister, you wasn't here last year when the Wobblies come through, blabbing eight-hour workdays—"

"You don't need the IWW to—"

"We did what they said. Went out on strike. Asked for decent wages, eight-hour shifts, an age limit for working the drifts. This was before the company store was up and running."

"I know," Andrew said. "I *was* here."

Kit groaned and seized his swollen knee.

"Then you remember what happened," another man said. "Osage threatened the grocers, and good old Frank, so they wouldn't trade with us regular. That's how they got us all on company scrip in the first place. End of sit-down."

Andrew rubbed his eyes. "All I'm saying is—"

"Fuck it. Here's to Kit!"

"Hear, hear!"

Someone blew into a harmonica with what sounded like his last good breath, and the singer, in the same red dress as before, hugged herself and hummed. A man danced up to her, whispered in her ear. "Scrip's no good," she said. "Cash only."

"Company *took* my cash!"

"And your passion with it, sugar."

His mouth dropped. She put her arms around him and swayed. "That's nothing," she said. "See what the bastards've done to me? Since Billy died in the Number Three I've . . . well, I've *got* to have cash. I have two little girls to raise."

The man lowered his head on her shoulder and they danced.

Harry watched them instead of his plate. He was sick of eggs. He could still taste the musty air of the mine; he couldn't swallow enough water to quell the dust-itch in his throat.

Dugan appeared in the doorway in a pressed green suit. Same bowler hat he'd worn last night. "Anderson!" he yelled.

Kit looked up from his stretcher, on the floor by the bar. "Yo!"

People stopped talking. Someone dropped a bottle. It rolled several feet across the grainy wooden floor, a lonely, imperfect sound from a flaw in the glass. Everyone, including Dugan, Harry saw, pretended not to hear it. To acknowledge it, he realized, would be to snap a delicate understanding between management and labor—words he'd learned studying the speeches of Oscar Ameringer.

"Collect your pay in the morning and go," Dugan ordered.

"Why?" Kit said.

"The company can't afford incompetence." He stressed the word "company" the way some preachers said "God" as if it were the only sound in the language. Harry, still thinking of Ameringer, heard other words in it: *companions* working for a *common* good. That wasn't what he'd seen today in the mine.

"Damn right! So fire that kid Fawkes brought in," Kit said. "He's the one who—"

"Ewing's fine. Fawkes has confidence in him."

"Fawkes doesn't know his ass from a wet powder charge."

"You shouldn't have been down there."

"The hole boss said our shift wasn't over!"

"It's over now, boy. Your check'll be waiting—four weeks' worth minus eighteen bucks for the equipment you lost."

"*I* lost?" The shock on Kit's face shook Harry; his throat tightened and he started to cough. Like the soiled men around him, he was full of the earth.

The singer said to Dugan, "I'll bet it excites you so much to kick a man, you don't have nothing left for a woman."

"Shut up, Sherrie," Dugan said. "What's a whore know about the drifts?" He looked angry enough to hit her. Andrew waved his cane to get his attention. "Mr. Dugan, your safety codes—"

"Shaughnessy, we had this talk last night, didn't we? I thought we'd reached an agreement."

Andrew stood there, silenced by the man's pointing finger. Harry coughed again; his chest heaved. Everyone turned to see if he was all right. Adrenaline shot through his body. His instinct, honed by years of practice, was to hold the attention he'd grabbed, to cast a net of words across the crowd. It was a feeling akin to the danger and excitement he'd experienced in the mine. He swallowed his cough. "Sir, you say this man's shift was done." He walked over and placed his hand like a blessing on Kit's tousled hair. His father had always taught him the value of "specific examples to make a point—use people from the crowd if you can." "Yet your company has failed to define shifts, legally speaking. Last year the workers asked for an eight-hour day. They were denied."

"Shaughnessy, is this your kid?" Dugan said, tapping his foot. "You tell him to can it."

Andrew didn't move.

"Therefore, this man cannot be held responsible for any infraction. He was simply doing his job," Harry said. "Your contention that his shift was up, when in fact shifts *do not officially exist*, would be laughed out of every court in this state."

"That's right!" Kit said. "Hell yes!"

"The way to prevent future misunderstandings, of course, is to set a daily work limit. Say, eight hours?"

The miners erupted in laughter and shouts. "Go get him!" someone said. His father's smile encouraged him. He felt again an intense physical intimacy with the men around him—a far cry from the embarrassment he'd known with Zeke Cash and his friends in the hills, from the humiliation that surrounded him at school, from the shame he felt at home whenever he let his mother down. He felt right, and in control—speaking, he could shape the world *his* way. "I was in the hole today," Harry said, raising his voice. "I saw, myself, the dangerous and unsanitary conditions." The words flooded past the tickle in his throat. "To be blunt, Mr. Dugan, I witnessed a shameless operation. A farmer treats his mules better than Osage handles its men." He squeezed Kit's shoulder. "I think the local newspapers would be very interested in that fact."

Dugan shook his hat in Harry's face. "I better not hear any more talk like this," he said. He looked around the room. "Nor any union talk, either! As for you, little man . . . I've seen you before . . ."

"In the papers," Harry said. "They dote on me." This wasn't true, but it had the intended effect. Dugan's knuckles turned white around the brim of his hat. He glared at Harry but didn't say another word. When he left, the miners cheered. Sherrie put her arm on Harry's shoulder. "You *are* old enough," she said. "For anything you want. *Twice* the man these others are." She kissed his cheek. "Don't weaken."

Roberto and the other Italians doused him with beer. They stood in a line and saluted him. "A song!" Roberto said. "We'll sing you a song. What would you like?"

Harry glanced at his father, who smiled and shrugged.

"A love melody?" Roberto teased. "An Irish lullaby?"

"How about 'Happy Birthday'?" Harry said. Weeks had passed without a proper celebration; Andrew's wounds had demanded the family's full attention. He glanced at his father again. Andrew's head was bowed.

"Is this your birthday?" Roberto asked.

"No," Harry admitted.

"A *real* song, then!" Roberto led his friends in an up-tempo drinking number. The Italians whirled Harry around the room. He remembered his father telling him one night, not long ago, that "character" always mattered more than a fellow's background or age.

Later in the boardinghouse he couldn't sleep. He felt he'd just run a race. His heart rushed; he shook with pride. He'd delivered these men from their worries, at least for tonight, and he'd done it with no set speeches, no memorized lines, just his breath and his mind and the need of the moment. The faces of the miners! The fear and the hope! The thrill of *seizing* the room! Now he knew more than ever what his words, words with the force of a freight train, meant.

"I'm glad you came," Andrew said, propping his cane against the wall. All day Harry had been aware that his father didn't actually need him here. The young miners who'd gone with them into the hole could easily have managed Harry's tasks. Warren Stargell or one of Andrew's other friends could have driven the wagon for him.

His gift to me, Harry thought, is the world around us.

"Me too," he said. In the field behind the dining hall the married miners stoked fires beneath small pots, bathed their kids with rough cloth rags. Their wives' dresses were faded and torn at the seams. The pregnant girl he'd seen earlier stood in line again in front of the outhouse, behind nine or ten dirty men. She cupped her belly with her arms, bit her lip. As he watched through the window, Harry felt his stomach drop. He hadn't delivered these people from anything. He sagged against the wall. Even if the company agreed to an eight-hour shift, this girl would still be pregnant, still be waiting in line. She'd probably end up like Sherrie, in a bar, he thought.

Songs and beer could give a single man a kind of courage, but parents didn't have any choice. They had to feed their kids. How could you ask them to join a union? Telling them to sacrifice their pay and defy the company, even for a day or a week, was like telling them to kill their babies.

This thought kept him tossing all night. He heard his father snore. To his left a man trembled with fever. Another was sick in the corner—too much whiskey. The building creaked in a chilly wind, like a battered old barge in a river-gale.

He'd just begun to doze when a hot light scared him awake. Someone had shoved a lantern at his face. A boot poked his ribs. "Get up, damn it!"

"Who—? What time is it?" Andrew mumbled.

"Never mind," Dugan said. "Just get your ass up."

Andrew couldn't find his cane in the blinding spot of light. The rest of the room was dark. Men groaned awake, then hushed when they saw what was happening. Harry helped his father stand.

"I'm Lester Fawkes. I hear you caused quite a stir this evening," said a man next to Dugan. He wore a heavy gray coat and a tie. His mouth was lost inside a bristling white mustache.

"No, Lester, this one," Dugan said. He jabbed Harry's chest. "He's the one who made the speech."

"Him? He's just a kid."

Dugan fished inside his coat for a torn piece of paper. When he unfolded it Harry saw his own round face. "I was there in Anadarko that day," Dugan said. "I knew I'd seen you somewhere before. It finally struck me. He was soapboxing, Lester, cursing the mines—"

Harry shook his head. "That's a bald lie," he said. "I had an audience of farmers. No respectable speaker would talk mines to a bunch of farmers."

Fawkes chuckled, raised the lantern in a swelter of moths. Harry heard whispers all around him in the dark. "Hell, Dugan, I'm not afraid of kids. Are you afraid of kids?"

"He's a fist-waver, Lester, I'm telling you, he—"

"I think my partner's afraid of you." Fawkes laughed again. "Come on, there's nothing this boy can do to hurt us." He tugged Dugan's arm. "Let him sleep. It's all right, boy. You can stick your thumb back in your mouth."

It was all Harry could do to keep from hitting him. He wasn't able to help the miners but at least they took him seriously. They cheered him and sang him a song. These men, Dugan and Fawkes, these *capitalists*, wouldn't know character from the big fat bunions on their feet.

Fawkes swung the lantern to light his path, sending dizzy shadows up the walls—men kneeling, scratching, rubbing their arms. Phantoms again, as they'd been in the hole: present in an instant of weak illumination, then gone. Harry smelled the lantern's bitter trace in the air, the sweet straw at his feet, the frailty of flesh all around him.

Andrew patted Harry's back. "Get some rest," he said. Rats *scritch*ed in the dark.

Laughter, faint singing outside. Through the window Harry saw a couple of fires, miners clapping and dancing with their wives. Their capacity for joy at the end of a day like this amazed him. People were strong; they could survive almost anything. That didn't bode well for the union either, he realized. One way or another, folks always learned to live with their limits.

A man on horseback rode through the miners' camp. He barked something Harry couldn't hear. The songs stopped, the fires went out. So many ways to be silenced. Beatings, threats. Coal dust. Comet tails. Earth and air. Shaken by the miners' harsh lives, the company's strength, the invisibility of being a kid, he promised himself, as he curled up to sleep, he'd speak and speak and speak.

4

Whenever a speaker came around, the farmers built a brush arbor. They'd go into muddy bottomland forests near East Cache Creek where oaks and elms and mighty pecan trees twisted out of black waxy clay. They'd cut about twenty poles—chinquapin oak, usually, or Shumard—and haul them back to the field where the meeting was set to take place. They'd sand and hew the wood, hammer the poles into the ground five or six feet apart, and cover the top with honeysuckle, sumac, mesquite. Torches tied to crossbeams cast late evening light. At Baptist revivals women placed ironweed and goldenrod around the arbor in pots, to brighten the space and attest to the glory of God.

In a vacant Baptist arbor, Annie Mae, Mahalie, and their friends organized a dinner for Andrew and Harry the day they returned from the mines. The arbor was handy. Beet greens and spinach had come into season; yellow squash was ripe. Andrew had bought a slab of salt pork in town, along with flour and syrup. Annie Mae made biscuits and gravy, and slow-cooked a pot of molasses.

Harry's shoulder had swelled and he was running a slight fever. Annie Mae spoon-fed him a new product Avram had sold her—

Greene's Chill Tonic, carbonated water and cherry-flavored quinine. A hellfire-and-brimstone meeting would occupy the arbor a week from now but tonight it was quiet and pleasantly cool, even to Harry in his fevered state. He watched salmon-colored scissortails chase insects through the limbs of a rusty viburnum. The white blossoms of Chickasaw plums flashed in the evening light; the woody smell of bluestem mixed with the scent of his mother's lemon meringue.

Annie Mae asked him to watch for people on the road. She didn't want the Baptists to catch them on their property. Usually in early summer Andrew built a tiny arbor in their yard for outdoor meals but he was too weak to work on one this year.

He hadn't seen a paper since he'd left. When he learned from Annie Mae that Governor Haskell had moved the state capital from Guthrie to Oklahoma City he cursed the state's "new money." "Damn railroad men," he said. "They've been lobbying all along to steal the governor's seal—God knows what kind of deal they made with him." He was fond of Guthrie's old Masonic Lodge, he said, whose chambers had housed a number of legislative offices. "It's a respectable place—for a Protestant outfit—full of grand old tradition. Now, the judiciary might as well move into the bank that bought it."

"Honey, please, can we just enjoy our supper?" Annie Mae asked, placing her hand on his. "I've missed you."

He touched Mahalie's arm. "I'll tell you what. If I were of the darker persuasion, Indian or black, I wouldn't be sitting here. I'd rush to the city and try to put a stop to this. If they get away with it, you know what'll happen two months from now. With the special election?"

Mahalie stared at her beets.

"They'll pass that Grandfather Clause, that's what—the literacy requirement. That'll keep a lot of your people from voting. City's bragged for years it has fewer 'dark' officials than any other town in the state. If *that's* the kind of attitude loose now in the House and Senate—"

"I can't vote anyway," Mahalie muttered.

"Politics! Politics! I'm sick of it," Annie Mae said, shielding her ears. She looked at Harry as if she'd just watched him vanish. Andrew reached for her.

"Excuse me?" someone yelled from the trees at the edge of the field. "Excuse me, but I believe you good folks are trespassing on church property."

"Uh-oh," Mahalie said. "Bab-tists."

Two men approached them through the thick understory, scaring up grasshoppers and flies. Their clothes were damp with sweat. "It's the Shaughnessy family," one said. "They're Papists."

"I'm afraid we'll have to ask you to leave," said the other.

Andrew protested, "My family's having a nice, simple meal here." Harry heard more anger in his father's voice than the situation deserved. Andrew was fuming about the capital still, looking for a fight. "We'll clean the place. We know how persnickety your grouchy old God is."

"Andrew!" Annie Mae gasped.

One of the men whipped off his hat. "Listen here, you sorry, genuflecting son of a—"

"Gentlemen, please," said Annie Mae. "Let's not be un-Christian. We're leaving now." Mahalie was crouching, ready to run. Annie Mae asked her to gather the dishes.

"You're welcome back on Sunday," said the man with the hat. "Might do your miserable soul some good."

Annie Mae hushed Andrew before he could answer.

The rest of the week, when he'd finished his chores, Harry walked to the field and watched the preparations for the meeting. Several young men built a stage and a series of pews to add to the dozen they already had. They brought a mahogany podium, highly

86

polished, slick and smooth, from their little country church. The top was gently angled with a thick, ridged lip to hold a written speech. Harry watched two men position it under the arbor; he envied them, touching it, putting their weight on its frame. He'd never spoken from behind a podium. Its severe lines and deep, swirling color conveyed a strict authority, a gravity of purpose. He pictured himself onstage, grasping its edges, rocking to the rhythm of his words. Breath caught in his throat when the men rammed it clumsily against the corner of a bench, nicking it. He couldn't believe they were going to leave it here in the open for the next few days, protected only by a light gray tarpaulin. Clearly, they didn't recognize its beauty the way he did.

At home he practiced his speeches in the mule pen, straddling the slats of the fence. "Friends, with the Republicans and Democrats in Congress, the capitalist class is in the saddle," he shouted at the peak of the barn, "riding the backs of workers!" His mother hadn't mentioned Kate O'Hare or Warren Stargell or the speakers' circuit, but she looked worried each time she glanced Harry's way. She made a point of complimenting him on the work he did around the farm—he'd caught three gophers since his first fiasco with the trap. She even listened to him speak, clapping when he finished. "Did you really like it?" he'd say. "Of course," she answered automatically as though he'd done a simple cartwheel. She may have told Avram he had a gift, but to Harry she seemed unimpressed, indulgent, at best merely polite.

Patrick Nagle was a better listener, patiently swatting horseflies with his tail, but even the old mule's loyalty wasn't enough now to inspire Harry. In the dining hall with the miners his words had had consequence, he thought, however small. He couldn't change people's lives, but for a few minutes that night some men thought he might. And for a few minutes he believed it too.

He'd wanted to lead them out of the hole. Oh, how he'd wanted that power!

Remembering the excitement, he lost his balance on the fence, scraped his arm on a spike. His mother dressed the cut, checked his swollen shoulder, and told him not to play so hard.

SHE WAS SNORING GENTLY the night Harry slipped out of bed, dressed quietly in the dark, and made his way to the brush arbor. The podium was there, wrapped in its tarp. Dew glazed the grass and pews; the honeysuckle thatch smelled fertile and rich. Now and then on the western horizon, above the slopes of the Wichita Mountains, flash-lightning darkled, damp and smudgy, like palm prints on a pane of glass.

Halley had followed Harry from the house. He sat on the stage, head cocked, while Harry lifted the tarp. The past few nights Harry had seen the podium in his sleep; in his dreams it was as tall as a lighthouse, imposing but safe, a steady source of clarity and wisdom.

He touched the dark wood, lightly, as if combing Patrick Nagle. The cover had kept it shiny and warm. He felt its solidity and weight, the dignity of its reddish-brown burls . . . local lumber cut and shaped by workers to hold the peoples' desires. From it, expressions of charity, freedom, and hope might ring—promises a man in a mine or on someone else's land needed to keep himself going.

Rake. Straighten. Hammer. Plow. Farm-words. *Plant. Water. Scrub.* Noble terms, Harry thought, but he longed to fill his mouth again with sounds of greater resonance. *Pride* and *unite* and "Follow me!"

These last words he'd said aloud, lifting his arm above the podium (he was too short for it, and stood on his toes). Lightning burst overhead; a sudden wind stirred the leaves, and several drops of rain, spitting through gaps in the arbor-vines, sprinkled the pews. "Why?" someone called from a stand of trees beside the field.

Harry, startled, backed away from the podium and nearly fell off the stage. He squinted, expecting to spot a giant Baptist waving a Bible and a gun.

"Why should I follow you?" the voice insisted. It belonged to a girl. Harry could see a patch of white among the trees; dark, flowing hair. Then she disappeared in a shadowy swirl of leaves. Halley crouched and growled at the edge of the stage.

"Hello?" Harry said, circling the podium. "Who's there?" Rain and dust scented the air. The storm was gaining strength. Against the stage's steps a breeze swept tangled duff. He began to wonder if he'd imagined the figure but Halley had seen something too—yes, and there she was again! Brown-skinned, tiny in a long white dress. Small, sandaled feet. Now he *knew* he was conjuring things.

"Sue-Sue?" he whispered.

"If I follow you, where will you lead me?" she said. Challenging? Teasing? Beside her, a dark animal growled at Halley.

This wasn't Sue-Sue, of course. He could see her better now that she'd stepped from the trees: an Indian girl about his age, carrying a wicker basket. "Who are you?" he asked. His shoulder ached. His forehead was hot.

"Mollie. Are you the preacher?"

"No, I'm . . . a Socialist," he said. "Practicing."

"What's a Socialist?"

Halley had crept from the stage and slowly approached her dog, sniffing vigorously.

"A Socialist . . . well, a Socialist believes workers should own factories and farms and all the means of production. We believe in equality, even for Indians." Except for Mahalie and her friends, though (who were usually too busy talking among themselves to pay Harry much attention), he hadn't stood close to many Indians. Now, as with Avram, he felt a little wary, curious but self-protective.

Mollie laughed. "Oh. A dreamer. That's why you're out here in the middle of the night talking to no one."

The dogs were whimpering amiably now and wagging their tails. "Are you a Baptist?" Harry asked, stepping closer. "I mean—"

She shrugged. "I come sometimes to listen to the preaching."

Her cheeks were as wide as copper pennies flattened on a railroad trestle. Odd, but attractive. Harry felt shy but he was compelled to try to engage her—in part, to overcome his fear of people different from himself. How could he be a good Socialist—how could he say the word—if he recoiled from anyone, even those with dissimilar customs? His father would be disappointed in him if he didn't make an effort.

He pointed at Mollie's basket. "What're those?"

"Wax myrtle leaves. They're just beginning to thicken on the trees." She lifted one from the basket, a tiny olive-green spear, crushed it between her forefinger and thumb. "Smell." She opened her hand beneath his nose. A dusky, spicy scent. The warmth of her skin. "They make a good air freshener," she said.

"You pick them in the middle of the night?"

"Lil and I couldn't sleep. The coming storm." She looked at her golden dog, muzzle to muzzle with Halley. "They like each other." She glanced back up. "Isn't the lightning beautiful?"

"I think maybe you're a dreamer too," Harry said.

Mollie smiled. "You better practice some more, Socialist. You're going to have to be real good to convince people." She made a kissing sound at Lil, who turned and followed her across the field.

"Wait!" Harry said. "Mollie *who?* Will you be here on Sunday?"

She waved without turning and disappeared into the trees by the road, as quietly as she'd arrived. Halley followed Lil a few steps until Harry whistled him to stop. Halley sat forlornly.

The raindrops increased. Harry rushed to pull the tarp across the podium. Stupid Baptists, he thought. The wood would rot out here. Didn't they know that? He supposed, to them, the podium was a simple prop to help the preacher deliver his message. But a message needed presence; it had to be embodied. A skillful speaker would use this wood as a badge, a *wedge* to drive into the crowd.

He'd return on Sunday, not because he cared to hear a sermon (especially after sitting through Mass) but because he wanted to see the podium perform.

And because Mollie might be here. The strange encounter had unsettled him. He didn't understand his powerful response to her, a pleasure that had escalated after his initial fears—the surprise of being overheard, perhaps; the delight of her features; the echo of Sue-Sue (such dark, sharp *beauty*—so much livelier than the pale little girls Harry knew at school, who teased him, anyway, about his speeches).

By the time he reached the yard his skin was hot. He crawled through his window, swallowing a cough so as not to wake his folks. Halley ran to the mule pen, stirring Patrick Nagle. Harry hushed them, then drew his curtains against the searing lightning. Wind flung grit against the wood and glass of the house. He dried his hair with the thin cotton blanket on his bed, tiptoed to the kitchen for water. The floorboards creaked. The chicks in their pen peeped groggily, hungrily.

The following morning he was too sick to leave his bed. Annie Mae fed him chicken soup and Greene's Chill Tonic. She kept a damp washcloth on his forehead, chipped a block of ice, and wrapped the shards in a towel on his shoulder. He shivered. "I swear, it's like you spent the night in the barn," Annie Mae said. Harry sneezed. "You were feeling poorly after your trip to the mines. I shouldn't have worked you so hard around here."

Forced to stay indoors all day, he was more aware than ever of the changes in his father since their trip to Anadarko. Andrew had left unfilled the timber orders from Osage. He'd never been an indecisive man but he hesitated now before starting any chore. Constantly, he asked Annie Mae's advice, even on tasks as simple as lighting the kerosene stove. He demanded coffee, tea, food—not harshly, but often. Harry saw how weary his mother had become.

One morning she said, "Andrew, will you fix Harry some oatmeal while I run down the road to Mrs. Smithers's and get us some fresh brown eggs?"

"Oatmeal?" Andrew said.

"I'll be right back."

"Can't he make it himself?"

Annie Mae stopped and turned in the middle of the kitchen. "No he can't, Andrew. I asked *you.*"

Harry was sitting at the table. He gripped his glass of milk. The scorn in his mother's voice, a swipe like a rusty blade, frightened him. "It's all right," he said. "I'm not really hungry."

"Yes, you are. And your father's going to feed you."

Harry glanced sheepishly at Andrew, who still hadn't moved.

"Aren't you, Andrew?" Her words seemed to draw the air from the room. Harry's chest hurt.

"Hand me that box of matches," Andrew told Harry.

"Thank you," Annie Mae said softly, then walked out the door.

As he watched his father at the stove, Harry wondered what he could do to make things right again around the house. When I'm well, he thought, maybe I should cut some trees. But he knew the hand briar saw needed more strength than he'd developed in his arms. The simpler crosscut he could manage with a partner, but he didn't know how to use his father's gauge for setting the length of the raker teeth, or the steel spider for setting the cutters' angles.

"Here's your oatmeal," Andrew said. He sounded angry.

"Thank you," Harry said, staring at the table.

WARREN STARGELL CAME BY early one afternoon and asked to speak to Andrew. Annie Mae let him in but she was silent and brusque. He wouldn't look at her. He fiddled with his hat.

From his bedroom Harry heard the men talk. He didn't catch every word, but he understood that Warren Stargell was arranging the Socialist speakers' circuit. Andrew mentioned "tagging along." His friend discouraged him. "With your leg and all," he said, "you need your strength." Harry felt certain his father couldn't survive the road right now. He'd been worn to a nubbin by the mines; he seemed befuddled in his very own home.

Before he left, Warren Stargell popped his head into Harry's room. "Get healthy, Harry boy. Rest your voice," he said. "Soon you'll be spreading the word." He winked with his lazy left eye.

Throughout the day Harry slept. In fever-dreams he saw Mollie and Sue-Sue. Bob Cochran hit Mollie with a rubber mask. Something stung Harry's ear. A man with scars on his face tried to smother him with a pillowcase. Then he was naked onstage. The crowd booed and wouldn't let him speak. Voices closed all around him, drilled his head. He woke with a buzzing in his ears. His bladder ached. The ice in the towel had melted and soaked his pajama top. His parents' voices were loud and angry in the kitchen.

"—bad enough you expose him to the dangers of a mine shaft— a *mine shaft*, Andrew—"

"I was with him every step of the way."

"Yes, and look what it did to you."

"Annie, this is just a speaking tour. He's done it dozens of times."

"He's never traveled for a month. Unsupervised."

"Warren'll be there—"

"Warren. Oh, *now* I'm relieved—"

"With other adults."

"You know what I mean, Andrew. He's never been anywhere without one of us—except that day in Walters."

The floor chilled Harry's bare feet. He rubbed his eyes and smacked into the back of a kitchen chair.

"Harry, honey, what're you doing up?" said Annie Mae.

"I have to go outside."

"Oh. Here, then, let me help you with your shoes. How's your fever?" She felt his forehead. His future had been tabled for the day.

The next morning his vigor had returned and he wasn't burning up. He fed Patrick Nagle but ignored the rest of his jobs. He helped his mother measure flour for a cake. "Mama?"

"Yes, Harry."

"Is it true I have a gift?"

She lowered a spoon into a bowl of sugar and stared at him.

"The Jew Peddler—Avram—told me you'd said so."

"He did, did he? When did you talk to him?"

Harry blushed. "The day I went to town."

"I see." She cracked an egg. Squares of muslin, cut to fit the windows, covered the kitchen table; pots of sumac berries, roots, and bark, mixed with old iron shavings, sat near the stove. Boiled, they'd make a dark violet dye in which to dip the muslin: for days now, Annie Mae had been making new curtains. "What else did he say?" she asked, nudging the pots away from Harry with her foot.

"He said you worried whenever I was gone. But if I have a gift . . . isn't it my duty to use it? Wouldn't God be mad if I wasted it?"

Annie Mae wiped her hands on her apron and touched Harry's shoulder. She *was* proud of him. He saw it in her eyes. Still, he knew, she couldn't help but fret. The world outside her window she didn't understand very well—Andrew had said so, on his trips with Harry. "What about those men, the kind who hurt your father?" she said.

"I'll be careful, Mama." He grinned. "I'm younger than them. I can outrun anyone."

"Not always."

He realized how much he loved her face. Patient. Soft. He knew from the gentle set of her mouth—frowning, but not harshly—that, behind her fears, she wanted him to have whatever he needed. "Please."

"This is important to you, isn't it?"

She had to hear it. "Yes, Mama."

She turned and looked at the chicks in their pen as if she could fix them where they stood, young and helpless, forever needing her care. "Harry, Harry, Harry."

"Mama—"

"Go on, then. I can't stop you."

"I'll be all right."

She brushed a tear from her face. Harry wrapped his arms around her waist. The road! Kate O'Hare! A breeze from one of the windows lifted the sheer corners of the muslin. The odors of the berries and the bark, of the moist balls of flour on the counter, dizzied Harry. I'll never again feel this safe, he thought, even as pleasure whipped through him, raising the hair on his neck. He tightened his grip on his mother's small hips until she said, with a knot in her voice, "Here now, let me finish this cake."

ON SUNDAY AFTER MASS he ran to the brush arbor. The Baptist women were setting plates of potato salad and platters of fried chicken on benches in the middle of the field. Whenever a preacher passed through—Baptist, Methodist, whatever—all the chickens in the county were killed, cooked, and served to the reverend and his crew; the Holy Spirit had quite an appetite, always cleaned His plates. Harry was ten years old before he knew there was anything more to a chicken than feet and a beak.

Kids in their Sunday suits played catch with rubber balls in tall grass by the road. Harry looked for Mollie but didn't see her. He'd spent two hours before church polishing his shoes, mixing chimney soot with molasses to make a thick black paste. The shoes looked great, but a couple of horseflies had lighted on them before the paste had dried. The flies were stuck fast. Still, his mother was pleased to see him taking such care with his appearance.

When the preacher took the arbor stage Harry laughed. The man was as thin as a crusty old railroad spike, hook-nosed and bald. The podium seemed to shrink beneath his gangly arms. "Friends! Have you met Jee-sus?" he called, his voice a high, whiny chirp. "Brothers, sisters, I'm here to tell you I was lost, oh yes I confess it to you today, before I knew Jee-sus was my friend, I scoured these valleys and hills and the filthy back alleys of our cities looking for any comfort I could find." It's not about comfort, Harry thought. God wants you to rise from your chairs and strike a blow against the banks. "My burdens weighed me down, *ground me down* something fierce, my friends, a miserable beggar, that was me, Lord, lonesome and low—" His head shone like a peeled turnip in the arbor's dappled sunlight. "Sound familiar, my friends? You know it does. I'm talking to *you!*"

Often, Harry's father had taught him, "The speaker doesn't matter. He's just a vessel for the message. The minute you start feeling good about yourself, the minute you start strutting, the message is a goner." But Harry couldn't help but feel cocky, standing here in his well-polished shoes, knowing he could outtalk this fellow up the road and back. It disgusted him to watch a man with so little talent for rousing a crowd pound and sweat on the podium. Someone should save it, he thought.

"Let's steal it," Mollie said.

He whirled to see her in her long white dress. Lil panted at her feet.

"You have that look in your eye, same as the other night," she said. "You want that thing, don't you, Socialist?"

His cockiness vanished. He coughed. He wasn't completely well. His mouth was dry; he tasted his mother's chill tonic. "My name's Harry," he said. "And no, I don't want it. It wouldn't be proper for me to covet—" Her beauty confounded him. It *was* beauty, despite the width of her cheeks, the slightly flat nose. In part, it was the strangeness of her features that drew him. Her eyes were dark and her long hair smelled of the fresh wax myrtle leaves she'd picked. "Property should be shared—"

"Tools should be used by those who know how to handle them."

Even God's tools? Harry thought. Once again, he found himself retreating from her surprising aggressiveness. Were all Indians this blunt?

"You didn't bring your dog," Molly said.

"No."

"Lil's lonely."

"Friends! Since Jee-sus stepped from His cloud of glory and took me by the hand, I've walked the paths of righteousness in His loving shadow, a brand-new man. That's right, brothers and sisters, I stand before you today, chastened—"

Harry and Mollie walked down the road, away from the arbor, in the direction of the sun. Lil chased butterflies from the shrubs' stiff limbs. Harry's body tingled, but not like it had with the fever; this was a liquid sensation, warm and smooth and pleasantly scary. He could feel Mollie without touching her: she was vibrant and warm. She set the air around her humming. She lived about a mile from here near Cookietown, she said, in a shotgun house her mother and father shared with seven other Kiowa families. She was two years older than Harry; she didn't go to school. Her days were spent in the kitchen or the yard, stirring beans or baking bread for the men and younger children.

Harry told her about the speeches he gave, Kate O'Hare and the upcoming circuit. "The other night," he said. "You shouldn't walk alone so late. It isn't safe."

"Of course it is. What do you mean?"

"There are men . . . the Klan . . . a pretty girl like you . . ."

Mollie stopped and looked at him. "What did you mean when you said you believe in equality for Indians?" she asked.

"I meant Indians shouldn't be treated any differently than anyone else." The words came easily, from old speeches he'd given, but he felt ashamed of his own doubts, his hesitation. He knew she saw him blush.

"Does that mean you'd just as soon kiss an Indian as a white girl?"

Harry stopped in the shade of a stately pecan tree. He didn't know what he felt, or what to do. Sunlight made confusing patterns on the road, through the shadows of the leaves. He ground his toe in the dirt, flattening one of the flies stuck to his polish. "I guess so," he said.

Her stare was intense. "Well?"

He looked around. A quail rose from a holly bush. A strip of cloud blew across the sun. No one. He bent forward and pressed his lips to the slight copper rise of her cheek.

Mollie smiled. "Now," she said. "When are we going to steal that thing?"

HARRY HAD NEARLY OUTGROWN the latest suit his father had bought for his trips. Annie Mae, silent, let out the pant cuffs and sleeves, tightened a couple of loose buttons, mended some seams. Andrew lectured his boy. "Remember: make a good family, make a good life. Whatever else your topic is, that's the basic theme. Keep it simple. Lord, I wish I was going with you."

Annie Mae frowned at him.

When his chores were done of an evening Harry ran to the fields to meet Mollie. Halley and Lil romped through sprawling pink blooms of Heart's Delight—the flowers dusted their coats, sweetly— and the leathery bells of scarlet clematis. Mollie let Harry kiss her cheek now and then but pulled away whenever he tried to hold her. "You're so pretty," he said.

She laughed. "And what do Socialists think about girls? Do they believe girls should be shared?"

In moments like this, her directness still stunned him, but the elation he felt with her now—a physical swirl and an ease, all at once— suppressed most of his doubts. "You're making fun of me."

"No, Socialist. I think you're sweet. Would you ever share me with anyone?"

"Never." He reached for her hand but she snatched it away.

She made plans for kidnapping the Baptists' podium. "We'll have to act soon. The revival's over this week and they'll be locking it back in the church."

"No no no, I can't take something that doesn't belong—"

"We're sharing it."

"Mollie—"

She placed a finger on his lips.

Annie Mae saw them together one day. "Who was that little Indian girl you were walking with?" she asked him at supper.

"Mollie Weryavah. I met her . . . on the road one afternoon."

"Weryavah, Weryavah . . . where have I heard that name?" Her brows furrowed but Harry wasn't troubled. His mother had Indian friends; she couldn't object to Mollie.

Meanwhile, plans were jelling for the speakers' circuit. Warren Stargell would call for Harry in his wagon a week from Friday and take him to Waurika, where they'd meet the rest of their group. The league was counting its money to see how many rallies and encampments it could arrange in a month's time.

Annie Mae laid handkerchiefs and extra pairs of socks on Harry's dresser so he wouldn't forget them; she told him how much tonic to take each day if he felt a fever or if his throat turned sore.

"Weryavah," Andrew said at supper the following evening. "You asked me if I'd heard the name. It just came to me . . . he's that fella who manages the shooting range over there south of Walters. Big man. People call him 'Butterball.'"

"Oh Andrew, that's right!" Annie Mae said. "That awful place by the creek where men go to . . . oh Harry. I think it's best if you don't have anything to do with that family."

Harry blinked. "Mama—"

"They're trouble, son. That's all there is to it. Andrew, how many times has Sheriff Stephens been called out there to bust up a card game or a—you know what I mean—"

"More'n a few times," Andrew answered.

Harry laughed. "Mollie doesn't gamble," he said.

Annie Mae shook her head. "I'm sorry about your little friend. She may be very nice, but her family has a reputation, Harry, and you don't want—"

"You said you believed in equality."

"This isn't about them being Indians. I'm talking about character. Andrew . . . ?" She looked to him for help.

"Oh, let him have his playmate," Andrew said. "I don't see anything wrong with it."

Annie Mae threw her napkin on the table. Her mouth was strained and her eyes looked sad. "If he's going to go gallivanting all over the countryside telling folks how to live their lives, he's got to be beyond reproach, Andrew. It matters, the company we keep!" She swept up all their plates, though they hadn't finished the meal, and left the table.

Later, Harry heard his parents in the kitchen. "I give and give and give, Andrew, and I don't get anything in return. All I ask for is a little support with Harry . . ."

"You're holding him back, honey, he's not a baby anymore."

"He never had a chance to be a baby. He was barely out of diapers when you had him on the road."

Harry was usually intrigued, as well as frightened, hearing his parents fight—the power of words!—but tonight he didn't want to listen. Everywhere he went their voices followed. The house had become too small for him.

That night he lay awake in his bed wondering if Mollie was trouble. The stirring in his stomach and groin—that was upsetting. But it was pleasurable too. He felt gripped by a power greater than he was, a force capable of unhinging his life, and that was part of its dark attraction.

He didn't sleep for another reason: he'd promised Mollie he'd meet her in the arbor at midnight. He waited until he heard his mother's even breathing and his father's snores (they'd finally kissed and made up, drying dishes. "Okay?" Harry had heard his father say. "Okay," said Annie Mae wearily).

Harry slipped out of bed, dressed quickly, and crawled through his window. Halley followed him, nuzzling his hand. Harry had forgotten his jacket. The summer nights were cool. He pulled his flannel shirt tight across his chest.

Mollie in her white dress—was it the only one she owned?—stood behind the covered podium: the angel of all speech. Harry was so captivated he couldn't swallow. He trembled. "Don't be frightened," Mollie said. She placed her hands on the collar of his shirt and pulled him toward her. Her right knee slipped between his legs and he felt the warmth of her thigh. She parted her lips, breathed sweetly in his face. "Are you ready?" she whispered. Harry nodded. She moved quickly away from him then and threw the tarp off the podium. Harry nearly swooned, as if Mollie had torn off her dress and stood before him naked. The red wood shone darkly in the moonlight like firm, ebony skin. "Hurry," Mollie said.

They grappled with the podium, each on one side. It was heavy and slick, hard to hold. They stumbled with it off the stage.

Halley and Lil chased each other under the stars. Crickets made music in moist blackberry brambles in a far corner of the field. Mollie, laughing, slipped and fell. Harry dragged the podium through wet heavy grass, gouging a deep furrow in the earth. Mollie had said there was an abandoned farm shed about half a mile down the road where they could hide their prize, but it was clear to Harry that they couldn't carry it that far. Mollie was laughing too hard to be of much help, and he was wondering why he'd let her talk him into this in the first place. He left the podium upright in a flat patch of rye grass; twigs and leaves clung to its base. He ran for the shelter of trees. Mollie followed with the dogs. "Wait!" she called. "Socialist! You can't just leave it here. You need to practice—"

He grabbed her around the waist and spun her until they fell to the ground, laughing and panting. The dogs licked their necks. Harry found her mouth with his, briefly, bumping noses with her, and started to kiss her the way he'd caught his parents kissing in the kitchen one morning, last year, when they thought he was doing his chores, but he didn't know how to hold his face. How had they managed it? Giggling, Mollie tried to twist away. Beneath his hands her small breasts heaved up and down. "You're trouble," he said, smiling. He elbowed Halley out of the way, rubbed a smudge of dirt from Mollie's cheek.

"You haven't had *enough* trouble in your life," she said. She locked her hands around his neck. "Socialist?"

"Yes?"

"Do you love me?"

He couldn't tell if she was playing or if she was seriously asking, and he couldn't judge his own response when he answered, "Of course."

"There's another boy who loves me. My cousin Anko."

"I'll beat him up." He didn't know what he was saying anymore.

"Have you ever been in a fight?"

"I've battled men twice my size. Tell me, is your father a gambler?"

She ignored his question. She kissed his eyebrows. "We can't just leave that thing in the field," she said. Just then they heard a car motor, close. Lil turned and barked. Headlights swung their way from the road, grazing the podium, which looked like a giant tombstone in the field. "What the hell—?" someone yelled from the car. Halley darted from the trees; a gunshot popped in the dark. Harry jumped up to see that his dog was okay, on the far side of the road. "What's happening?" Mollie said, shaking.

"Rabbit hunters," Harry said. His father had told him about this crazy new "sport" made possible by the Model T: night-hunting, freezing jackrabbits in the glare of the lights. The sudden, artificial beam had a paralyzing effect on the animals just long enough for a skilled marksman to squeeze off a shot. "Poor things don't have a chance," Andrew had said. " 'Cept most of the boys who go in for it aren't real hunters. Drunk kids, mostly, in their daddies' new cars."

"Get back home," Harry whispered to Mollie. "Through the trees here—and stay low. I'll see you tomorrow."

"What about the podium?"

"We'll have to leave it." He bumped noses with her again, then ran, crouching, down a narrow path behind the field.

"Bud, swing the car around! I saw something!" one of the hunters shouted. Harry tripped on a tree root, scraping his knee and the flat of his palm. A shot whizzed behind him, splintering tree bark? The podium? He couldn't stop to look. A spider web, invisible in the crook between two poplars, hit him and stuck like cotton candy to his lips. When he woke in his bed the following morning, sore from running, rank with sweat and mud, the web was still in his mouth. He tried to spit it out, and finally brushed it off on his way to the kitchen to wash. He heard his parents dressing in their bedroom, cleaned himself quickly. His throat ached and he felt his fever had returned.

Later that morning, as his mother was stirring a pot of beans in the yard, Harry saw through the newly curtained kitchen window Mollie and Lil approaching the house from the road. He laughed— they were safe!—but right away his relief switched to panic. His mother had told him to avoid the Weryavahs. He rushed out the kitchen door, waving his arms to catch Mollie's eye. She smiled when she saw him. He motioned her down the road, tried to signal her he'd meet her in their usual spot in the field. Annie Mae bent above the beans, sniffing the rising steam. She hadn't seen anything yet.

He was stupid. How could this girl make him do such silly, dangerous things?

Halley in the kitchen doorway thrilled to Harry's swift gestures. He yapped loudly twice, drawing Lil into the yard, leaping and barking. "Harry?" said Annie Mae, looking up. She saw Mollie. Mollie halted in the road, alerted by Harry's face. Playfully, Lil and Halley wrestled in the kitchen, smashing the barriers of the chick pen, scattering the frightened birds who ran in all directions in the yard. "Harry, the babies!" Annie Mae yelled, putting her hands to her head. "Shoo, shoo!" she screamed at the dogs. Startled, Halley and Lil veered toward the mule pen, jumped between the slats of the fence, and nearly ran into Patrick Nagle. The sleepy old mule twitched, suddenly wary and, sensing danger, jerked forward, stumbling over Lil, who'd tried to squeeze between his legs. The unexpected contact sent a wild shiver through the mule. He leaped the fence but he was too old and slow: one of the spikes snagged his belly. Harry heard a sickening tear. Patrick Nagle stumbled and squealed and ran toward the woods. Harry followed, watching through tears as intestines spilled, steaming and slick, from the hole in the mule's belly. Patrick Nagle trampled his guts and fell, finally, in a clump of sticker burrs. Harry dropped beside him, not feeling the ground's needles, and cradled Patrick Nagle's head in his arms. The fright in the animal's eyes eased into quick, numb calm. His breath turned cold, swelling goosebumps on Harry's flesh. "Patrick Nagle," Harry said. His voice cracked. "Patrick Nagle."

Halley trotted around the edge of the sticker patch, wagging his tail, then whimpered, confused, when neither Harry nor the mule ran to play with him.

Mollie stood on a small rise nearby, watching quietly. "Socialist?" she said finally. "Socialist, are you all right? Can I help?"

He looked up, but didn't answer her. He thought he saw her kneel in the grass. Tears blurred his sight.

Patrick Nagle smelled rancid, ancient. He seemed to be attentive as Harry delivered one final speech to him, his most faithful listener. "Be brave, brother," Harry whispered. "You fought the good fight." Patrick Nagle relaxed and buried his nose in Harry's lap.

WARREN STARGELL HAD LOADED his wagon with water pails and jerky, soda crackers, candies. "Got to keep the Boy Orator happy on the road," he said, clapping Andrew's back. "We'll take good care of him, Andrew. Don't you worry."

Annie Mae buttoned Harry's shirt collar tight around his neck. He still had a cough and he was pale. He'd never seen his mother so worried, but she kept her promise to him and didn't try to hold him back. Neither of his folks had said much about Mollie or the mule, maybe because they knew how awful he felt about Patrick Nagle, maybe because he was leaving and they missed him already.

Annie Mae had only found two of her chicks. The rest had probably perished in the woods somewhere, during the cool summer nights.

She kissed her boy and told him not to forget his tonic, to go to Mass when he could, then she turned to the house and disappeared inside.

Andrew shook Harry's hand. "Carry the message, son."

"I will."

"I'm proud of you." They hugged quickly, then Harry climbed onto the buckboard seat beside Warren Stargell.

They didn't talk. Warren Stargell concentrated on the road, Harry gazed at the fields. He hadn't seen Mollie to tell her good-bye, and he felt a pang of regret. But he was carrying the message now and he'd decided his mother was right: he had to be a responsible young man. Whatever he felt for Mollie—and he wasn't *sure* what he felt, though it was powerful and strange—he didn't act responsibly when he was with her. He had to focus on the task at hand; the country needed the wisdom he and his fellow speakers could offer.

He wondered if the Baptists' podium had survived the night of the hunters. Someone had removed it from the field. He hoped it had weathered the cold and wind and dew, prayed the boys' bullets hadn't touched it. For the rest of his life, he knew, before every important speech, he'd imagine that glorious pulpit all alone on the Oklahoma plains.

PART THREE

Barnstorming

5

Kate O'Hare wore a light cotton blouse with ruffles down the front, and a red bow tie around her high collar. Her deep green skirt swept the speakers' stand as she paced in front of the crowd. She was a tall woman in her mid-thirties. Harry loved her face: long and narrow with a short, thin nose and a generous mouth quick to smile. Her red hair curled across her neck and ears. She raised her arm, waved a fistful of newspapers. "When we're done here, folks, take an *Appeal to Reason*—it lays out our philosophy for you. We ask you to subscribe if you can, but if you don't have the pennies, that's all right, tuck one of these in your overalls or your jumpers, take it home and share it with your neighbors. Those of you who can read, light the lamps for your less fortunate friends."

Her timing was perfect, honed in over a decade of public speaking. She knew when to lift the mood with a joke or startle her listeners with fire. Harry admired the way she used her plain dress and humble manner to draw people close, then grabbed them by the ears and wouldn't let go.

J. T. Cumbie, the Socialist candidate for governor, topped the bill with her. A distinguished old gentleman with a bright bald pate and

a flowing beard—he called himself the "gray horse of the prairie"—
he sparked the crowd, denouncing the "monstrous atrocity of a very
few men controlling the means of production" and led a chorus of

> The coming of the jubilee
> When workers of the world are free.

When it was his turn to talk, Harry was so excited, so inspired, he
rushed to the edge of the stand and stammered, "Brothers and sisters!
Here's to the collective ownership of . . . of . . ." He worked up a small
river of spit to soothe his scratchy throat. ". . . the *entire earth!*"

Men and women waved the red flags that league members had
passed around the encampment. Parents handed the flags to their
children, hoisted the kids onto their shoulders, and danced across the
low hill, beneath the shade of tall maples. J. T. Cumbie raised his
arms like a vulture ready to swoop and urged everyone into song, to
the tune of "Onward Christian Soldiers":

> Then raise the scarlet standard high;
> Within its shade we'll live and die.
> Though cowards flinch and traitors sneer,
> We'll keep the red flag flying here.

He nudged Harry back to the center of the platform. "Tell 'em,
son. Go on."

The pine boards were flimsy. They bent and bowed as Harry
lunged back and forth to engage each row of the crowd. His throat
was weak, sore from his late-night meetings with Mollie. He coughed,
spread his hands. "Human rights take precedence over property
rights," he croaked. "So the Bible says, and so said the patron saint of
American agrarianism, Thomas Jefferson." He spoke softly to protect
his faltering voice. "Believe me, friends, when men and women work
together instead of competing like jungle cats, laughter instead of
tears, joy instead of sorrow, health instead of pain will overflow our
lives. With a cooperative spirit, we can vanquish every evil!"

Scattered applause. Red flags. He had to raise the volume. "It doesn't matter if a man is Catholic, Baptist, Heathen, or Jew," he said, ignoring the pain in his throat. "If we're wage workers, our interests are all the same. And who represents the wage worker in the halls of the state capitol? The Democrats? The Democrats are a motley circus of landlords and parasites, huddling in luxury in their *towns!*"

The clapping increased. He was building up steam. Word passed through the crowd that the speaker was just a little boy; those who hadn't been watching or who were eating picnic lunches or changing their babies' diapers looked up. Flies pestered Harry's forehead. Sweat glued his shirt to his skin. "The Republicans and the Democrats don't seem to hear it, but everywhere in this great state of ours there's a sweeping call for righteous government. The earth's burden-bearers demand it!" he yelled.

Several men shouted "Yes!" and shook their fists. Kate O'Hare clapped in the front row, Warren Stargell beamed.

"Friends, the Socialist movement is the concrete expression of this demand. It's dedicated to the conscious organization of a just society. With the coming of Socialism, children can enjoy their childhood, women can be womanly, and men can be men. From conquest to victory!" He pumped his arm in the air. The crowd shouted, "Victory! Victory!"

He wiped his face with his sleeve. His throat was tearing apart but he couldn't stop now. These people were his; every muscle in his body tensed with awareness and control. "Now the highfalutin bankers and the rich, fat lawyers, they'll tell you we're the worst bunch of scoundrels ever to come down the pike. Oh yes indeed, they'd have you believe Socialists aren't real Americans. But let me tell you, friends, a real American stands by his brothers and sisters. A real American doesn't sell his neighbors out for a quick profit! You *know* who I'm talking about, don't you?"

"Hell yes!" "'Ataboy!" "Tell it!"

"Our road isn't easy, though."

"No no." "That's right." "Lord help us."

"We'll all be called to sacrifice." He patted his chest to break up the phlegm in his lungs. "Socialism will succeed only if working people of all races and religions unite to fight the property owners. I know and you know that most of our fine communities are based on religious and racial identity." He placed his hands on his hips, challenged the group with a frank and sober stare. "It goes against all we've been taught to merge our individual personalities and our small holdings with larger, cooperative land units, but that's the road to prosperity for all. It's the *humane* road, the road to a true democratic America. Make a good family, make a good life—for *everyone*. How do we do that? Wave the red flag, my friends, wave the red flag!"

The audience jumped up and down, hooting and shouting. Harry staggered a little, dizzy and weak. He stumbled toward the platform steps; J. T. Cumbie stood there with his arms crossed. He was scowling. Was he angry at something Harry had said? Jealous of the enthusiasm Harry had pulled from the crowd? He stroked his beard, moved aside. The field was a sea of red shirts, red hats, red flags.

Warren Stargell patted Harry's back. "Nice job, son. Rest up a little. In a while we'll rustle up some grub."

Kate O'Hare caught Harry's eye, smiled, nodded, then disappeared into the crowd, passing out copies of the *Appeal.*

Harry made his way to the tent he shared with Warren Stargell. People shook his hand or hugged him. Some had tears in their eyes. They thanked him for his message of salvation. In the tent he swallowed a bit of his mother's tonic, washed his face in a bucket of water, and napped for a couple of hours.

When he ventured back out the sun had set. Families huddled around campfires, grilling rabbit or chicken or squirrel. The dusky sky and yellow flames accented every scar or bruise on their bodies, the wear and tear of life on the farm. Webworm silk drifted like lace in the trees. Scorpio rose in the south.

A group of men sat on logs at the top of the hill discussing the effects of industrialization on the life of the worker. A few yards away, another group argued the "race question" and the Grandfather Clause. Still others listed "divine" correspondences between the New Testament and the Socialist doctrine.

Harry, still groggy from his nap, drained by the speech he'd given, found himself irritated by the words, by his inability to concentrate and sort them out. His neck ached—he missed his bed, his mother, his marbles, his room. He was glad to be here. He was. But just for a minute, he wanted to see his mother's face, her gentle, sloping shoulders.

He spotted Kate O'Hare and her husband Frank, dark and handsome, with their oldest boy, their baby daughter, and twin sons. They were sitting at a fire with a man Harry recognized from photographs as Fred Warren, the managing editor of the *Appeal to Reason*. He had big ears and a wide mouth that made Harry want to laugh. Next to him were J. T. Cumbie, Warren Stargell, and two men Harry didn't know, one of whom was saying, "Jefferson himself believed that man had an innate moral sense. So did Emerson: 'Look with the eyes of the spirit,' he said."

"Yes, but Darwin's done away with those ideas, don't you think?" said his friend.

"For a few dissolute Frenchmen, maybe, who can't wait to embrace every new fad—"

"If you accept the basic premise of evolution—"

"Then you *have* to believe life's progressing from incoherence to clarity—"

"You've misread Darwin, John. It's not a straight line to perfection."

"Harry, have a seat," said Warren Stargell. "We're frying up some frogs' legs." Behind him, a man Harry had just noticed was busily skinning a squirrel, peeling away the fur with a long gray knife, stretching the white, marbled skin.

Fred Warren scratched his huge right ear. "In any case, it's clear to me that the United States is an evolutionary peak. It's moved from chaos into a system of laws; *our* beliefs'll take it to the next level, from brutal competition to self-regulation—"

"The rule of love," whispered Kate O'Hare. She brushed a horsefly from her daughter's nose. The little girl crawled into her lap. J. T. Cumbie stared at Harry, still with a sour face. In the gauzy light of the fire, his shadowy eyes seemed to move back and forth like collapsible telescopes. Harry wondered what he'd done to offend the old man. Again, he longed for Annie Mae.

Warren Stargell laughed. "My Christian friends used to tell me God was a ruler in the sky, like old King George. Nowadays they tell me He's a force in Nature, working—like evolution—to perfect eternal Good."

"I'm not surprised," said Frank O'Hare. "As our colonial experience recedes—"

"*And* as scientific thought progresses," added Fred Warren.

"—naturally, our conceptions of God, not to mention national destiny, change to fit the latest models."

The man who'd skinned the squirrel cut off its head, rammed a stick through its body, and held it over the fire. The meat began to glisten and spit. Warren Stargell handed Harry a frog leg. It tasted like catfish, sharp and ashy.

"Well, despite our differences, we all agree that America under Socialism is Earth's best hope for moral order, right?" Fred Warren asked.

"I'll drink to that," said J. T. Cumbie. Everyone raised a cup. Harry lay on the ground with his food and watched the stars through the trees. He began to relax, imagining his mother's voice. *Harry*, he heard her say, *Harry, I'm with you.*

The Northern Cross, Cassiopeia, Leo with its sickle-shaped head all hung like dewy nets in the limbs. The air, full of smoke, smelled gamey. The grass was moist and cool. Babies laughed and cried in tents on the hill; lanterns hissed, pots banged, men and women lowered their voices, surrendering to the evening.

Frank O'Hare said Dora Mertz and Stanley Clark would join them at the next encampment, and maybe they'd get to meet Patrick Nagle, Oscar Ameringer, Gene Debs. All of Harry's heroes! (The name "Patrick Nagle" saddened him briefly.) Excited again, he felt his strength return. His head hummed with thoughts of God, morality, national destiny—these people knew so much!

Frank O'Hare stood and picked up his boys. "I'd better get these Short Hares to bed," he said.

They all finished eating and wished each other pleasant dreams. As Harry turned from the fire, J. T. Cumbie grabbed his arm. His beard, like the tail of a mare, brushed Harry's hand. "Warren here tells me you're Irish Catholic. Is that right?" he said.

"Yessir."

The old man nodded, dropped Harry's arm, then walked away. Kate O'Hare slipped by him, carrying her daughter. "You spoke real well today," she said.

Harry blushed. "My throat was sore. I can do better."

"Oh my. I can't wait." She nodded good-night.

In the tent he brushed grass and dirt off his bedroll. Warren Stargell rolled a cigarette. "Harry, my boy, by the time we're done this month, a red tide'll sweep the cities and the plains! Your pappy would've been proud of you today. Cigarette?"

Harry hesitated. Warren Stargell laughed. His left eye, drooping, glimmered in the lantern light. "Here, I'll help you roll it. A little victory smoke. You've earned it." He pulled the pouch of Bull Durham out of his pocket again. Harry smiled, feeling tonight like a grown-up. He reached for the paper and a match.

* * *

HE AND WARREN STARGELL hadn't gotten along well, their first week on the road. The schedule and the pace were both more strenuous than Harry had expected—much busier than the trips with his dad— and Harry tired easily. Exhausted, he slipped into bad habits Andrew had once drummed out of him. He forgot to button his coat. He picked his nose onstage. "Harry, stop acting like a baby!" Warren Stargell yelled at him. "Straighten up, son!"

"I'm not a baby!"

"Then get your finger out of your nose."

"You're not my dad. You can't tell me what to do."

"Your dad asked me to look after you. He told me you'd developed into a fine little man—"

"Leave me alone!"

"Harry, now—"

"Shut up!"

One morning, Warren Stargell tried to straighten Harry's tie.

"You're choking me!" Harry screamed.

"You think Oscar Ameringer walks around looking like he just fell off a hog train?"

"I can do it."

"All right, then."

Harry relooped the knot. "Does Oscar Ameringer look like he does in newspaper pictures?" he asked.

"Handsomer, in person. Almost as handsome as you." Warren Stargell patted Harry's shoulder. "I'll tell you a little secret, though."

"What's that?"

"He's not the speaker you are. No one in this camp can hold a candle to you, kid, once you get on a roll."

Harry knew the man was just buttering him up, but he preferred this kind of talk to being called a baby. After that, he and Warren Stargell didn't fight so much. Harry grew accustomed to the daily pace. He took more care with his coat and his tie. Warren Stargell joked with him; he said Harry was trying to look like Oscar. Actually, Harry imagined Mollie whenever he dressed. It helped him do his best, knowing she'd be impressed if she could see him.

WHEREVER HARRY WENT—ANTLERS, McAlester, Coalgate, Tishomingo—Andrew mailed him telegrams and letters full of good luck wishes, prayers. His correspondence said nothing about the family's money troubles or the national events Harry was learning about every day: the burgeoning of the garment workers union, the growing power of the American Federation of Labor, the energy of the Chicago Renaissance. Andrew never mentioned the bold Socialist challenge to Samuel Gompers for control of the AFL, or W. E. B. DuBois's doubts about the movement.

Little by little, Harry realized, he was beginning to outgrow his old man. In the encampments he met the movement's intellectuals—planners, talkers, readers who brought to life for him all the history and thoughts behind the words he'd spoken for years. They knew not only politics, but art and literature and fashion. They mourned Mark Twain, who'd died with the appearance of Halley's Comet ("What's the difference between a dog and a man? Twain said, 'If you pick up a starving dog and make him prosperous, *he* won't bite you.'"). They quoted Walt Whitman and William Dean Howells. They gave Harry copies of the *Nation*, *Harper's*, *Scribner's*, the *Independent* and the *Outlook*, magazines so vivid and venturesome he couldn't imagine ever using their pages in an outhouse.

One man he met even had advance copies of articles and political cartoons that eventually appeared in a brand-new monthly called the *Masses*.

It's happening, Harry thought. The Red Tide. And no one can stop it. His head throbbed with excitement, with curiosity, and the pressure to learn.

Tough lessons, too: for example, he discovered that Socialists often bickered, like everyone else. There was rarely a united front. When he asked Warren Stargell why J. T. Cumbie seemed mad at him, Warren Stargell replied that Cumbie didn't trust Catholics or Jews (whom Harry had mentioned in his speech); he didn't favor voting rights for Negroes.

"He's crazy, then," Harry said.

"He's our candidate for governor, Harry."

"Bad choice."

Warren Stargell shrugged.

"I'll support him publicly," Harry said, growing in confidence—he felt it in himself, surging and rising—maturing rapidly in the heady swirl of the circuit, "but I'm going to stay away from the old coot."

One day, Kate O'Hare bravely challenged her female comrades. Harry had gone with her and a few other speakers to address the Chautauqua Literary and Scientific Club of Guthrie, a powerful women's organization. He was overwhelmed by the combination of thick, sweet perfumes in the downtown meeting room, the secretive rustling of petticoats beneath long black skirts. He thought of Mollie: her mysteries.

Two or three times since leaving the farm he'd noticed pretty young ladies in the streets of the towns, and tingled to touch Mollie again, or the girls in the streets, or *any* girl, and he marveled at the force, the new constancy in him, of this impulse.

Now, he sat by the stage, watching Kate O'Hare pull herself erect, smile, and open her arms. She praised the club and others like it for raising library funds, establishing kindergartens, lobbying for better child labor laws. "I've watched ragged children weave youth and health into shining silks," she said. "I've followed children into mine and mill and sweatshop, into the cotton fields, and over to the sunny fruitland slopes. Oh, I know where the icy blasts chill blood and marrow, where fires scar body, mind, and soul, and sisters, having seen all this, I hate it as only a mother can!"

Harry thought of his own mother, of Mollie, of the ladies in the streets: the thrill of the pitch, the billowing shocks of the body. Comfort. Excitement. Desire. They were all mixed up in him now, like a fresh and potent marmalade.

Kate O'Hare commended the efforts of woman suffragists. Her voice was a steady drumbeat of sense: "Today, everything used in a home is produced *outside* the home in a factory; without the power to vote, to effect change in the workplace, a mother has absolutely no control of the conditions existing there. If a textile mill is unsanitary, operated by sickly women and children, a veritable breeding place of disease, a mother who buys the fabric made there is helpless. If a food factory is reeking with filth and germs, and sends poisoned food to the family table, a mother is powerless to protect her own."

The club billed itself as an open forum for ideas. It allowed interested men to attend her speech. When she mentioned woman suffrage, a skinny fellow shouted, "My mother wouldn't have been any better if she'd had the ballot! She found ample opportunities *at home* to exercise feminine virtue."

Another man, a chubby clerical-type, chimed in: "Supper's a part of everyday life. I suppose you ladies would like to change that, wouldn't you? If you get the vote, you'll all be running for county commissioner, and no one'll be home to fix our meals—"

"Exactly," said the first man. "Woman suffrage and Socialism will ultimately lead to the destruction of our marriage vows. Do we want our daughters raised on the doctrine of free love? I think not!"

The women in the audience were stirring, tugging at their bracelets and puffy sleeves, waiting for Kate O'Hare to respond. Harry feared the anger of men, but by now he'd learned its shapes: the sudden boasts, the strutting shows of power. With women he didn't know what to expect. His mother usually went silent and asked to be alone when she got upset. What did she do by herself? What would the Chautauqua ladies do here in public, in the middle of the day? Their whispers made him nervous. Their perfume sailed in clouds. He felt closed in, he couldn't breathe: like sitting in a mine shaft again.

Kate O'Hare patiently raised her hands. "I agree with you," she said.

Several of her listeners shook their heads in disbelief.

"Women shouldn't be given special treatment."

The men nodded at each other.

"The issue is the oppression of the working class. *That's* the battle we're fighting. If we separate the sex struggle from the class struggle, we've lost sight of our ultimate goal."

Women rose in their seats, shouting at her and each other. She stood calmly on the stage, smiling, supremely at ease with her principles. Harry thought he was probably in love with her.

"Where you're wrong," she called, addressing the men, "is insisting that Socialism will destroy the institution of marriage." The audience hushed. "I agree wholeheartedly that a woman's place is in the home. But in a capitalist economy, poverty is so rampant, many of our best young women are forced into the streets, pushed brutally into prostitution, abortions . . . far from harming the family, Socialism will promote better relations between men and women by giving them greater security."

She spread her arms, a gesture of appeasement. "Look at the people you know," she said softly. "Look, perhaps, at your own lives. Women are exploited at home. We all know it. A farm wife is just a hired girl. Despite what the ads say in the big city newspapers, it's not lack of cosmetics that ages women before their time. It's the treadmill, the life of hard, incessant labor without reward. Inevitably, a young girl ruins her health dragging big, heavy sacks up and down cotton rows day after day after day. Moneyless, she lives without power, without individuality. In time she weakens, grows bitter and dull."

She wiped a film of light sweat from her brow. "Is her husband to blame?" she said. "Certainly, certainly—up to a point. But is he any better off? Isn't his back also bent and sore from the loads he carries? Gentle women—friends—I ask you, I beg you, to consider the larger issue. The *real* problem is that we're landless people. Our homes aren't *really* our homes. We're all of us—men and women both— slaves to the bank."

The women nodded and murmured. The men fiddled with their shirt collars. "One step at a time," said Kate O'Hare. "I absolutely support forcing a referendum on woman's suffrage onto the ballot this year. But that can wait if it has to. More important right now, because it affects *all* of us, is a statute declaring that use and occupancy are the only title to land."

Brilliant, brilliant, the way she worked the crowd, Harry thought: first agreeing with her opponents on a minor point, setting them up, snaring them later with their own strict logic. She never raised her voice unduly, never got ugly, never lost her patience.

Day after day, he watched her charm miners, schoolmarms, merchants; heard her teach frugality and hope. In the country or in town, on a pinewood platform or in the grandest carpeted hall, she was equally at home.

"Never speak *at* people," she told Harry. "Speak *for* them. You and me, blessed with this little gift of words—we're servants, that's all. We're not here to rise through the ranks of labor. We're here to rise *with* them."

And their ranks swelled daily. They traveled in a ragged caravan of horse-drawn wagons and jitneys, Ford touring cars owned by various communities. Each week Harry and a few other young men would run into town ahead of their comrades with posters announcing the festivities:

MAMMOTH SOCIALIST ENCAMPMENT
Tell Everybody
Come Join the Merry Throng

~

Daily addresses by different orators who know and will tell the truth. They will prove that Socialism can give every man an equal opportunity to labor and receive the full product of his toil undiminished by legalized robbery.

•

Picturesque grounds one mile west of town.
Bring all the folks, camp and spend a day or two of instructive and entertaining pleasure.
Meals and supplies at regular rates.

•

The brainiest and ablest statesmen in America will positively attend!

~

GOOD LOUD SPEAKERS
GUARANTEED!

One day while unloading equipment, one of the organizers told Harry his philosophy of a successful encampment: "Shade and water—essential. Good concessions—food, pinwheels—to keep the kids happy, and enough adults willing to supervise the little brats. Musicians are okay, but never hire a brass band. They drown out the speakers. And never put a merry-go-round too near the speakers' stand."

That summer, the biggest attraction, aside from the speeches, was a gas balloon leased from an Oklahoma City circus. Chester Leeds, the man Harry had watched skin the squirrel his first night out, gave the public free rides in the giant contraption. He let Harry feel the balloon's rough fabric as it lay pooled on the ground, unfilled, between rides. Chester was a puppy of a man in his twenties, exuberant about the crowds that streamed into the camps, helpful and kind to the sunburned families who traveled many miles to receive the benediction of Socialism. He was engaged to a friendly young girl named Sally. At supper every night Harry split his time between the O'Hares and Chester and Sally, who adored him.

After a while, the towns, noisy and dry, blurred in Harry's mind. Durant, Atoka, Ponca City. On the first leg of the trip he heard, every night, Fort Sill's big new army cannons practice firing on a distant range. The dull booms echoed in the hills to the west; occasionally a scent of gunpowder drifted into camp on a breeze. The wind was always hot. His dreams were ribbons of images pulled from newspapers he scanned while Warren Stargell drove the wagon from place to place.

One day, he had so much time to read, he memorized a whole editorial from the *Walters New Herald*: "With the death of Geronimo the curtain was rung down on the life of a human being who lived but to curse mankind," it said. "The reading public for years has been nauseated by the publicity given to the affairs of this most cruel and vicious character whose name has ever made a blot on the pages of human history."

Andrew had always admired Geronimo. "He loved his people," he'd once told Harry. "That's the most you can ask of a man."

"Make a good family?"

"Right. 'Family' means all of us."

"Even the capitalists?"

Andrew had paused. "We have to hope they'll come around. For their own sakes."

In the paper Harry also read articles about Chief Crazy Snake, whose band of Creeks refused to settle on their tiny reservation. Each day, editors warned white families in Okmulgee County to look after their scalps. In his sleep, Harry kicked and groaned, escaping vague screams. He heard his mother warning, "Trouble."

In mid-July, a three-day encampment was scheduled two miles north of Ada. Ninety-two men had been murdered senselessly in Ada since statehood; it was a rough and lawless place, and everyone knew it.

On a sticky, dusty Monday, Warren Stargell, half-asleep, leading the caravan to the campground, was nearly thrown from the seat of the wagon when his horses stopped abruptly. Harry had been reading a paper and he, too, almost tumbled to the ground. The horses had come upon a plowed-up patch of road south of town. Beside the road, ankle-deep in strawberry vines and rows and rows of sunflowers, nine or ten young men with shovels and hoes shouted, "Turn around! Goddam Reds! We don't want you here!" "Bellyachers!" "Communists!"

Warren Stargell started to protest but one of the men yelled, "Cracker, shut up! We've heard it all before."

"Instead of talking all the time, you ought to listen for a change. Listen to a preacher, listen to a banker!"

"Hell, if you sorry sons of bitches had any initiative you wouldn't be so poor!"

This last remark pierced Harry; blood raced to his head in waves. His vision shrank to the size of a shirt button. He pictured his father stooped in a field, miners trapped in a hole. He stood in the seat, red-faced and shaking. "Let me tell you something!" he hollered. "Capitalism is an evil that *feeds* on the initiative of good people, and like all evil it's going to devour itself."

"Harry." Warren Stargell tugged his sleeve. "Harry, hush up. Let's just get out of here."

Harry shook him off. "Your town is a center of despotism, boys. I can smell it from here. My friends and I, we'll just wait till it fattens itself and bursts, then we'll come in and bury the corpse!"

His words so enraged the men, they squatted, reached for stones, and tossed them at the wagons and cars. Warren Stargell leaped from the buckboard, finding cover behind a big spoked wheel. Harry saw Kate O'Hare, in a wagon behind him, hustle her kids to safety behind a scrawny mulberry bush. He'd developed a strong arm in the rock fights at school. He jumped from the wagon, scrabbled for ammunition in the road, and hurled it at the men. Mostly he found his mark: a soft upper thigh, a fleshy forearm. He was outnumbered, but the townsmen didn't have his accuracy, and after a couple of minutes they retreated into the woods. "Harry! Harry, let's go!" yelled Warren Stargell. He climbed into his seat, reversed the wagon, and led the group out of danger.

They canceled the encampment, followed Rock Creek to the town of Sulphur. There, they rested and relaxed in the natural hot springs. Stress, hasty meals, and Warren Stargell's cigarettes had upset Harry's stomach. The healing waters did him good. Sally spoon-fed him Peruna, a digestive remedy, and Cardui Tonic. Harry had seen Cardui advertised in the newspapers. In the ads a smiling woman said, "For seven years I suffered from female troubles. I took twelve bottles of Cardui and now I'm fat, healthy, and strong!"

"What are female troubles?" Harry asked Sally. "That's not anything I have to worry about, is it?"

"Just take it, honey. It'll settle your nerves."

Chester laughed and ruffled Harry's hair. "Believe me, we *all* have to worry about female troubles."

"Chester!" Sally blushed.

"It's alcohol," Chester said, reading the bottle's label. "Eighty proof. You know, now that I think of it, I believe *I've* been having troubles."

"Give me that," Sally said. She sounded angry but she was grinning at him.

That week, while the organizers planned new campsites, Kate O'Hare decided to visit the Confederate Veterans' Home in nearby

Ardmore. She said she fervently supported the United Daughters of the Confederacy, who'd founded the home, and wanted to commend them in person. Harry, Chester, and Sally went with her.

The place wasn't finished. Boards lay scattered on the grounds. The main building was made of gray brick; four large pillars supported a double-decked porch. The nursing staff and the Daughters of the Confederacy were thrilled to have a visitor as famous as Kate O'Hare. She told them she was proud of the work they did. She introduced Harry and Chester and Sally. A young woman toured them through the dining area, the barns out back, the orchard, and the vegetable gardens. She explained to them that all "Johnny Rebs" were welcome here, especially those who'd lost their families and homes in the war, and had nowhere else to go. "We have about eighty-five valiant old warriors here," she said proudly. Harry saw tears in her eyes and understood that the South's defeat grieved her deeply.

While Kate O'Hare and the others took the tour, Harry wandered back into the house. He'd smelled something wonderful in the kitchen: peach preserves or some other sweet boiling fruit. Sally's medicines seemed to have done the trick. He felt better, and he was hungry. He tried to follow his nose but he wound up in a narrow corridor leading away from the dining room's light and the pleasant smell. He inhaled a whiff of Mercurochrome, of damp, sour clothes. He turned into an open doorway and nearly ran into a man on spindly crutches. The man was old, naked from the waist up. The flesh of his breasts sagged like saddlebags. He had a wispy beard and smoky white eyes. "Whoa there, Private," he said to Harry, smiling, then hobbled on past, down the hall. He left a faint scent of boiled milk in his wake. He moved in obvious pain. The gray pantaloons he wore made loud scratching noises.

Harry peered into the room. In buttery light from a single tall window he saw old men in high-backed wheelchairs, old men in narrow iron beds, old men hunched over rickety tables playing dominoes. Coughing. Raspy breaths. The smell of onions, unguents, urine. Harry kept to the wall.

He heard *Manassas, Antietam,* strange names whose exotic sounds thrilled him so much he felt his scrotum tighten. Drawn by the music of the words, he stepped cautiously toward a pair of beds and a conversation there. One fellow said to another something about "sizable corn." The listener had no arms. He lay propped in his bed like a damp bulky box. The speaker's left leg was memory and air. As he spoke, his red stump thumped his sheets. "I's crouching there, thinking how good the sun felt on my skin," he said, "thinking I'd never seen ears of corn this juicy and big, when all of a sudden I's blinded by a splash of light, then another, in the rows ahead of me. I took a step and just as I realized what I'd been looking at, a lightning bolt burned my face. Bayonets," he whispered. "Points gleaming in the sunlight. We'd stumbled right smack dab into a Yankee platoon. They'd been waiting overnight for us in the field." He hawked and spit into a cracked tin coffee cup on a table by his bed. "Blade went right through my cheek. Five minutes later the day was as still as you please. Three hundred men in my unit. Only four of us left moving."

The armless man shook his head, then, startled, spotted Harry near the foot of his bed. "Say, boy!" he grumbled. "Whatcha doing, lurking there?"

"Nothing," Harry said.

"Nothing? What kind of answer is that?"

"I was just—"

"Staring at the war heroes?" He laughed, an ugly gurgling sound. "Eyes 'bout to pop out your head."

"You 'bout to cry, boy?" said the man with the stump. Harry's eyes *were* blurry; he noticed a long bandage on the man's right cheek. "Or are you a girl? I think maybe that's it. A little crybaby girl. They oughtn't to let girls in here."

His friend laughed and wheezed.

"I'm not a girl," Harry mumbled.

"Then get those tears outta your goddam eyes. You think I want your pity, boy? To hell with your pity!"

"I'm sorry," Harry said. The light from the window diminished. The sun had slipped behind a cloud. Harry had a vague impression, in the shadows of the room, of open sores, jaundiced flesh, bones and pieces of men.

"Sorry? *Damn* your sorriness, boy! Come here. I said come here!"

Harry walked carefully to his bed. "You know what they call me 'round here? Call me Hole," he said. "Know why?"

Harry trembled. "Why?"

The old fellow slowly pulled the bandage from his cheek. There was an empty space where his skin should have been. He grinned. "I can stick out my tongue 'thout opening my mouth," he said. "Watch." He pressed his lips together. His tongue wiggled through the hole in the side of his face. Harry's stomach lurched. The man with no arms laughed so hard he fell into a coughing fit. Helplessly, he thrashed in his bed.

"Want to touch it?" the old fellow said.

"No thank you, Mr. Hole, sir." Harry heard a squeak of shoes behind him on the dark linoleum floor. A woman's voice said, "What are you rascals up to? Tommy, Tommy, calm down." He turned to see a nurse in a stained white uniform. She raised the armless man by his squared-off shoulders and pounded his back. He stopped coughing. She looked at Harry's face and at the old man's absent cheek. "Randall, you been scaring this boy?"

He spit more phlegm into his cup. "He wanted to see the war heroes. We obliged him."

"Who are you here with, hon?" the nurse said to Harry.

He backed away, wide-eyed.

"Run along now, little girl," Randall said. Tommy laughed and began to cough again. "Run to Mama, boo hoo hoo."

Haltingly, in the wagon on the way back to Sulphur, Harry told Kate O'Hare, Chester, and Sally what he'd seen. Chester shrugged, flicking the reins. "Those weren't no war heroes, Harry. They're just bitter old men."

Kate O'Hare touched Harry's shoulder. "Losing an arm or a leg can *make* a man awfully bitter. Justice, fairness, democracy—men say these words when they go into battle. But what you saw today, Harry—that's what it *really* is."

He nodded.

That night, around the supper fires, his friends shared memories of the War between the States. Some of them had been children when the fighting broke out. Their fathers and grandfathers and older brothers had served the Confederacy. "None of the men in my family wanted to join," said one young man. "We weren't rich enough to own slaves. I remember my daddy saying, 'Why should we fight the rich folks' battles?'"

"Isn't that *always* the question in war?" asked Kate O'Hare.

"I must have been ten or eleven when the war ended," another fellow said. He set his plate of chicken at his feet, wiped his hands on his pants, and though the night was warm, held his fingers near the fire. Harry heard crickets in the tall, moist grass. "I remember traveling to Atlanta with my family, trying to find my father's brother. He'd been wounded, and we'd got word he'd ended up in a hospital there. I can still picture it all, clear as a bell. The streets were full of rats. Garbage had been piled to the sky. Everywhere I looked, I saw kids squatting in filth. My father wept. I'd never seen him do that. He'd been raised in Atlanta. He couldn't believe what the war had done to it."

Fred Warren picked his bottom teeth with the tip of a stubby knife. "The seeds of the Civil War were planted in the very womb of this nation," he said matter-of-factly.

"How d'you figure?" Chester said.

"Some folks trust majority rule, nothing else. They don't believe in specialists. Or politicians. Others say the voters think with their hearts, not their heads—you need strong leaders to push the national will. Finally, there's the localists, who'll swear to you our representatives in Washington are blind as one-eyed moles to whatever's happening back home—"

"They *all* sound smart to me," said Chester.

"Exactly," Fred Warren said. "That's what I mean. The Civil War was inevitable. And the tensions behind it, they'll never go away."

Harry's head was cobwebbed with the horrors he'd seen that afternoon. He couldn't eat his dinner; the scent of sickness, of decay, lingered in his nostrils. What did Fred Warren's flat words have to do with the mutilations or the anger he'd witnessed today at the home? He couldn't sit and listen any longer to the talk. He jumped up and asked Sally where her medicine was. "What's the matter, sweetie?" she asked.

"Female troubles," Harry murmured, turning to hide his tears.

PATRICK NAGLE WAS A GENTLE man, generous and kind, ardent, full of conviction, but a poor public speaker. He stood onstage with Harry just long enough to mumble, "If present economic conditions persist, years from now we won't be asking this boy, 'What business are you in?' but 'Who do you work for now?'"

He was more comfortable behind the scenes, he admitted, writing articles, drafting speeches for others. "I don't really have what it takes to be a hand-shaker or a baby-kisser," he said. Harry liked his presence, his striped suit and slick, black mustache. He was disappointed when Nagle rushed off "to other party business."

As he stepped into his jitney he winked at Harry. "You're a good Irish lad," he said. Harry was glad his father had named their mule for him.

Dora Mertz and Stanley Clark were charismatic leaders, but around the supper fires at night they were loud and a little too friendly with the bottle. "It's always a shock to learn your heroes are human," Warren Stargell whispered to Harry one night, registering the boy's reaction to the pair.

But Oscar Ameringer, the great Oscar—he *exceeded* his billing. He *knew* so much! He'd read all the primary Socialist works, both European and American. He was a fine speaker but he didn't try to whip the crowd into a frenzy. He was more of a teacher, Harry saw, patiently explaining political principles. Some of the party faithful thought he wasn't fiery enough—he didn't support an all-out revolution. He believed capitalism would inevitably fail, and that democratic Socialists would gradually take the reins. Harry believed him. It thrilled the boy when Ameringer told a crowd one day, "The word *Socialism* indicates association, organization, and cooperation." After that, Harry would have followed him anywhere. He was just plain *good*.

One afternoon, while Warren Stargell and others were watering the horses, J. T. Cumbie complained to Ameringer about the "religion nuts" gnawing steadily away at the party.

"Who do you mean, J. T.?" Ameringer swept a lick of thick brown hair off the tops of his ears. His eyes were steady and gray.

"This boy, for one." Cumbie pointed at Harry, who was kneeling by a stream, washing the dust from his face. "He's been telling the crowds it's okay to be a Catholic or a Jew and still be a Socialist."

"I agree with him," Ameringer said with a precision, Harry heard, that dramatically thickened his heavy German accent. "The party considers religion an individual matter. You know that."

"And *you* know, Oscar, that preachers are the spiritual cops of the capitalists. If they gave a damn about the working class, they'd back our strikes instead of fretting about sinners."

"You don't need to orate, J. T. It's *me* you're talking to. And I think the boy's okay. Leave him alone, all right?"

Cumbie glared at Harry. It was best to let the moment pass. Cumbie had wronged him, but the old goat was a revered party elder.

To be a good Socialist, did you really have to like everyone? Or was it enough to *pretend* to like some folks?

Harry dried his face and climbed back in the wagon.

"Treasures?" he said.

"Oh yes," said Kate O'Hare. They were sitting by the embers of the supper fire. Warm night; slats of purple clouds ribbed the sky, as if the dome had been condemned, and the stars were flakes of falling plaster. Kate O'Hare was drying her hair with a gray cotton towel. The soap she'd used smelled honeyed, fresh.

"The French. The Spaniards. Even outlaws—Jesse James, Belle Starr. Anyone who's ever passed through this country is said to have buried silver and gold in it." She draped the towel around her knee. Her damp red hair curled like a cap of leaves. "As I've traveled over the years, I've heard several stories about a cave in the Wichita Mountains blocked by a locked iron door."

"What was in it?"

"Some say it was a storage vault for gold, and a prison for Indian slaves working Spanish mines in the eighteenth century. Others swear the James gang left over two hundred thousand dollars there after a Kansas bank heist. Frank James went back to find the booty after Jesse died," she said, "but the oak tree he'd marked with a railroad spike had disappeared, scorched by lightning one night in a wild thunderstorm."

"Are these stories true?" Harry asked, watching the gentle ridges of her face. Her small mouth glistened in the firelight.

"Who knows?" She leaned over, close to the flames, scruffed her hair. Her fingers were long, white as the early moon. "I met a man in Cooperton once who swore to me he'd ridden into the Wichitas from Cutthroat Gap early one morning, and somewhere north of Elk Mountain, he ran across the door. It was rusted and warped. With an oak limb he managed to smash the lock and pry his way inside. Gold ingots had been stacked like cordwood at the back of the cave, he said. Doubloons bubbled out of shredded baskets, surrounded by a dozen or so skeletons—Indian slaves, he supposed. He couldn't carry the gold—he only had a mule—so he hurried down the slopes to Indiahoma for some help. But the next day, when his little party wound into the mountains, the arroyos all looked alike to him, and he couldn't locate the spot. To this day, he's still searching."

Harry stared at her, fascinated by her disheveled beauty as much as by her story.

She looked at him, her elbows on her knees. "And what would you do if you found a treasure like that?" she asked him.

He chewed his bottom lip, then grinned. "I'd give it to you, to help you print the *Appeal.*"

Her laughter sounded rhythmic, like prayer. She tossed the moist towel so it covered the top of his head.

"You're a sweet boy," she said. "And you know what?" She reached across the flames, touched his wrinkled shirt above his heart. "Your strength's right there," she said. "Don't forget it."

IN A COTTON FIELD a few miles north of Sulphur, over thirteen thousand people showed up to be near the health resorts and to hear Oscar Ameringer, Kate O'Hare, and Eugene V. Debs. It was the biggest audience Harry had ever seen.

"I gave my standard speech—the one Cumbie doesn't like," Harry wrote his father afterwards. "And I got a standing ovation. Shoot, they would have saluted a sagging old milk cow, they were so worked up for Debs. He's a sweet dreamer, Dad. He truly loves the people, and they love him back. They know he's going to be the first Socialist President of the United States. When he speaks, you feel you're hearing a prophet. It's like Oklahoma shimmers, then fades, and we're standing in the land of Palestine, listening to the carpenter of Nazareth."

That afternoon, Harry watched Debs's every gesture, every move. The man, reedlike, tall and tan, took the stage at the end of the day, when the crowd's anticipation was at its height. He leaned toward his hearers, opened his swaying arms as if to embrace them all. "When you wend your way homeward, I want you to feel you've refreshed yourselves at the fountain of enthusiasm," he told them, using the setting, with its many hot springs, to illustrate his points. "And when you get there, deliver to your neighbors the glad tidings of the coming day! No one—not even the most class conscious industrial workers in our largest cities—is more keenly alive to the social revolution taking place in this nation than the farmers of Texas and Oklahoma. You, my dear friends, are the standard-bearers of the future!"

He unbuttoned his coat after about twenty minutes, loosened his tie, which gave him a more down-to-earth, yet intense, look than he'd started with. Harry glanced at Warren Stargell, to see if he'd noticed the effect.

After Debs talked for a while, he endorsed J. T. Cumbie's candidacy for governor, then quietly stepped aside, letting the old man bask in the glow he'd fanned. Cumbie didn't have the temperament or the discipline to maintain the good feeling Debs had built among their constituents. He launched into an attack on Governor Haskell, citing a recent land fraud investigation in which the governor had been implicated. The content was effective, but the tone of certainty and hope had been lost.

Harry took note: stress the positive. A bright clarity, like the edge of a morning cloud, followed Debs wherever he went.

Like Nagle and Ameringer, he was a busy man, and had to "rush off"; Harry experienced his absence, the loss of his energy keenly, and for days afterwards, he lolled around his tent, nibbling only fruit. He felt lonely, homesick again. The tension with Warren Stargell returned.

"Stop acting spoiled," the man snapped at him one afternoon. "We've been through this. I thought you said you weren't a baby."

"I'm not a *baby*. Leave me alone!"

"I'll tell you what you are. You're a foot soldier—"

"No."

"—in a righteous cause."

"No!"

Warren Stargell rolled a cigarette. "This sets you apart from other boys your age." He licked the dusky paper. "You have a responsibility to nurture your talent, son, share it with others. All right? You have to hold steady—"

Harry curled up in his sleeping bag.

"I know how it is. Most days you love to talk. Sometimes, like now, it's a burden, right? You get tired. You want to run and play."

Or lie down with Mollie. Harry didn't know what he wanted. Sometimes he felt like two different people, a kid and a man. The kid wanted to go home, eat his mother's food, chase his dog through a bright, blooming field, flirt with a girl. The man wanted to hold a stage as powerfully as the speakers he'd seen.

"Don't you think it's the same for Mr. Debs? Even now?" Warren Stargell said.

"He wants to run and play?"

"I reckon he does, sometimes. Here." He held the cigarette out. Harry took it between his fingers. "What say we rustle us up some frogs' legs?"

"I'm not hungry." Harry's knees ached, from many hours pacing a stage. His body felt stretched and twisted, as if the man inside him were trying to burst through the skin of the boy.

"Next town we're in? Maybe we can buy you some marbles," Warren Stargell said. "Or a drawing pad and some pencils. Would you like that?"

"I don't care," Harry said.

"All right then, suit yourself."

"Mr. Stargell?"

"Yep?"

Harry straightened his shoulders. Marbles, he thought. Yes, marbles might be nice. "Got a match?"

ONE HOT AFTERNOON, A week after Debs's departure, Cumbie was struggling to win a crowd's blessings. People liked his ideas but it was clear to Harry and to everyone else that his attacks on Governor Haskell were wearing thin; he sounded foolish and mean.

"Alfalfa Bill" Murray had joined the race for governor that year, as an "exponent of the militant progressive democracy of Oklahoma." "Alfalfa Bill," a farmer from Tishomingo, was one of the best-known politicians in the state. He had been one of the leaders of the Constitutional Convention, and a strong supporter of farmers' rights. A virulent anti-Socialist, he took to following the caravan that summer, dogging and harassing the speakers.

That day, as Cumbie sought to win the people's favor, Murray appeared in the field in a Ford touring car. He leaned past his driver and squeezed the horn. The audience craned to see. Cumbie sputtered. Murray rose in his seat, tried vainly to straighten his wrinkled tie. He fingered his walrus mustache. The driver wheeled the car slowly toward the stage. Families jumped up from where they'd been sitting and made way for it to pass. As it moved, Murray shouted at the top of his lungs, "Don't listen to these troublemakers! They'll steal your land away. They'll reduce you to the level of nigger hands on giant farm collectives!"

Cumbie was so angry he couldn't speak. He paced the stage tugging his grizzled beard, glowering at his opponent. Harry knew about Murray; many times, he'd heard his father talk about the man. Apparently, no one was going to challenge him. Harry listened to as much as he could take, then, guessing what Andrew would do, leaped onstage next to Cumbie. "And tell us about *your* platform, Mr. Alfalfa

Bill!" he yelled. "Isn't it true you support the disenfranchisement of blacks?"

Murray looked amused. "Just exactly what do you mean by 'disenfranchisement,' young fellow?" he said.

"I mean the Grandfather Clause."

"That I do."

"So why should we believe you when you say you're on the side of the common man?" Bull Durham had coarsened his voice. "If you won't support blacks, you won't support us. We're *all* wage workers *together.*"

"That's a distortion of economic reality—"

"Isn't it true you're against child labor laws?"

The crowd began to grumble. A smattering of boos.

"And safety for miners and other workers?"

"Too many regulations hamper the flow of capital. You're too young to understand these concepts, boy, go back to school—"

"J. T. Cumbie understands a racist when he sees one!" Harry shouted. He skipped Cumbie's own ideas. "J. T. Cumbie knows who's on the side of the worker and who isn't! And that's why J. T. Cumbie will be the next governor of the great state of Oklahoma!"

Thunderous agreement from the crowd. Cumbie smiled at Harry, took his hand and raised it in his own. Murray signaled his driver, and the Ford pulled quickly out of the field to shouts and laughter and jeers.

"I owe you one, kid," Cumbie said to Harry. He squeezed Harry's hand.

After that encounter, Kate O'Hare convinced Cumbie he should oppose the Grandfather Clause. "You ought to seek Negro support, J. T. Everyone else in the race is ignoring them. Murray, Lee Cruce . . . it's a waste of vital potential. Publicity—"

"Yes. The kind I don't want."

"On the contrary."

Kate O'Hare admitted to a fear of "nigger bucks," but she tried, always, to overcome her prejudice, and she knew what was good for the party. She talked the caravan into heading for Taft, an all-black town near the confluence of the Arkansas and Verdigris Rivers in the northeast part of the state. On the way, she and Cumbie drew steady crowds. Harry handed out the *Appeal*, Chester filled the balloon. One afternoon he gave Harry a ride. Heavy brown ropes tethered the passengers' basket to stakes in the ground (Harry thought of the ropes he'd seen on the mining platform, the day he'd worked the hole); hemp lines rose from the rim of the basket, attached to the red and yellow fabric filled with illuminating gas. Chester loosened the ropes; the basket jerked and swayed. He and Harry drifted, bobbed above maples. Harry laughed in delight. Oklahoma spread beneath him like one of his mother's quilts, rivers like ribbons of thread. He opened his arms to gather it all: gypsum, pecans, straw, and mesquite. Hills and plains collided in a quiet drama of textures and hues. A patchwork of farms. Crops in even rows, patterns of labor and love . . .

"You and me, Harry, we're the damn future, you know it?" Chester said. "Fred's right: we're the best hope this ol' country has. Look at it. So much land. So many people just waiting for something good in their lives . . ."

Harry spotted a tiny community, wagons and fences, ragged log cabins. "Is that the town we're going to?" he said.

"I s'pose it is."

"People live in those buildings."

Chester nodded.

"They look so small."

"The folks inside them, they'll grow and grow and grow once they hear Kate and J. T." Chester nudged his shoulder. "Once they hear the mighty Boy Orator."

Harry smiled. "Thanks for showing me, Chester."

Chester glanced at him as if to say *It's a gift, look after it.* "S'pose we better fold our wings," he said. "There's work to be done."

* * *

FREEDMEN HAD FOUNDED TAFT with the land allotments they'd earned at the end of the Civil War. Harry had studied all this in school; his lessons came back to him now.

In the Territories, the Indian tribes had all owned slaves. After emancipation, black leaders proposed that the area enter the Union as a series of "Negro states," and inspired a significant westward migration. Harry had once read how a large black exodus from the South helped populate Taft and other towns like it in tangled bottomlands, dense piney woods.

The Socialist caravan entered the town one rainy day on a dirt road paralleling tracks for the Midland Valley Railroad and the MK & T. Sagging shingled roofs, wild mushrooms poking through broken wooden walks, doorless, mildewed outhouses. Small black faces peered at the wagons from open windows in log cabins set back from the road several yards.

Warren Stargell was tense and grim. "Saw a young Negro put to death couple of years ago, over by Stillwater," he said. Raindrops slopped off the rim of his hat. "Some fellows tied him to a tree and lit his clothes with a torch."

"Why?" Harry asked, watching children run to the edge of the road to stare mutely at their wagon.

"Don't rightly know. Seems to me they didn't think they *needed* a reason. A bunch of us tried to stop them but the sheriff and his deputies held us back. Some folks, Harry . . ." He shook his head.

The town's railroad depot, gutted by fire, had nearly collapsed in a blanket of ashes. Harry learned, later, that a mob had burned it to protest segregated railway cars. Midland Valley refused to rebuild it. Trains didn't stop here now.

He read the tattered, hand-lettered signs on faded oak walls: Ford's Cotton Gin, Stout Ham's Hardware Store, Rockwell Grist

Mill, Hobart Sanders's Soda Pop Factory. On Main Street, men in dusty overalls and women in thin cotton skirts, shielding their heads with newspapers, stopped and stared at the white folks' blustery parade. Only the bank building, in a tall brownstone, looked to be in decent repair.

Warren Stargell parked the wagon in front of the bank's glass doors. He and Chester and Frank O'Hare went to check on lodgings for the night. Harry saw Kate O'Hare hug her daughter and smile at passing women in the street. A pair of small children, a boy and a girl, approached him. They patted the flanks of the horses and stared up at him in the wagon's spring seat. Harry felt awkward under their blunt and restless scrutiny.

"Who're you?" the little boy asked. He was soaked.

"Name's Harry." Be proud, he thought. You've come to help.

"Why are you here?"

"To give you good news." He smiled at the kids. "Your mama and your daddy, if they'll join us, well . . . they won't be mistreated any-more."

The girl laughed loudly. "My daddy? You seen my daddy?"

"No, I—"

"I ain't *never* seen my daddy."

"I'm sorry," Harry said.

"What do you know about it, *Harry?*" She spat on the ground. "'Sorry' count for *nothing.*"

The men returned from up the street, disgruntled, conferring among themselves. Harry leaped from the seat and followed Kate O'Hare to where they stood, shaking their heads. "What's the matter?" she said, hooding her eyes in the rain.

"They don't want us," her husband told her. "They're afraid we'll start trouble."

Kate O'Hare brushed a wet red lock from her eyes. "We're here to support them. Did you tell them that?"

"*Support?*"

They all turned to see a tall dark man in a gray suit and blue string tie. He held a small umbrella. "Excuse me, but you see this bank building here?" he said to the group. "Only place in town owned by a white man. Only place in town making any money. Can you guess what he said, the bank president, when he moved his vaults in here and took a lien on every business in sight? 'I'm here to support you.'" The man shook his head. "No thanks, folks. We got all the support we can stand. Good day to you." He turned to leave.

Frank O'Hare ran in front of him, introduced himself, and held out his hand. The man shook it warily. "We're not on the side of the bankers. Not at all. We're *with* you."

"I know who you're with," the man said. "Les, over at the hotel, told me what you said. You're with the Reds. Wellsir, we don't need any Red talk around here, stirring folks up, making 'em more miserable than they already are."

"May I ask your name, sir?"

"Bobby Springs, Deputy Mayor."

"Mr. Springs, we're here to offer hope."

He chuckled. "And you know what coloreds hope for, do you?"

"I think I do. A good living, a nice home for your wife and kids—"

Bobby Springs bowed slightly and said he was sure they meant well, but the last thing the town needed was to be linked with a bunch of Reds. "More than most folks, we got to keep our noses clean, if you know what I mean," he said.

Kate O'Hare told him there was strength in numbers. "The state legislature's liable to pass that Grandfather Clause next month. If you'll join us, Mr. Springs, maybe we can head it off."

"'Maybe' sound like trouble to me, Miss. I heard 'maybe' one too many times." He bowed again, politely, then walked away.

Warren Stargell and Frank O'Hare debated whether or not to set up the speakers' stand, anyway, despite the Deputy Mayor. "He didn't exactly order us out of town," Warren Stargell said.

A stern-faced woman walked quickly past them, gesturing with her fingers at the children who'd talked to Harry. They grinned at him, giggled, then followed her into a nearby dry goods store. Harry looked around. The streets were crowded when they'd first got to town. Now no one was about. He saw a gingham curtain flutter in a window, a newspaper scrap tumble in a gust of dust. It wrapped around a hitching post on the corner.

Warren Stargell reached for a bucket to water the horses. Harry heard a *click* somewhere above and behind his left shoulder. He cocked his head. A deafening *crack*—a rifle shot, he realized seconds later—splintered a wheel-spoke in front of him. Everyone dove for cover, splashing in puddles of water. Kate O'Hare's daughter kicked and squealed. After a minute, Harry peered around the legs of the horses but saw no one. No more shots. Finally J. T. Cumbie said, "I think *that* was our order to leave." He glared at Kate O'Hare. "Never should have come here in the first place."

They piled into their wagons and cars and bolted down the street. They weren't far out of town when Frank O'Hare told Warren Stargell to stop. "Let's just set up shop in this field for a couple of days," he said. "Word of mouth'll get around. Anyone in Taft who's interested'll find us."

And they did. By the second day, a throng of over two hundred women and men with their children had covered the soggy ground with blankets and picnic lunches. They listened to the speeches (J. T. Cumbie promised to "liberate" them from their "enduring bonds"), read aloud to each other from the *Appeal*. They laughed and sang rowdy spirituals, lined up for brief rides in Chester's balloon.

Late in the day, as Harry was leaving the platform after his speech, he ran into Bobby Springs in his gray suit and tie. "Very impressive, Mr. Shaughnessy. Passionate. Polished."

"Thank you, sir." Harry pulled Bob Cochran's yellow kerchief out of his pocket and wiped the sweat off his face. "I didn't think we'd see you here," he said.

"I was curious," Bobby Springs admitted.

"You know, Frank was telling you the truth. We really *are* on your side."

" 'With friends like that' . . ."

"I'm serious."

"I just hope y'all know what you're doing, son, that's all."

"You wait. When Gene Debs becomes President, it'll be the birth of a whole new nation."

Bobby Springs laughed.

"Are you the one who shot at us?" Harry asked.

The man frowned. Harry described the incident in the street the other day. Bobby Springs looked stricken, and only partly recovered when Harry assured him no one had been hurt.

"Thank Jesus. I'm terribly sorry such an outrage occurred in my town. Damn fools know better than to take potshots at white folks—"

"We didn't call the law."

Bobby Springs nodded. "You're carrying a powerful message—a *threatening* message, even to some of us who'd like to believe it."

"I know," Harry said.

"Good luck to you, son." He tipped his hat.

Harry rolled himself a cigarette; Warren Stargell had given him a pouch of tobacco. He watched Chester check the stakes in the ground around the balloon. Last night's rain had softened the turf. Now a new light drizzle had begun. Chester looked worried. He reknotted the ropes, turned and smiled at a group of kids. Just then, as Harry looked on, a stake tore from the ground; the rope snapped forward and snaked around Chester's right leg. He whirled to see what had happened, tugged at the rope. His sudden motion freed the other stakes, and the balloon began to rise, dragging Chester through a rugged thatch of grass. He worked his fingers into the earth; clumps of mud crumbled in his hands. The rope jerked him into the air.

Harry dropped his cigarette and ran, waving his arms. The balloon had drifted too high. He leaped, but Chester's hand was just out

142

of reach. "Harry! Harry!" he called, upside down. He clawed at the rope. It was soggy and thick, and clung, tightly wrapped, to his leg. Sally came running from her tent. The crowd gasped.

Chester flopped in the air, working the rope. He was a good thirty feet high by now. The rain picked up; a powerful gust snagged the balloon and carried it eastward away from the field. "Oh my God!" Sally yelled. "Someone—please—!" She sank to her knees in the grass.

Your wings, Harry thought. *Unfold them, man.*

Chester loosened the rope, unwrapped the coil, and tried to straighten up. He lost his grip and fell head first into a tiny stand of maples. Sally screamed.

"First time I ever watched a man die," Harry wrote his father later. "I hope it's the last. The next day, after Sally left with Chester's body in the wagon, the rest of us came on to Oklahoma City, to wrap up our circuit. We're a sad bunch, Dad. We've drawn some good crowds this month, but we've been shunned plenty, too. We haven't lost our optimism, but there certainly isn't a red tide waiting to engulf the capital."

That drizzly afternoon in the maple grove near Taft, as the men untangled Chester's body from the trees, Harry, shaken, cold to the core of his ribs, held Sally. Chester's arms bobbed recklessly, like a scarecrow in a windstorm. Sally trembled, wouldn't watch. Whispering, Harry told her Chester had simply run on ahead of them. He'd be waiting for them all on that glorious day when they learned, for a fact, that Heaven was painted red.

THE HUCKINS HOTEL, ON Broadway Street in downtown Oklahoma City, was the temporary home of the new state capital. It was a squatty rectangular building; from a distance it looked to Harry like a toolbox, each of its shaded balconies a hollowed-out space for storing washers and screws. Next to it, another hotel, the Skirvin, was under construction. Steel cranes reached into the sky, their cross-beams like tic-tac-toe games scratched across the clouds.

Electric lamps graced every corner: the future was here. Horse-carts, streetcars. A man sold hot dogs and cold fried potatoes from a card table on a sidewalk in front of the tall gray Pioneer Telephone Building (Harry had never seen a telephone but he'd heard about them); a flower-seller paced the steps of a massive Baptist temple. Harry smelled leather and sweat, perfume and hot rubber tires, asphalt, toasted bread, burning oil. Sparrows sang, engines wheezed, coins rattled in pockets, men whistled and women laughed, more easily than his mother ever had. Greens, blues, and reds looked sharper than ever before, splashed across the city's fancy metal signs, or expensive tinted glass in a few of the downtown shops. He could barely catch his breath.

He watched the legislators button their dark cotton suits in front of the Huckins, nod and gesture and slap each other's backs, then dis-appear into the lobby.

Kate and Frank O'Hare led their friends to the St. Nicholas Hotel on Eighth Street; the owners knew them and offered dis-counted rooms for a couple of nights. Harry had lunch with Warren Stargell and Fred Warren in Gus's Fish and Steak House in the ground floor of the building—a hot roast beef sandwich with pickles and a spicy kind of mustard he'd never tasted. Then he climbed the stairs to his room and, despite impatient horns shaking his streetside window, fell into a dreamless sleep. He hadn't been in a real bed in over three weeks.

Warren Stargell woke him around seven-thirty that night, told him to wash up and change. Everyone was going to dinner. The lights had come on in the city. Harry stood at the window looking down at the nearby buildings, the yellow strips of curtains, the giant words in ads for shoes and shirts and bottled Coca-Cola, the button-like headlights rolling down glistening gray streets. He whispered to himself the word "illumination" and knew what it meant for the very first time.

The group walked five blocks to the Evermonde Café, a small place that Frank O'Hare recommended. It was on the first floor of a large brick building trimmed with a thin wooden sign: "Carver Kiropractic College and Infirmary." Several buggies blocked the curb.

"What's . . . *kiropractic?*" Harry asked.

"Chiropractic medicine. That's where they twist your spine into crazy knots," J. T. Cumbie said. "Capitalist racket, like everything else in this town."

The café's proprietor, a big brown-haired woman named Rose, hugged the O'Hares as they walked in the door. "Don't think you're gonna eat here for free," she told them. "I don't share my food, I *sell* it!"

Frank O'Hare smiled. "You're forgiven, just for tonight."

Harry didn't think he'd be hungry after the sandwich he'd eaten at lunch but he inhaled a bowl of chicken soup and a flank steak, medium rare, with peas and potatoes. He decided he liked city life—as long as the league was paying.

After dinner, walking off their meals, they passed pawnshops, furniture stores, manufacturers, and business schools, each window a glimpse of strange, different lives Harry had never imagined. All these possibilities! In Oklahoma!

He noticed a Catholic church he'd return to in the morning. He'd promised his mother he wouldn't forget his prayers.

On the way back to the hotel, he saw a pair of cops give them all a serious once-over before moving on down the street. The policemen wore tall, rounded helmets and knee-length coats like the British bobbies he'd seen in books. Their polished black shoes reflected the lights of the street. One of them touched the bill of his helmet with his billy club, greeting Harry as he passed. Harry shivered. "I'm a Red," he almost told the man, just to see what he'd do. Just to see the real city.

HE'D AGREED TO MEET Kate O'Hare and the others in front of the Huckins Hotel at ten A.M. First he ran to the church.

The sanctuary was deserted, small and dark, brightened only by a series of candles near the altar. A large wooden cross hung in the nave, next to a painting of Mary looking pensive and sad. Harry saw a grimy alcove cut into one of the walls, big enough for a life-sized statue of a woman or a man. A statue *had* been there; he saw its outline in the wall, a blank where dust and soot had failed to collect: a robed figure with its right hand raised. Probably Christ. Where was He now?

Gears ground in the street outside. A newspaper boy screamed about scandals, robberies, bloody murder: "Authorities baffled! Latest details!"

Like every other laborer in this unforgiving city, Harry figured, Christ had probably packed His lunch and caught the streetcar to work.

He said a prayer for Chester's soul, and asked for the Holy Mother's help as he and his friends spread the truth. Lately God had sent them more trials than triumphs. It didn't seem fair to Harry. Oscar Ameringer, Patrick Nagle, Gene Debs—they all said God was on the movement's side. If so, His support was awfully subtle. "Faith," Harry exhorted himself. "Don't lose faith."

By the time he reached the Huckins, just after ten, Kate O'Hare was already wagging her finger at the passersby on the walks, and the legislators who hurried past her into the hotel. She wore a long linen dress, flaming red, with a cream-colored sash around her waist, and a white cotton bodice. Her lustrous hair was tucked into a yellow straw hat. Harry fell in love with her again, as he did each day.

"Woman labor!" he heard her shout at a pair of dour congressmen. "Gentlemen, when will the laws on your books match the facts? Why, in your very own city, just a few blocks from here, women weave the nation's clothing. The matron at her loom has long been the theme for the painter's brush and the poet's songs. But today she no longer inspires picture or rhyme unless it's the verse of misery and the portrait of human suffering!"

The politicians shook their heads and looked away. Streetcars clanged and people called to one another. Some of them stared at Kate O'Hare, but refused to stop and listen, apparently frightened of being implicated in something strange, troublesome, dangerous, or illegal. J. T. Cumbie strolled along the street curb, restless, grim about the meager response, but Kate O'Hare kept talking. Harry looked around, expecting to spot, any minute now, a cop on the beat, and was shocked to see Jesus. So *this* is where He'd gone! He was barefooted and He wore a pair of tattered overalls. His long hair and beard were matted and moist and filmed with chalky dust. "Got a quarter, brother?" He said to Warren Stargell. Then Harry noticed the fellow wasn't alone. Three other thin men, toothless and pocked with sores, moved through the line of Socialists, begging change. "Share the wealth, sister?" said the man who looked like Jesus, thrusting his open palm toward Kate O'Hare.

"The shame of it," she answered softly. "That a man can starve within a few steps of the state capitol. Tell me, if I give you money, will you buy yourself a meal or will it go for a bottle?"

He grinned. His weathered expression was both cocky and shy. His clothes smelled of urine and cigarettes.

"Socialism can cure your craving for drink, friend."

He rolled his eyes. "Here it comes," he said. "The sermon."

"No no. I don't agree with the churches that drink is a question of morals or sin," said Kate O'Hare. "Churches are built for the glory of God and not for the uses of man."

Harry felt himself blush.

"Drunkenness is a disease," she said. "I've seen miners afflicted with rheumatism and printers with consumption. Drunkenness, too, finds *its* proper culture in excess—of idleness or work, excessive cold or heat, too much speed or deadly monotony. Am I telling your story?"

Tears glistened in the young man's eyes. He stared, astonished, at Kate O'Hare.

"Here, friend. Take my hand. I won't judge you. Intemperance is the fruit of capitalism. I'm not concerned with material prosperity. It's the prosperity of the human spirit I cherish. Sit with me, relax, let me share with you—"

"No!" He pulled away. "I ain't joining no goddam cause!" Trembling, he brushed his salty cheeks. "I drink because I *like* it, lady, all right?" He laughed, a forced hack deep in his throat, and motioned his friends to follow him down the street. They lurched past buggies and shiny new wagons. Kate O'Hare closed her eyes for a moment, straightened her hat, and said, "I believe we've done all we can here for the time being. I think I'll go back to the room and lie down. Frank, can you take the kids to lunch?" She turned and, with great dignity, moved slowly beyond the shoppers and smiling storekeepers sweeping their walks.

AFTER LUNCH HARRY TAPPED lightly on her door. She looked sleepy when she answered. Soft. Warm. Her red dress was wrinkled. "Harry. Come in, come in."

"I'm sorry to bother you, but I guess Mr. Stargell and I are heading home tomorrow. I didn't know if I'd see you again." He looked at the floor. "It's been a real privilege sharing the stage with you."

"Likewise." She sat on her unmade bed. "I've heard a lot of fine speakers in my time. Oscar, Eugene, Kate Barnard, Caroline Lowe,

Mother Jones. But you, Harry . . . you're one of the best, and you've got a lot of years ahead of you. When I get home to Kansas City, I'll tell all my friends about you."

"Thank you, ma'am."

"When I first started barnstorming, I had a high, shrill voice," she said. "Frank used to tell me to tone things down, but I didn't believe him until we visited the St. Louis World's Fair a few years ago. They had a pavilion there where you could make your own phonograph records. Lord, when I heard how I sounded! I had to do a lot of work. But you're a natural, Harry."

He smiled. "Do you mind if I ask . . . ?"

"What is it?" she said.

"This morning. When no one listens. When changes don't happen fast enough. How do you—"

"Keep myself going?"

He nodded.

"I'll tell you, Harry, no matter what happens today, tomorrow, or the day after that, I'm content just knowing I've served. I've given the working class my girlhood, my young womanhood." She shrugged. "And now my motherhood. It's true. Changes don't always happen quick enough to suit me. But all we can do is spread the word."

Harry nodded again.

"Here. I've got something for you." She knelt beside her bed. "It's not a doubloon or a gold ingot, but I'd call it a treasure just the same." She pulled a thick, cream-colored book from a bag, turned to its fly-leaf, and scribbled something in it with a pen. She handed it to Harry: *The Jungle* by Upton Sinclair. "A few years ago we serialized part of this novel in the *Appeal*. Words *can* change things, Harry. If you ever doubt that, remember this book. Did you ever hear of the Pure Food and Drug Act?"

"No ma'am."

She smiled. "Well, it doesn't matter. Hold on to this. It might be important to you someday."

Harry said, "I love you."

She hugged him and told him she'd see him again down the road.

THAT NIGHT, SITTING IN the steak house after dinner, J. T. Cumbie told Fred Warren and Warren Stargell it had been a grueling month, full of triumph and tragedy, a long day, and he could use a little nightcap, how about them? They agreed and asked a young waiter to recommend a quiet place where Mr. Cumbie wouldn't be recognized (it wouldn't do for a gubernatorial candidate to be caught guzzling "demon rum"; he'd managed to promote himself, publicly, as a tee-totaler). The waiter pointed them toward Hudson Street. There they'd find a drab brick building attached to the rear of Swangaard's Waffle House. "Three rapid knocks on the door," he said. Warren Stargell thanked him and gave him an extra tip.

Harry asked if he could tag along. "Certainly," said J. T. Cumbie, buttoning his coat. "I'd say you've earned your stripes."

The "gray horse" led the charge to Hudson Street. It was just a few blocks away. Across an alley from the waffle house, beneath a dim electric light, two young women in thin black dresses stood smoking and talking. Harry thought of Sherrie, the dancer he'd seen in the miner's dining hall, and the pregnant girl in the camp waiting in line for the outhouse. He felt a sudden sadness and missed his mother. These women looked lonely and cold. He wished he could invite them in to talk without awkwardness or misunder-standing.

He wished he could touch them.

The night smelled of coal and oil. Train cars clattered in the distance.

The tiny room was filled with smoke, low voices, and laughter. Fred Warren ordered a bottle of grain alcohol for Warren Stargell, J. T. Cumbie and himself, and a glass of beer for Harry, his first since

Anadarko. The bartender didn't mention Harry's age; everyone knew that minors were the least of his problems if the law got wind of this place.

They found a round table in the middle of the room. Sawdust covered the floor. Kerosene lamps, hung on twisted nails in the walls, sputtered and hissed, casting more noise than light.

Warren Stargell raised his drink. "To fallen comrades," he said.

"Dear Chester." Fred Warren threw back his head and drained his glass. It was cracked and chipped and slightly discolored.

"To our next governor," Harry said, nodding at J. T. Cumbie.

"Thank you, son."

They toasted again. Warren Stargell reached into a pocket for his pouch of Bull Durham. Harry noticed a white-haired, black-clad figure enter the door in a flurry of commotion. The smoke made him dizzy. Then he heard a woman's voice: "There are just two crowds on Earth, God's and the devil's."

Warren Stargell lighted a match. "What the hell?" he said.

The figure in the doorway tossed off her light cotton scarf and raised her arms. Her dress was as black as a judge's robe. She was chunky and small. "It's plain to see, the devil makes this his stopping place when he's not busy down in Texas!" She stalked to the center of the room, grabbed the whiskery jaw of a young man chewing tobacco. He swallowed hard, choked. "You remind me of an old billy goat gnawing his cud," the woman said.

"My Lord," whispered J. T. Cumbie. "You know who that is, don't you?" Before he could say the name, she whirled toward the table and slapped the cigarette out of Warren Stargell's mouth. "Sucking on a coffin nail!" she shouted. "Are you in a hurry to meet the devil, my friend?" She spotted Harry. "Dear Christ, this boy's losing his soul already. Run, boy, run!"

Harry sat, astonished. She had a wonderful speaking voice, he thought.

The bartender snagged her arm. "Listen here, lady, you can't just waltz in here—"

She leaped away from him, reached into the folds of her enormous skirt, and produced a smart little hatchet. She swung it over her head then brought it down, mightily, on the table in front of Harry, spilling the whiskey and beer, sending long blond splinters twisting into smoke in the air. "The wrath of God!" she screamed.

All the drinkers dove for cover.

"I thought she'd retired," Warren Stargell said, scrambling under a table.

"I thought she was dead," Fred Warren replied. Bottles crashed, wood snapped, arms and legs splayed, twitching, in sawdust and bubbles of ale.

"God is a righteous cyclone," she yelled, "sweeping the Earth!"

"Who *is* she?" Harry asked.

"Carry Nation," answered J. T. Cumbie. "Saloon-buster and goddam pain in the ass."

Harry remembered the sign in the hills near Zeke Cash's still, but he didn't have time to think about it. She was heading his way again with the hatchet. Swiftly, he crawled behind the bar. A chair-leg sailed above his head. "I strike this blow against the brewers and distillers, the Republicans and Democrats and all the city's businessmen who've conspired to pickle the masses!" she wheezed.

Men rushed out of the room in twos and threes, squeezing past each other in the doorway. Harry followed Warren Stargell into the alley; the blade wasn't far behind. He heard its whistle, the groan of the doorjamb.

The two women who'd been smoking huddled by an overturned trash can. Drunks scurried past them, scattering garbage, ash, and gravel. "Smoke and booze and hoity-toity girls!" Carry Nation screamed. She set off after the women.

A minute or two later, half a block down Hudson Street, Harry met his companions and they walked back to their hotel. Sawdust garnished J. T. Cumbie's beard like strings of tinsel in a Christmas tree. "Man wants a quiet drink," he muttered, brushing off his sleeves. "Ends up with his head cut off."

The night air was cool. Harry took it gratefully into his lungs. His knees were sore from crawling around on the floor. Steam rose from open grates in the streets, smelling of water and earth and of families forced too close together: the crowded wastes of the city's full life.

In the bright lobby of the St. Nicholas Hotel the men exchanged their good-byes. Up in the room he shared with Warren Stargell, Harry stood at the window savoring one last view of the avenues. He didn't know if he'd ever see Oklahoma City again. He stared intently, then closed his eyes, seeing the lights—memories already—etched against the slippery darkness of his lids.

The crowds, the dusty roads, the speeches of his heroes: the month had been blessed with excitement and event, but now that it was over, a thought he'd long been trying to ignore swamped his mind once more.

Warren Stargell told him good-night.

He mumbled, "Sleep well," and turned to the window again. He'd be up for a while. With his little finger he scribbled on the glass a faint and smudgy "Mollie."

6

He woke, and for a moment he didn't know when or how he'd got to bed. It was his *own* bed, with the faint lemon smell of his mother's homemade soap in the folds of the sheets. Halley slept at his feet. He remembered stumbling into a flat, ordered field at twilight—yesterday? the day before that?—unbuttoning his pants to relieve himself and being surrounded by bison; they rose all around him like mossy stones unearthed in a sudden upheaval. Warren Stargell shooed them away, whooping, waving his hat. After that, the journey home was a swell of dust in his mind. He vaguely recalled his father lifting him from the wagon; now here he was in his room.

He sat up and scratched Halley's ears. The dog sighed and burrowed deeper into the quilt. Harry didn't hear his father's snores. When was the last time his father had slept without snoring? He got out of bed, tiptoed to his bedroom door and, with the certainty learned from long familiarity with a place, knew he was alone in the house.

He pulled on his pants and shoes and stepped outside. The gate to the empty mule pen swung aimlessly on its hinges, creaking and rubbing the wood by the open latch. Starlight silvered the leaves of the trees, the distant fields' tight rows. Cotton season soon. He didn't want to think about it.

Clover, mint, and honey weighted the lazy air. The night's silence seemed loud and profound after the constant hammering of voices and noises in the city. The sounds of his own breathing seemed clamorous in the stillness.

His father stood next to the barn, hands in pockets, unmoving.

"Dad?"

"Harry. Thought you'd sleep at least a couple of days." He laughed and held out his arm. Harry slipped under it, toward the warmth of his father's chest. Andrew squeezed his shoulder. "I was just thinking we got to ride into town tomorrow. Buy some boots and gloves. It's that time of year."

"Dad?" Harry blinked sleep from his eyes. "Where's Ma?"

Andrew stepped away from him. He didn't have his cane but still he moved slowly and with care. "Your ma," he said. "She's tending to some business in Walters."

"What kind of business?" Harry had never associated this word with his mother.

"We'll talk about it in the morning. You need your rest now." He patted Harry's back. "Before he left, Warren told me you'd brought a lot of converts into the fold. I'm real pleased."

Harry nodded and yawned, gave up and said good-night when it was clear his father wasn't going to say any more just now. He jumped back into bed next to Halley, comforted by the dusty smell of his fur, the light flapping of the curtain in the midnight breeze. Home. But something was wrong. His mother had never been away before. Tired as he was, he lay awake all night, anxious for dawn and his father's explanation.

ANDREW LOOKED LIKE HE hadn't slept, either. His face was puffy and pale, his thin hair stiff. His eyebrows, bushy, seemed ready to spring into his eyes.

He set a bowl of oatmeal in front of Harry. A scorched smell hung in the kitchen. "I may have overcooked that a little," he said. "Eat up. I'll get the wagon. We got some errands to run." He limped toward the door.

Harry tongued the oatmeal; it was spongy. He set it aside. He brushed some baking soda over his teeth, dragged a hand through his hair. His mother usually cut it twice a month, but now it was long and tightly curled.

They were halfway to town before his father finally leaned back in the wagon's seat and looked at him. "Don't be alarmed now, Harry, but your mother's in jail."

Harry sat up straight. *"Real* jail?"

"She didn't do a thing wrong, not as *I* see matters—"

"What happened?"

A bitter laugh. "Liquor, if you can believe it." He told Harry that Annie Mae and three other women from the church had slipped five dollars to an Atchison, Topeka, and Santa Fe Railroad man so he'd deliver a barrel of sacramental wine to them Monday night, on the late run.

"I don't understand," Harry said.

"While you were gone, the county tightened its prohibition laws. The new 'bone-dry' statute says you can't bring out-of-state alcohol here unless you can prove it's for medicinal purposes." He shook the reins; the horses speeded up. "For years now, St. Mary's wine has come from Kansas City. The county says no more."

Harry thought for a minute. "But that makes the Mass illegal."

"That's exactly what Annie said."

"They can't do that!"

Andrew shrugged. "They got her on a bribery charge."

The jailhouse in Walters was musty and small, flooded with cold gray light through grimy windows set in a patchwork of bars. When Harry and Andrew arrived, Annie Mae, in a tiny cell with three other women Harry didn't know, was complaining to the sheriff. "I know you know it's not right. You're a good Christian man, Sheriff Stephens."

"That I am, ma'am, but—"

"Then you realize it's indecent to keep the four of us here without partitions or curtains of any kind. When we need to change clothes or tend to our toilet—"

The sheriff, a short, balding man with bowed legs, scratched his head. "We never had women in here before, Miz Shaughnessy. I didn't rightly know how to prepare—"

"Andrew! Harry!" Annie Mae reached between the bars in the door. She wore a pink blouse and a gray cotton skirt. "Harry, oh Harry, I'm so happy to see you, sweetheart!" But then she frowned and pulled her arms inside the cell before Harry could touch her hands. She dipped her head. "I'm ashamed for you to see me like this," she said.

"No, Mama, no." He whirled on the sheriff. "*You're* the one who should be ashamed," he said. "Locking these fine ladies up . . . this is a direct violation of the Constitution of the United States, which, in case you didn't know it, Mr. Stephens sir, guarantees freedom of religion. I demand their immediate release or we'll have you in court!"

Annie Mae grinned.

"I don't make the laws, young man."

"Don't you have a conscience? Can't you spot impropriety when you see it? This statute will never stand up—"

Andrew poked his arm. "That's enough now. We'll handle this the proper way, through the proper channels." The smile on his lips reassured Harry. "Do you have everything you need?" he asked Annie Mae.

"Except my dignity."

"As soon as they set bail, we'll get you out."

"Don't worry, Mama," Harry added. The haggard look on her face made him cry.

She smiled at him. "My little politician."

Andrew kissed her through the bars then led Harry back outside. "Well," he said quietly. "The road toughened you, son. You've got more authority now than ever. More presence."

"Dad, isn't there something we can do?"

"You had a good argument in there, but Sheriff Stephens is the wrong man to make it to. We've got to go higher up, and we will, we will."

They walked across the street to the hardware store. Andrew bought two new pairs of gloves for cotton-picking, and a thick set of boots, but later that day, when a county judge set bail for Annie Mae at twenty-five dollars, Andrew sold the items back to the store and went to the bank for the rest of the money. "Looks like we'll be picking bare-handed this year," he said.

At home, in the kitchen, Annie Mae sponge-bathed over a tin tub for nearly an hour—"I've felt dirty for days"—closing her eyes and letting the warm water relax her, then set about baking cornbread and a peach cobbler, steaming red beans and rice, pouring sugar into giant tumblers of tangy iced tea. Except for the night in the arbor, when the Baptists chased them away, the family hadn't eaten a meal this abundant all year, and for the balance of the evening they laughed and forgot their troubles.

Later that night Harry was awakened by a glare beneath his bedroom door. He heard his father's snores. He got up, stirring Halley who sighed and turned on his back, dangling his legs in the air. The dog still had digestive problems; he smelled like the gas in Chester's balloon.

Harry got dressed and walked into the kitchen, where his mother sat at the table sorting bills. "I didn't mean to wake you," she said.

"That's all right." She brushed hair from her eyes. She looked so tired. "What is it, Mama?" He touched her wrist. "They won't send you back to jail, I promise."

She shook her head, spilling tears. "Oh Harry. I don't know if we're going to make it." She rattled the papers on the table. "Your father still can't work at full strength, and the chores around this place are just too much for you and me—"

He squeezed her fingers. "I'm sorry. I shouldn't have left," he said.

"It's not that. But I don't know how we're going to pay our debts. Now, on top of everything else, the county won't let us worship, and foolishly, *foolishly* I've crossed the law . . ." She stiffened, and rubbed her back.

Harry hugged her tightly, whispering that everything would be all right. She patted his arm. "Well. These aren't your worries," she said. "School'll be starting again soon, and it'll be cotton season . . . you'll have plenty on your plate. We'll all just do the best we can."

She kissed him good-night. His room was hot and he slept badly. Each time he woke, he noticed the light still burning in the kitchen.

He wanted to find Mollie—she probably didn't even know he was back—but in the next few days he stuck close to home, gauging his mother's moods, helping her sweep and wash and cook. He fed the chickens and watered the horses. He avoided the mule pen. Andrew slept late each day, limped to the barn in the early afternoons and just stood there, gazing at the stark line where the sky capped the furrowed edge of the land. He didn't mention the coal mines. He wasn't planning any business trips.

One day they did go into Walters, all three of them, to talk to the county commissioners. Annie Mae pleaded with them to reconsider their position. *Squawking like turkeys*, Harry thought, *the only way to change a law.*

One of the officials, a big man named Boyd, bit the end off a fat black cigar, wiped his bottom lip, and said, "If we allow Catholic communion wine, we'll have to make special exemptions for all the other denominations, and that means our 'bone-dry' law would spring a pretty big leak."

"Surely you recognize the difference between a bunch of

bootleggers in the hills and good people worshiping their Lord," Harry said.

"And surely, young fellow, you recognize the need for tough measures in this area. Sometimes, for the greater good of the majority of the people, a minority is called upon to sacrifice. That's as good a working definition of democracy as you'll ever hear, and if you have any political ambitions—as I understand you might—you'd do well to heed it."

Harry tugged his shirt to smooth the wrinkles, and stood as straight as he could. "Suppose for a moment that the majority of the citizens in this county were Catholic," he said. "Would we even be standing here discussing this? I think not. You wouldn't have *thought* of passing such a careless, narrow law. It's one thing to speak of reasonable sacrifice, Commissioner Boyd. It's quite another to punish a group of people out of prejudice and ignorance of their beliefs."

"Now hold on a minute—"

"The anti-Catholic sentiment in this county is quite well-known, and you'd better believe we'll make it an issue in fighting this preposterous legislation."

Annie Mae and Andrew stared at him, stunned, as if the governor himself had just walked into the room. None of the other commissioners said a word. A young man with a press pass jammed into his hatband began scribbling hasty notes.

"Now then, Mr. Boyd, I think you'll agree the laws of God supersede the laws of man. With that in mind, if you don't want to be dodging lightning bolts anytime soon, I suggest you release that barrel of wine you impounded to Father McCartney over at St. Mary's, and let him say the Mass while this new law is being reevaluated. Because it *will* be reevaluated, I assure you." He stepped closer to the man, in the foul haze of his cigar. "Democracy, Mr. Boyd? Absolutely. And that means freedom to worship as we please, a right accorded us by the wisdom and the law of this land."

He turned and walked out the door with his parents in tow. The reporter followed, checking the spelling of "Shaughnessy," grilling Harry about his next plan of attack.

"Mother, what's the name of the Chancellor for the Diocese of Oklahoma?"

Annie Mae nearly tripped in the street, running to keep up with her son. Andrew, favoring his bad leg, straggled far behind. "Father Urban de Hasque," she said breathlessly.

"And our bishop? Theo—?"

"Theophile Meerschaert."

"A friend of the governor's, as I recall," Harry said. "I saw a picture of them together in the paper one day. They'll be notified. And we'll publicize our plight in the Catholic press. Once we're all mobilized, we'll just see who's a majority."

The reporter asked, amused, "Is this your first big campaign, ah . . . Mr. Shaughnessy?"

"Not at all. I just came off the road with J. T. Cumbie, the next governor of this fine state of ours. Mark my word, the people's revolution will soon sweep bigoted bureaucrats like Mr. Boyd out of office . . . and when you quote me, you can call me the Boy Orator."

HIS MOTHER WANTED TO know where he'd learned such words as "supersede" and "impropriety" but he really couldn't tell her; he'd picked them up, traveling. At the end of the week, the *Walters New Herald* published the journalist's account of Harry's showdown with Boyd. It concluded: "At twelve, Mr. Shaughnessy is already a stirring speaker, a promising young statesman, perhaps the best native politician our infant state has produced. We will certainly keep an eye— no, both eyes—on this budding new leader."

THE KIOWA COMMUNITY EAST of Cookietown, several hundred acres of hardscrabble leveled by harsh plains winds, sudden floods, merciless velocity and force, was virtually unreachable by wagon or car. The paths into and out of the region were rocky, winding and narrow, poor even by the low standards of the rest of the county's roads. Walking, switching a stick to keep flies off his face, Harry remembered the smooth paved streets surrounding the Huckins Hotel. The farther you got from the city, from the congressmen's haunts, he thought, the sorrier the highways got, the schools, the working conditions of women and men. The life of a congressman: that was the way to go.

A thunderstorm the night before had stirred up pollen and dust. A scent of rank water clung like skin to the shimmering heat in the air. Plants, scorched, closed up; mosquitoes circled their drooping stems.

He left the road when he saw four or five whitewashed shacks and a tepee made of canvas and oak. He didn't know where Mollie lived; he'd have to ask.

As he tramped through brittle brown weeds, huffing and sweating, he began to sneeze. By the time he reached the first shack, and a group of small children playing with straw dolls and sticks, he figured he looked to them like a hideous animal from deep in thickest Texas, with his red, watering eyes, puffy nose, and twisted mouth. Thin white moths rose from tangled vines at his feet. He said, "Hello." The children stared at him as if they'd just witnessed an accident.

"Weryavah," he croaked, wiping his nose with the back of his hand. "Mollie Weryavah. You know her?"

One of the girls pointed downhill, toward a swirling, muddy river. Harry thanked her and set off across the field. Pheasants and doves and wild turkeys roamed the banks of the river; Harry had been there once, years ago, with his father hunting Thanksgiving dinner. Past brambles and bees he ran. Shouts rose from a dogwood and mulberry thicket. Cedar waxwings lifted in a big spooked bunch above the water. Among the trees Harry glimpsed a soft flash. "Mollie?" he called, sneezing.

The white figure stopped abruptly. Her dark face peered through the leaves. "Socialist?" she said.

He beamed.

"Damn you," she shouted, turned away, and trudged across the wet, waving grass.

"Mollie! Mollie, wait!" The mud by the river's high bank slowed his steps, but he ran and caught her arm. Just then a growl burst from the shadows on the other side of the water. "Oh no!" Mollie said. She covered her face with her hands. A gold shape rushed from the bushes followed by three tall teenaged boys. Harry could see it was Lil they were chasing, but the dog looked broken, mad. Foam-strands hung like folded wings from the corners of her mouth. "My God," Harry whispered. Mollie knelt in the grass. Her hair was longer than he'd seen it last, wavy and fine. The summer sun had red-dened her skin. She smelled of coming rain, of river stones, of sun-flowers and ivy.

Harry dropped beside her, held her shoulders. "How did it happen?" he asked.

The boys had lost sight of Lil and were standing now, tired and uncertain, by a fallen limb jutting several feet into the water.

Mollie wiped tears from her face. "A rabid wolf, down from the hills . . ." She twisted out of his arms and looked at him. "You bastard, you didn't tell me good-bye!"

"I know, Mollie, I—"

"Too late," she said, rising. "It's too late now." The tallest of the boys had splashed across the river and stood behind her, muddy and wet. He didn't have a shirt; his chest was as flat and glistening as the prehistoric glaciers Harry had studied in school, that had smoothed America's plains. With his long fingers he flicked soggy hair off his shoulders. "This is my cousin Anko," Mollie said. "Anko, this is Harry."

Anko grabbed Mollie's arm. He kissed her mouth. Then he stepped away from her and glared at Harry. "She can't get far," he said. "We'll track her. In the meantime, we'd better find a madstone."

Mollie nodded. Harry looked at her, questioning. She shook her head. "You should go," she said.

"Yes," said Anko.

"Can't we talk?" Harry asked. "For a minute?"

Anko stepped forward and tugged his shirt. The sudden movement made Harry's nose run again. "Go," Anko hissed. "Go *now*." His heavy breath smelled of fresh fish and dill.

Angry, humiliated, Harry started upriver, glancing back at Mollie. Katydids popped against his pants. The mud smelled like something old and dying. Suddenly Mollie was behind him, panting. She kissed him quickly. "Socialist, do you love me still?"

He plunged his face into her hair, felt the curve of her hip through her dress. "Yes," he said. "Yes. That's why I came to find you."

She looked around. Anko had disappeared downstream. "Then come tonight, here by the river. At eight. That's when the Elder wakes. We'll go to her for a madstone."

"What are madstones?"

"Shhh. Just meet me here, all right?"

"What about Anko?"

She shrugged. "I'll slip away from him."

Father McCartney had planned a special Mass tonight, to rally the Catholic community. Somehow, Harry would have to sneak off. *You've got more authority now*, his father had said. *More presence.* But standing here with Mollie he didn't feel any different at all.

The craziness was blossoming again.

ST. MARY'S, ON THE south side of Walters, was a small, clean chapel with a red carpet inside, and a coat of lime green paint on its square oak walls. Candles and kerosene lanterns lighted the altar. Men unknotted their collars and ties in the stifling heat, women fanned themselves with hymnals. Harry watched a clear drop of sweat roll down the lovely long neck of a woman beside him in the pew and disappear above the top button of her dress, where the rise of her breasts began in earnest.

The priest placed the chasuble over his white linen alb and led the congregation in a recitation of the Angelus: "The angel of the Lord declared unto Mary—"

"And she conceived of the Holy Ghost. Hail Mary—"

"Behold the handmaid of the Lord—"

"Be it done to me according to Thy word—"

Once the prayers were finished, Father McCartney raised the chalice, but instead of offering the blood and body of Christ, he paused. Then he said, "Friends, as you know, some local men of power have tried to separate us from our Savior, from our Almighty Lord's supreme sacrifice on our behalf." The sacramental wine the sheriff's men had impounded had mysteriously disappeared; Father McCartney had accused them, the mayor, and the county commissioners of drinking it all. "So we cannot receive the blessing of Christ tonight." He urged his fellows to pressure the town leaders so that Righteousness and the Spirit of Forgiveness would once again grace "this parched and sinful land."

The Baptists had printed an open letter in the *Herald*, commending the commissioners for "banning liquor from our lives" and warning them not to be fooled by the "pagan rituals" of those who "call themselves Christians, but who will surely be cast into Hell for their wanton ways come the glory of Judgment Day."

At home, before the Mass, Andrew had grumbled about the Baptists' "shoddy Christ." "You know what *they* use at communion? Grape juice and pie crust. I mean, what kind of Savior is *that?*"

"Depends on what kind of pie," Harry had said, grinning. Andrew swatted his rear.

When Father McCartney ended his service, the parishioners

stood in the chapel discussing their missing wine, wondering what in Sam Hill the world had come to. The priest slipped into the confessional; Annie Mae insisted Harry take his turn. He hadn't done penance since before the summer encampments.

The wood inside the booth was cool and dark. The seat was hard. He heard the priest slide back the little door in the wall between himself and Harry, and shafts of light, thin as pencils, filled the tiny space where Harry waited. He could see the vague outline of Father McCartney's head through the wire grating in the wall. The priest was young—thirty, maybe, more like an older brother than a father, which made it hard for Harry to confess to him, or to take their exchanges seriously.

He coughed. "Forgive me, Father, for I have sinned." Oh Lord. Cigarettes and beer. Concealing the truth from his folks. Yelling at those who opposed him. And Mollie. Sweet Mollie. The heat of her skin. Her soft, moist lips. He squirmed, then knelt on the hard, gritty wood.

He told it all but the priest seemed not to listen. He said distractedly, "Say a hundred Hail Marys and fifteen Our Fathers. I absolve you of your sins in the name of the Father and of the Son and of the Holy Spirit." Harry rose to leave, relieved and a little confused. "Harry," said the priest. "Stay a moment longer."

Startled and afraid, Harry sat back down. Never had Father McCartney broken the spell of anonymity inside the confessional. What could this mean?

"I saw your name in the paper," the priest began.

"Yessir," Harry mumbled.

"It seems you're well on your way to a certain . . . celebrity."

"I don't know, Father."

"No need to be modest. You've confessed your sins and Pride was not among them. Harry?"

"Yes, Father?"

"I appreciate your efforts on behalf of St. Mary's. It was very brave of you to stand up to the county commissioners and say the things you did. But Harry?"

"Yessir?"

"You and your family—you're Socialists, aren't you?"

"That's right, Father."

The priest paused. "You're aware of the strong prejudice against Catholics in this state." He cleared his throat. "It could damage perceptions of us even further if the press associates us with radical politics. Therefore, I'm afraid I'm going to have to ask you to step into the background."

"But—"

"Surely you see the problem."

Harry sighed. Faith, he told himself. Don't lose faith. "I think I should go now, Father."

"Harry, listen to me. We both want what's best for the Church, isn't that right?"

He remembered the small mob on the road to Ada, the men who beat his father. "Yes, but I don't believe silence advances any cause," he said softly.

"I'm asking you. As a favor to your Lord."

Now he pictured Jesus throwing stones. He burst through the door of the booth. His mother was standing on the church's front steps with several other women in silk dresses and big round hats. Smiling, Harry tried to look calm, unburdened by sin. Annie Mae told him that Mrs. Riordan and Mrs. McIlhenny had prepared a few dishes and were inviting people to dinner. "Find your dad for me," she said.

He didn't know when or how he'd escape to see Mollie. Father McCartney, stepping from the confessional, nodded gravely at him from several yards away.

Crammed with Catholic bodies, the Riordans' small home sweltered and seemed to roar with the heat. Harry looked for the woman he'd sat beside in church, but didn't see her. He nearly choked on the smell of aftershave. Squash and okra steamed in dishes on a long walnut table draped in pink linen. He stuck his finger into the chocolate icing on a cake and licked it clean.

At one point he looked around the house, unable to locate any men. In the absence of sacramental wine, he figured, they'd found another "blessing." Mr. Riordan probably had a healthy stash. In the parlor someone began to play a tinny piano. Women's laughter rang in his ears. He told his mother he was dizzy and a little sick to his stomach. "I think I'd like to walk home," he said.

She placed a hand on his forehead.

"I'm fine," he said. "I need some air."

"It's a long walk, Harry."

"It'll do me good, Ma." He kissed her cheek. "I'll see you later."

Before she could say anything else he'd bolted out the door. He ran under gnarly apple trees throbbing with cicadas. Sweetness filled the night, tinged with a whiff of decay: late summer, soon to be gone.

This time, when he left the road near Cookietown to cut across the fields, he pulled a handkerchief from his back pocket and covered his face to keep from sneezing. He was early. Mollie wasn't here yet. He sat and watched the moon rise above the water, whitening the trembling reeds and muscular ripples in the shallows. In the morning he'd tell his parents he'd gotten sleepy walking home, and crawled into a neighbor's barn to nap. He'd need to do penance again, but he didn't want to talk further with Father McCartney.

He waited half an hour. The water's smooth sounds relaxed him but he grew suddenly alert when something rustled in the bushes behind him. He turned and Mollie fell into his arms. Her hands explored his face, his hair, the curve of his ears; her tongue circled his, surprising him. "Mollie, Mollie," he whispered. "You're not still mad at me, are you?"

"Yes," she said. "I didn't think you'd come back to me."

"I did. I'm here now. I missed you."

168

"Socialist?" Tears, milky in the moonlight, streaked her cheeks. "They've killed my dog."

"I'm sorry, Mollie. I'm so sorry." He brushed the wetness from her face. "Where's your cousin?" he asked.

"With my father." She grasped his hand. "Come on."

"Where are we going?"

"To the Elder."

"I want to hold you."

"Later. We have to hurry." She led him downriver. "The Elder is the only woman of our tribe who's allowed to be a keeper of medicine," she explained. "It's a very rare honor. Her family has always been gifted with the secrets of healing."

In a tarpaper shack by the water an old woman sat on a bed beneath a dim kerosene lantern. Moths attacked the glass around the flame. Frogs bellowed in the high grass just beneath her window. Her eyes were hard, white as limestone deposits. Harry couldn't tell if she saw anything. She never moved her head, not even to nod hello. She sniffed the air. "You know the taboo against guests," she told Mollie.

Mollie bowed her head. "Yes, Elder. I'm sorry. We were in a rush. I—"

"The healing may not work now. I cannot guarantee it."

"I understand."

"Who was bitten?" she said, her voice faint and hollow: wind inside a cave. Harry stood rigid, quiet.

"My cousin Anko's little brother. On the hand, when he tried to capture the dog."

The old woman pointed to a worn pouch, a skin of some kind, on the floor beside the door. Mollie opened it and pulled out a round shiny stone about the size of a silver dollar, but thicker and coated with light gray fuzz.

"I have treasured this madstone since I was a little girl," the Elder explained. "Do you know the story?"

"No, Elder."

"When I was six, I was bitten in the woods one morning by a skunk. That night my father hiked into the Arbuckle Mountains and shot an arrow into the heart of a small white deer. From its belly he pulled this powerful gem. He came home, pricked my wound to make it bleed, and applied the stone to my broken skin. It stuck, which meant the poison was in me. I shook my arm, but the stone wouldn't move. All night it sucked the death from my veins—I could feel it drawing. In the morning it fell to the floor and I was cured."

Harry shook his head and started to say something, but Mollie silenced him with a sober look. The frogs stopped for a while, then started up again, a deep bass chorus in the grass. He looked around the shack: a shield, the kind a warrior might raise in battle; three small, faceless dolls, tall as ears of corn.

"The boy who was bitten," said the Elder. "What is his name?"

"Tawha," Mollie said.

"If his bite is not still bleeding, open it with a razor blade or a knife. Sprinkle corn starch on the cut and apply the stone. If it doesn't stick, there is no poison in Tawha's blood. If it does, leave it until it falls to the ground on its own."

"Yes, Elder. Thank you," Mollie said.

"Return the stone to me when it has done its work. There are fewer white deer in the mountains now than there used to be— hunting is too easy with guns." The old woman grimaced; her face collapsed into fleshy crags. "Madstones are getting harder to find."

Mollie paused in the doorway.

"You have another question for me?"

"Yes." Mollie touched Harry's shoulder.

The Elder's lip twitched. "You know the answer already."

"Yes." She pulled Harry's hand and led him outside. "She's crazy," he puffed, running behind her through bull thistle and tall, silver goatsbeard. "Your friend needs a doctor."

"She's a very wise woman," Mollie said. "She's saved several lives."

Harry snatched her arm. They both nearly fell. "Mollie, superstitions may be fine with cuts and colds, but—" His chest heaved; he could barely catch his breath. "If that boy was really bitten—"

Mollie frowned at him. "Is that what we are to you?"

"What do you mean?"

"Superstitious children?" She closed her eyes for a moment. "Maybe Anko was right."

"I didn't say . . . what? What did Anko tell you?"

She looked at him fiercely. "He said I shouldn't go outside my people. He said white boys . . ."

"White boys what? What about us?"

"He said you'd use me, Socialist, that I'm nothing more than a child to you, someone you'll play with then throw aside when you're bored."

Harry ran his hands down her arms. "Mollie, Mollie, is that what you think?"

She lowered her head. "I don't know. Am I a child to you if I say I believe the Elder?"

"Of course not."

"You heard what she said about you."

"*Me?*"

"Usually, when someone's old, especially a woman, the tribe abandons her. It isn't cruelty, it's just . . . the proper thing to do. Blankets, food—they're all limited. They're needed for the young, the healthy and strong. We all understand this. But the Elder is an exception. She's a very powerful woman. She's never wrong."

"All right, all right, maybe I don't understand your laws," Harry said. "I'm worried about this boy, that's all. I didn't mean you were—"

Gently, she raised a hand to his lips. "It doesn't matter," she whispered. "It doesn't matter anyway."

"Why not?"

"I can't see you anymore."

He tightened his grip on her arms. "Mollie, that old lady doesn't know anything about me."

"Do you love me?"

"Don't you know I do? Yes. Yes."

She shook her head. "I love you too," she said. "But it doesn't matter, Socialist. It's too late. You shouldn't have left me when you did."

She wouldn't tell him anything more as they headed uphill away from the river, holding hands through brambles and the weeds of the fields. She stared at the ground. When they came in view of the shacks Harry had spotted the other day, Mollie stopped him, her body tight against his. She pointed at four slender sorrels grazing in a square of light near one of the houses' dingy windows. "See those animals?" she said.

"Yes."

"A gift from Anko's family to my father."

"So?"

She squeezed his fingers. "A dowry."

Harry's feet and hands went cold. "You don't mean—?"

Mollie nodded.

He touched her chin, turned her face toward his. "You're too young to marry."

"Am I?"

He shrugged.

"Usually, girls in my family wed at sixteen. I'm a little early, but Anko says he loves me, and my father likes him."

"Marry *me!*" Harry said.

She kissed his cheek. "I have to go now. My father and Anko and Tawha are waiting for the madstone." She leaned her head, briefly, on his shoulder. "I'm glad I got to see you once more. Don't forget me, Socialist."

"Mollie, don't marry him."

"My father has already given his approval. So has the Elder."

"I don't care."

"You don't understand. It's already been arranged. There's nothing I can do."

"You can run away with me."

Mollie smiled. "How can you save the world if you're hiding in shame with an Indian girl?" She kissed him again then wriggled free of his grasp. He watched her run across the field toward the dirty windows, the hem of her skirt stirring poppies. He stood for a long time without moving, cursing Anko, cursing himself, wishing he had a madstone to stick on his skin, to suck the bitter blood from his heart.

THE FIRST DAY OF school in the fall was always confusing and loud. Mrs. Altus, the teacher, a big, imperturbable woman in her early forties, had to divide a roomful of children of various ages and accomplishments into compatible groups, check their grooming (head lice, sores), get them started, often without pencils or paper. The day went smoothly if only half the kids were punished for shoving or shouting.

This year Harry had even less patience than usual with the opening rituals. His classmates, even those his age, seemed silly. Since he'd seen them last, he'd campaigned with Kate O'Hare, grappled with his father's injuries, his mother's arrest, their mounting debts; he'd got his heart broken. The other kids were scrawny and *young*. And the subjects! Algebra, geography—they had nothing to do with the worlds he'd discovered. Sitting in the classroom, he felt he'd dropped into a hole.

He'd tried to read *The Jungle*, the novel Kate O'Hare had given him in the city, but the prose was tortured and dense. He asked Mrs. Altus if she'd explain the author's references, the workings of the stockyards and the meat-packing plants in Chicago, a place he could barely imagine. She looked suspiciously at the book, frowned at Kate O'Hare's inscription: "For Harry, who can make a difference." "We can't engage in special projects," she told him. "We must stay within our age group and stick to our assignments." He asked her if she'd ever heard of madstones, if she'd seen any medical reports on the healing properties of deer. "Harry, you're wasting my time," she said. "Don't get sidetracked with novelties. You *do* want to grow up and be a productive citizen, don't you?"

At recess, Randy Olin told Harry to crawl into the new textbook box, as his prisoner. In the spirit of friendship (his mother had stressed this again!) he got on his hands and knees, opened the cardboard flaps. He paused. He remembered the summer crowds near Guthrie, near Sulphur, the shy hope on the faces of hardworking women and men. *He* had sparked that hope. Harry Shaughnessy, the Boy Orator. "No," he said, standing up, brushing the grass from his pants. "I won't. This year I'm the sheriff."

"Says who?" said Olin.

"Get in that cell," Harry said. "You're under arrest."

Eddie McGarrah stared at the two of them as if a cosmic calamity had suddenly knocked the world off its axis. Randy Olin always got his way.

"The charges are as follows: immaturity, predictability, lack of ambition." Harry squeezed Olin's neck and heaved him into the box. Olin struggled and kicked; Harry rolled the box over and over to keep him off-balance. Their classmates laughed, even Eddie McGarrah when he saw and heard the others. "You know what a *real* jail's like?" Harry said. "Small and filthy and cold. It's even more humiliating than being tossed in a box." He stepped back and clapped the dirt off his hands. Olin scurried free of his confinement, started to stand, but stopped when he saw Harry's face. "This is a stupid game for stupid kids," Harry said, glaring. No one bothered, or even approached, him the rest of the day.

The next morning, he brought his bag of marbles to school and gave it away to a gleeful little boy.

Harry longed to see Mollie but knew he wouldn't be welcome by the Kiowa shacks. She was probably married. Whenever he thought of her, he felt like crying.

Before cotton-picking, the Baptists staged one last revival south of town. On Saturday Harry went to hear the preaching, hoping to spot Mollie in the arbor, just to see how she was. After the sermon, the crowd wound through a field toward a muddy diving hole. The preacher waded into the swirling brown water (he could afford plenty of dry clothes, Harry thought, after passing the collection plate). He dunked several people, also fully dressed. Harry didn't find Mollie. He started to leave when he heard a commotion in the pond. The preacher was leading Jimmie Blaine into the water. Everyone knew Jimmie, a man of thirty or so whose head was too big for his body, and who spoke with a lisp. People said he was "slow," but he was friendly, a good worker on his father's farm, and a good hand in the cotton patch. At least once each year he reaffirmed his Christian faith by getting baptized again. He was frightened now by a long, sleek water moccasin gliding toward the preacher and him. He flapped his arms, splashing the preacher's face. Clearly, this annoyed the man, who tightened his grip on Jimmie's neck and forced him deeper into the pond. "Ain't you thee 'at thnake?" Jimmie said. The preacher started to immerse him. Jimmie shouted, "Ain't you thee 'at 'oddamn thnake?"

Now everyone saw it. "Reverend, reverend!" someone called. The preacher lunged for the shore. Muddy arms helped him out of the water. The crowd huddled around him, protectively. Jimmie still stood in the middle of the pond, shivering and bawling as the snake circled, flicking its head and tail. Harry picked up an old oak twig and plunged into the ripples. With the stick he flipped the moccasin onto the bank, next to the preacher and his flock. They screamed and scattered.

The rest of that month, in the cotton fields, Jimmie stuck by Harry, doing a good deal of Harry's work as well as his own. A bumper crop this year: over thirty inches of rain had fed the ground, and the plants were healthy and rich, three to four feet tall. The creamy white blossoms had quickly turned pink and decayed, leaving a sweet scent in the air that intoxicated the bees, giving way to soft green bolls that hardened then burst into five-spiked burrs. They were dark brown and brittle, filled with airy cotton.

Mrs. Altus canceled classes at the height of the picking. She did this every year, under pressure from the children's parents. Every hand in southern Oklahoma, old and young, large and small, was needed in the fields. Harry helped clear his father's acres, then hired himself out to other tenant farmers. No one worked for himself. The bank owned it all. Black men and women, invisible the rest of the year, always appeared at cotton time, ready for labor. Sheriff Stephens strictly enforced the "vagrancy law": anyone caught loitering on the streets of Walters was arrested, no excuses, and forced to pick for the county.

Harry liked to start early each morning—he competed with Randy Olin and Eddie McGarrah to see who could harvest the most—but the weighers wouldn't take wet cotton. "Ain't paying for dew," they'd say. "You wait'll that's dry, so we can get an accurate measure." They paid the boys thirteen cents a pound; on a good day, when his back wasn't screaming and he could still bend and stretch at sunset, Harry averaged two hundred pounds in just under twelve hours.

The first day school was out, Randy Olin appeared in the fields wearing a white mask beneath his battered straw hat. To avoid sunburn, everyone wore long sleeves and hats, though fall temperatures still topped ninety degrees. As Olin approached, Harry saw it wasn't a mask at all, but a whorled cream spread liberally across his cheeks and the back of his neck. "Buttermilk and cornmeal," Olin explained. "So's I don't freckle and end up looking like a damn ol' *Irishman*."

"You look like an ass," Harry said. "Careful, or they'll hitch you to that wagon over there."

"Shaughnessy, is it true all Catholics are drunks?"

Harry ignored him; he adjusted the straps of his croker sack so they wouldn't nip his shoulders. Eddie McGarrah, trailing Olin, giggled and spat in the air.

"I heard they had to pass a law so's the Catholics wouldn't fall over tipsy in church."

"You don't know what you're talking about," Harry said. "You might learn something if you read the papers."

"Damn papers write about the damn Irish all the time. Mr. Boy Orator. So what?"

"So what?" Jimmie Blaine echoed, approaching Harry, dragging his long empty sack.

"Oh look, it's Shaughnessy's friend, the simpleton," Olin said. McGarrah laughed. "Finally, there's someone on Shaughnessy's level."

Jimmie tried to smile but he only looked confused.

"Olin, you're pathetic," Harry said.

"I hear your daddy got so soused in church one day he ran outside and tried to fuck a cow, thinking it was the Virgin Mary."

Harry nearly swung at him, and would have if his arm hadn't snagged in his sack as he turned. Jimmie saw Harry's anger and, apparently trying to help, reached for Olin's arm. Olin jumped back—"Stay away from me, simpleton!"—bumping McGarrah, who fell against a sharp cotton stalk. Its limbs stuck out at right angles to the ground, and ripped his long checkered sleeve.

"You boys!" yelled a foreman from the road. "Time's a-wasting. Snap to it!"

Harry looked darkly at Olin, then turned and began to pluck at the bolls. He didn't have gloves. The family's bills and Annie Mae's bail had eaten up the supply-money. At thirteen cents a pound, he wasn't going to relieve his parents' debts anytime soon.

It was impossible to avoid being jabbed by the bolls' prickly edges, even when he was careful, and he wasn't careful today: he was furious at Olin, more than ever determined to outpick him. He told himself Olin wasn't worth the energy it took to be mad at him, he was just a baby; he understood, then, that this loudmouthed kid wasn't the only fellow troubling him. The "drunk Catholic" talk brought him right back to Father McCartney.

As Harry had warned Commissioner Boyd, the local courts were now reviewing the "bone-dry" statute, questioning its efficacy in light of the Catholics' anger. Last Sunday, Father McCartney had told his congregation he was "sure this abominable law was going to be repealed, with the Lord's generous help." What did the Lord have to do with it? Harry thought. Did the Lord speak to Boyd, the *Herald*? Immediately, he was ashamed of his immodesty, but the priest had annoyed him just before Mass. He had thanked Harry for "staying out of the fray" while he, Father McCartney, in agreement with Chancellor de Hasque and Bishop Meerschaert, negotiated with the county leaders. Harry hadn't stepped back on purpose. No one had come to him; for all his big talk when the reporter had asked him his plans, he didn't know how to take the next step. He was still just a kid. A powerless little boy.

His helplessness infuriated him; county laws, tribal laws, marriage customs. He wanted the knowledge and the ability to change them all. Irritably, he pulled at the bolls. They punctured his hands until he bled. By noon, his spine and his knees ached. He reeked of sweat, a deep, earthy musk. Boll-needles and thin, nuggety seeds pinched his skin beneath his nails. His fingers throbbed, swollen and red. His throat crackled, deep inside, like wallpaper ripped from sticky boards.

He dragged his sack, eight or nine feet long, through the field toward the water-wagon and the weighing scale. Sunlight hammered his face. Little green bugs peppered his forehead and cheeks. A small girl, happy to be helping the adults, very serious and self-important, dipped a tin cup into a barrel of water and handed it to him. While he drank, two men lifted his sack onto the scale, a shiny metal pan hung on a chain attached to a raised wagon tongue; it dangled six or seven feet in the air. "Forty-five and . . . one-half pounds," said one of the men.

He'd have to do better than that if he was going to beat Randy Olin. He reached toward the little girl who was standing in the wagon and gave her the cup, a small movement that seemed to tear every muscle in his back. He limped into the field. Children walked steadily along the rows, carrying dripping water dippers to several of the pickers. The white kids were fascinated by the big black men. They tried to catch rides on their sacks, trailing the ground as the quiet workers moved up and down in a line. Harry could see the frustration, pain, and annoyance on the faces of the men; they couldn't snap at the kids for fear of upsetting the whites and losing their jobs.

Randy Olin was laughing at Jimmie. "That's right, there are snakes here too, all over this field!" he said. Jimmie had been telling his snake story to everyone. "You can try to kill them, simpleton, grab a hoe from one of those wagons and chop them in two, but you know what happens then? *Both* halves jump to life! So you chop and chop and chop. Pretty soon there's *ten* snakes slithering after you, rattling their tails and gnashing their fangs!" Jimmie screamed.

"Shut up, Olin," Harry said. "*You're* the simpleton. That butter-milk on your face has seeped through your skin and into your brain, and there's nothing left in there but a soggy mess of cereal." He grabbed Jimmie's arm and led him away.

"Ith that true, Harry? The ten thnaketh?"

"No, Jimmie. Randy Olin's a liar. Don't believe anything he tells you."

"Hey Shaughnessy!" Olin called across the field. "You pick like a girl! End of the day, I'll have you beat by a mile!"

Harry's jaw clenched. He dropped to his knees and began to tug at the cotton. Right away, his joints burned again. Tears streamed down his face with every pluck and pull. Jimmie noticed his distress. "Harry, you all right?"

"Just exhausted, that's all."

"Let me help."

Harry shook his head but Jimmie said, "It'th okay, my thack'th full. Take it in. I'll finith yourth."

Jimmie was big and seemed not to tire. Too dumb to know he was hurting, Harry thought: the kind of thing Olin would say. He smiled, then carried Jimmie's sack to the wagon. "This is Blaine's," he whispered to the weighers. Olin, in the field, stared at him, astonished. Harry took a drink, watched several women, including his mother, in the shade of two maples weave ducking for extra sacks. She waved at him.

By the time he returned to his spot in the field, Jimmie had nearly filled his sack. "Take a break, Harry," Jimmie said merrily. Harry sat behind a thick clump of stalks, out of sight of the foreman and Randy Olin, kneading his muscles, catching his breath. He rolled himself a cigarette. Twenty minutes later he hauled his sack to the scale. Olin had a fit, his face as red as a sting. Harry could see him squint from several yards away, and pound his thighs with his fists.

Back in the field, Harry said, "Jimmie, I appreciate your help, but—"

"It'th okay, Harry. You're a good friend to me."

So the rest of that afternoon Jimmie regularly spelled Harry; by sunset, he'd picked enough for each of them to top three hundred pounds. The weighers counted out the money. Olin accused Harry of cheating but no one listened to him. People were tired and ready to leave for the day. "It's politics, Olin," Harry told the boy. "Expediency. Finding, and appealing to, the proper constituency."

"Huh?"

"Exactly the response I expected from you. Which is why you'll never beat me."

He turned for home. There, against the sky, surprising him, was Avram's dark profile, the big black hat and flowing shirt. The peddler passed in his noisy hack, nodding hello to the pickers. Harry tasted lemonade deep in the back of his throat, remembering the flask Avram had given him the day they'd moved the wagon. Thin clouds, purple and gold, streaked the yellow horizon behind the salesman's head. Watching him all alone in his seat, bobbing, flicking the reins, Harry was overcome by loneliness, the ache and the loss he'd felt since parting with Mollie. Did Avram have a wife? A child? How did anyone survive this windy, rocky world on his own? Avram turned a corner at the edge of the field before Harry could say anything to him. The weighers called good-night. Harry brushed dark seeds from his sleeves, tried to shake the sadness from his mind. He folded up his sack, and followed the ruts in the road.

FATHER McCARTNEY MURMURED, "AMEN," then gave a lesson from the Pentateuch. "Good tidings" closed the evening service: "Friends, just this morning I was contacted by Sheriff Stephens. He told me that the 'bone-dry' statute will be repealed as of the first of next week, and all charges against our neighbors"—he indicated Annie Mae and her three co-conspirators—"have been dismissed."

A burst of applause from the pews. Afterwards, on the church steps, the priest shook Annie Mae's hand and told her she'd been very brave. He ruffled Harry's hair as if petting a dog. The next day, when he got home from the fields, Harry saw a picture in the paper of Father McCartney shaking hands with Commissioner Boyd. The caption read "Faith in Compromise."

Harry tried to squelch his jealousy and his feeling that he'd been outmaneuvered by the priest, who seemed to crave celebrity of his own. His mother was free—that was the important thing—and besides, at least this was a triumph in a season of defeat. The Democrats in Oklahoma City had passed the Grandfather Clause, killing the Negro vote. The Democratic candidate, Lee Cruce, had been elected governor on a promise of attracting new investment capital to the state. In the end, J. T. Cumbie pulled over twenty-four thousand votes, an impressive showing, but not enough to change politics-as-usual. Warren Stargell had told Andrew, "Cumbie's taking it hard, I hear, but he swears he'll rise again to fight another day." Harry heard little conviction in his voice. Cruce was a disastrous choice, Andrew said: a banker by trade, he was an overly cautious man, deliberate and without a shred of humor. He supported black disenfranchisement. He swore he'd block the Socialists' attempts to distribute textbooks, free, in all the public schools. Andrew, Warren Stargell, and the other members of the league sat for hours in their meetings, barely moving or talking.

Their lethargy affected Harry's work in the fields. He was grateful for Jimmie's help. Following the incident in the pond, Jimmie had decided to convert to Catholicism. He liked Harry and Harry was Catholic, he explained; priests didn't go anywhere near muddy old swimming holes; and he enjoyed Confession. It was like telling stories, he thought, so over and over he told the story of the snake to Father McCartney, who emerged dazed from the booth each time he'd blessed and forgiven Jimmie. Harry enjoyed the priest's annoyance.

One afternoon in the fields Jimmie leaped into the air, wringing his arms. He called Harry's name. "Thnake!" he said. "I think I heard a thnake!" Harry knelt. Beneath a thick clump of stalks he spotted a cinnamon-colored foot, a long, twitching ear. "Come here, Jimmie."

"I don't think tho, Harry, I—"

"It's not a snake. Come look."

Jimmie crouched beside him. A waxy whisker poked from a cloud of cotton. Small squeaking sounds, muffled, rose from ribbed furrows in the dirt. "Rabbith!" Jimmie shouted. "Harry, it'th rabbith!"

A mother cottontail had given birth beneath a flat canopy of bolls, fat and hanging close to the ground. Jimmie reached for one of the babies, sending a shower of seeds into the soil and into the animals' fur. The mother bristled but didn't attack. Jimmie rocked the tiny rabbit in his palm. Its eyes were barely open and it tried short thrusts with its stunted hind legs.

That day, Randy Olin outpicked Harry by nearly fifty pounds. Jimmie's production dipped considerably; he couldn't be pulled from the rabbits. Harry loved Jimmie's delight and didn't mind losing the race except for Olin's taunts. By midafternoon it was clear that Olin had established a faster rhythm. "By a mile, Shaughnessy!" he called across the rows. "I'm going to beat your Irish ass by the length of this county!"

Harry tried to cap his anger but it swelled inside his chest, like the soft, throbbing heads of the blisters on his fingers. At one point, with the sun burning holes in everything in sight—or so it felt—he and Olin approached the weighing scale side by side. Olin's white grin burst through streaks of buttermilk and dirt, grit and sweat. "How much did the little girl pick this time?" he said to Harry.

Harry jumped on the wagon and drank from the barrel of water.

"Two pounds? Three pounds?"

"I've beat you every day this week," Harry said. "My arms could fall off and still you'd never catch me."

"You're a cheater, Shaughnessy, that's why."

"Take it back," Harry said.

"Tricking the simpleton—"

Harry flung the water dipper at him, leaped off the wagon, and grabbed Olin's shirt. Olin's sack slipped from his shoulders; ragged tufts of cotton sprayed the scale. "Take it back!" Harry shouted, shoving Olin to the ground.

"Or what?" Olin spat, gasping for breath.

"Or I'll—" Harry stiffened. A glimmer of white. A faint, familiar scent. Pungent. Sweet. Wax myrtle leaves?

He released the boy's dirty shirt. Olin, lying on his side, scrambled past him, kicking at Harry's shins. "Damn fool Irishman!"

Harry slapped away Olin's feet. All of a sudden he felt no trace of physical pain—not from the grueling hours of stooping in the fields, not from sunburn or Olin's flimsy kicks. The numbness he felt spread quickly from the center of his chest, from his heart.

She was walking down the road in the same white dress she'd always worn. Her hair was longer; she wasn't as skinny as before. Calm, unsmiling, she held her husband's hand.

Take it back, Harry thought. Oh God, take it back.

Olin, the weighers, the women weaving croker sacks, including Annie Mae, all stared at the Indian couple as they passed. Harry ran to catch them. "Mollie," he said, ashamed of the dirt and sweat on his clothes. He tried to smile but the effort was just too much. "How are you?" he asked.

Anko, wearing a dark hat and a striped vest, frowned and tried to move past him. Harry stood his ground. He had plenty of anger left from his collision with Olin. "I'd like to know how Mollie is," he said in a low voice. Mollie stared at the pebbles in the road.

"She's fine," Anko said. "Now get out of our way."

"I want to speak to your wife for a moment," Harry said. "Excuse us." He touched Mollie's arm, nodded toward the edge of the field.

"You have no right to touch her!" Anko said. From his faded khaki pants he pulled a gleaming silver object. He held it close to his body so only Harry and Mollie could see it: a thumb-sized knife.

"Look around," Harry said evenly, disguising his fear. "You're surrounded by my people. You harm me in any way, they'll be all over you. You won't stand a chance. Now. All I want to do is speak with Mollie for a moment. That's all." He walked her down the road a few yards. He was keenly aware of his mother's stare, of Olin's taunting face, of Anko's cold and obstinate fury. He didn't care. He asked Mollie again how she was.

At first she wouldn't look at him. She folded her arms at her waist. "I'm pregnant," she said softly.

Harry couldn't speak. Flies circled his sweaty hair. His fingers ached.

"The Elder says it's a boy." She smiled faintly, as if to herself. "In some ways, my father's a very modern man. He trusts the keepers of medicine, but he also insists I get up-to-date care, so Anko's taking me to the doctor in Walters. We have an appointment. We shouldn't be late."

Harry wanted to touch her hair; he closed and opened his hands at his sides. "Are you happy?" he whispered.

She smiled again—sadly, he thought. "I'm Anko's wife," she said. "That's all."

He nodded. His neck, his whole body, hurt. "How's Tawha?"

"Cured. I told you, the Elder's never wrong." She turned away from him and took her husband's hand.

"I love you," Harry said. He didn't care if Anko heard.

"Good-bye, Socialist," Mollie answered. Anko glared at him, then led her away. As Harry watched them shrink with distance, he was aware of Olin shouting, "Shaughnessy loves an Injun!" and laughing. He turned to see his mother. Annie Mae pretended to concentrate on her weaving, ignoring the other women's stares, Olin's chant. "Shaughnessy loves an Injun, Shaughnessy loves an Injun!" Olin was rude enough to say the awful things that occurred to everyone, Harry thought. Most people had the good sense to deplore base impulses in themselves, but that didn't change the fact that we're all Olin inside. He saw the faces of the weighers, the other pickers. Every last one of them felt the shock, the disgust with him for touching an Indian girl, the sneering superiority to which Olin gave voice. They wouldn't look at Harry.

He turned to see the couple round a bend in the road and wink out of sight. He felt a twinge, a hard spasm in his chest; he hated Kiowa customs, all Indian laws.

A fourteen-year-old, pregnant! His Mollie!

"Shaughnessy loves—"

Embarrassed, ashamed, heartbroken, and revolted by his own harsh thoughts, Harry pushed Olin into the dirt. "I *hate* Indians," he said. "I hate them, you understand?"

COTTON FILLED THE WAGONS. Harry and Jimmie lay atop a swollen mound. Their arms and legs sank into soft white clouds. They'd go into town with the weighers and the foreman, to help them unload.

No one had said anything after Olin had picked himself up, walked quietly away from the fields. Harry thought the men might shun him, but they accepted his offer of help. Work came first.

He told Annie Mae he'd be home late. A silky strand of cotton floated in a breeze, wrapped his mother's hair as she stood in the road.

"I'm sorry if I embarrassed you, Ma," he said.

"Didn't I tell you to stay away from that girl?"

"You did."

"Then why didn't you listen to me?"

"I love her, Mama."

"Oh Harry. You're twelve years old. How can you—?"

Tears blurred his eyes. "I want to be with her. I want to see her every day."

"That's not the same as love."

"How is it different?"

Annie Mae softened, reached up and gently tugged his hair. "Your father's pushed and pushed you, ever since you were knee-high to a cotton stalk. You've grown up far too fast."

"How old were you when you fell in love with Dad?"

"A lot older than you are now." Her hand left his hair and cupped his moist, gritty cheek. "I'm sorry, Harry. I know the kind of hurt you're feeling, love or no love. It doesn't help to hear this, but it'll pass. I promise."

Harry smiled weakly. "Thanks, Ma."

"I'll save you some supper."

The wagon pulled away. Jimmie held one of the tiny rabbits in his hand. He laughed and stroked it all the way into town. Grasshoppers ticked across the cotton, past Harry's face. He watched a praying mantis cling to a boll, bobbing up and down, swiveling its vigilant head. It looked deeply intelligent, bored.

"Harry, do you want to pet my rabbit?" Jimmie asked.

"No, Jimmie, thank you."

"I love my rabbit, Harry."

"I know. Be careful with it."

Fireworks soon, and dances and a big market to celebrate the end of the season. The joy in finishing and the relief on everyone's faces drove Harry's sadness even deeper, so deep he couldn't loose it with a scythe.

Jimmie cradled the rabbit close to his chest.

"Careful," Harry said. "Be very, very careful, okay?"

ALWAYS, AFTER THE FALL harvest was in, the remainder of the year seemed quick and uneventful to Harry. Classes droned on until the Thanksgiving break. His father asked him if he wanted to go with Warren Stargell to the river, to hunt a tom for the feast. At first Harry wasn't sure; he feared he'd encounter Anko, but then he decided that wasn't likely. The river was cold this time of year. There wasn't much reason to go near it unless you were looking for a turkey, and Kiowas wouldn't eat the birds. It was one of their laws, their damned, silly laws. He didn't know how he knew that, but he did. Had Mollie told him? He'd thought he'd never forget a single word she had uttered, a single twist of her mouth. Now, memory's bitter betrayals dismayed him daily.

Annie Mae and Mahalie cleaned, stuffed, and basted the bird; Andrew and Warren Stargell toasted each other with cider (a concession to the ladies), bemoaned the Socialist League's sorry luck. "We'll get 'em next year," Warren Stargell said.

He was still saying it at Christmas. "Just wait. Next year the people's revolution will sprout like a weed."

A poor figure of speech, Harry thought.

And a poor Christmas it was. His parents didn't talk about it when he was around, but Harry knew the family was in danger of losing the farm. He saw the stack of bills on the kitchen table each night. It had mounted as the months passed and Andrew had remained idle. Harry's income from the harvest had already dried up and blown away.

On Christmas morning, Annie Mae took his face in her hands, warmed by the fire, and kissed him on the cheek. "I wish I had more to give you than that," she said. "Merry Christmas."

"Merry Christmas, Ma."

That afternoon, Jimmie Blaine dropped by with a baby rabbit. "*My* baby grew up to be a mother and now *thee'th* having babieth," he said. "Happy 'olidath, Harry." He said he couldn't stay; he had dozens of sweet bunnies to deliver to friends. Rabbits had replaced snakes in Jimmie's confessions to Father McCartney. Jimmie told him this, and Harry laughed.

Annie Mae wrapped the rabbit in a blanket and kept it in a box by the kerosene stove so Halley wouldn't bother it. This is where she'd kept her chicks, and Harry couldn't look at the box or the mule pen without a melancholy pressure settling in his stomach and his legs.

Andrew spent much of the holiday season standing by the barn, watching the swirling gray skies behind the silos, which moaned and creaked with each new frost. Harry knew not to bother him. He stood with Annie Mae at the kitchen window, studying Andrew's silent struggle with the losses they all knew were coming. The house was falling away, familiar no longer.

On New Year's Eve, Annie Mae surprised Harry by arranging three nice glasses on the table and pouring wine from a jug. "We need to put 1910 behind us," she said. "It's been a hard one. Call your daddy in."

"Is this real?"

"Of course it's real."

"Where'd it come from?"

Annie Mae grinned. "The night we made the deal with the railroad man, we opened up that barrel of sacramental wine and set aside about three jugs' worth—just in case the county stood firm."

"Mama!"

"I can't think of a better use for the surplus. Now call your daddy."

Andrew was even more shocked than Harry. "Liquor, Annie? You?"

"It's been blessed, Andrew." She smiled and winked at Harry. "'Wine maketh glad the heart of man'? Don't tell Father McCartney."

"You'll have to do penance, Ma."

"You let me worry about that." She raised her glass. "To a better year."

"To the people's revolution!" Harry said.

Andrew simply nodded and swallowed his wine. At midnight, the winter's first snow brought the new year cascading gently into their yard.

PART FOUR

Battlefields, 1917

7

The year had begun with bombs in Europe. Ever since the sinking of the *Lusitania*, Americans had been outraged and confused. President Wilson urged "friendly feeling" toward the poor German people, and toward German Americans in general, but each new talk he'd given had moved the country closer to intervention overseas.

Finally, in April, he called a special session of Congress and declared, stirringly—reluctantly, it seemed to Harry—that it was a "distressing and oppressive duty," a "fearful thing to lead this great peaceful people into war."

Harry read the text of Wilson's speech in a week-old copy of the *New York Times* he'd found scattered in a chair in the lobby of the St. Nicholas Hotel. Since the first of the year he'd stayed in Oklahoma City, on a stipend from the league, helping plan antiwar rallies.

He sipped his tepid coffee, smoothed the page. Some of the war news appeared next to a long feature on the rope tricks and cowboy jokes Will Rogers performed on Broadway, in the *Ziegfeld Follies*. While he was making people laugh and forget their troubles, Wilson was swearing to Congress that "we shall fight for the things which we have always carried nearest our hearts, for democracy . . . for the rights and liberties of small nations . . ."

Harry tossed the paper aside. That's it, he thought. America's first step into this vile and bloated carnage. Saddened, angry, he pushed past the lobby's glass doors, onto the street. Spontaneously, he shouted, "Shall our boys become cannon meat? My fellow Americans, the blood-stained currency of war is sorry business, sorry business indeed!" Women and men scurried by him, staring. "Let's demand of our leaders an embargo on the exportation of war munitions, demand mediation rather than struggle—and, like dew from the heavens above, peace shall blanket the earth!"

A man with a briefcase and a wide felt hat spat at his feet. Through tears Harry watched pigeons strut precariously across roofs of dirty brick buildings, dodging paper and flecks of ash in the air. He stuffed his hands in his pockets, ducked back inside the hotel.

His small room felt cold and harsh, as if the planet's thin atmosphere had suddenly soured, spoiling all of Earth's goods. He looked at his frightened face in a wall mirror. One month shy of his nineteenth birthday, he still had a pert, childlike appearance, freckles, and thick wavy hair. The league's posters still proclaimed him the "dynamic" Boy Orator.

Restive, he paced the room, tugged at the curtains of his second-story window, gazing at people on the streets. There were far fewer horses and buggies, many more cars, now than he'd seen only a few years ago when he'd come here with the speakers' circuit. Merchants, shoppers, children moved with much greater speed than they used to, with a confident recklessness that fragmented the city. The avenue itself seemed to roll and spill like a cresting ocean, but going nowhere—or everywhere at once. Prosperous, preoccupied, this looked too busy to be a nation at war.

Federal law would require him to register for the draft. He wondered if he could refuse on principle? What would happen then?

He'd write and ask his father. Andrew wanted to be here, but the livery stable demanded all his energy.

For two years now, since around the time of his seventeenth birthday, Harry had been in touch with his family mostly through letters and telegrams. Soon after New Year's Day, 1911, when things were at their worst for the farm, Andrew had received a telegram from Oklahoma City, informing him that his brother, Lee, had been hit by a streetcar and killed. No one had heard from Lee since he'd left his wife and kids in Lehigh and disappeared into the Indian Territory years ago; apparently, he'd been in the city all that time, and had made quite a success for himself in the garment business.

Lee left a nice sum for his brother; with that and the money he earned selling off all his farm equipment, Andrew moved his family into Walters and made a down payment on a boxy little house. Within a couple of months, he'd partnered up with another investor in town and opened a livery stable.

Harry had felt funny, living there after the farm. Closed in. Too many buildings, too many people.

One of their neighbors had a phone. People walked for miles just to see it. Two short rings, one long, got you the sheriff. But the novelty of that wore off quickly, and nothing else in Walters held Harry's interest. The circuit, his speeches, the love of the crowds had made him restless.

So one spring, after he'd lasted as long as he could confined by narrow lanes, boring routines, he'd decided against both his parents' wishes that he belonged on the road. The farm was gone. School offered him nothing. He was a man now, ready to be on his own. His heart beat to the rhythm of the pitch.

When the league could afford to sponsor him, he spoke full-time. Otherwise, he took odd jobs wherever he could find them, hiring himself out during cotton season, haying and baling, stacking lumber.

In McAlester, he'd worked for the MK & T as a station clerk. He swept the waiting rooms at the depot—separate spaces for "Coloreds" and "Whites"—tagged baggage, hung the mail sack on a platform so the conductor could snatch it with a long iron pole as the train whisked past.

Occasionally—usually on holidays—he visited his folks. His mother was lonely in town. She missed Mahalie and her other friends. Now that Harry was gone she longed for another child to care for; shortly after the move, she'd had another miscarriage. Her back hurt her worse than ever. She was in her early forties, and knew the dangers of continuing to try to have a baby, but her need was strong. Harry always hated to leave her, though he was eager to get out of town. It had never felt like home. Halley, big now, lanky and lazy, followed him partway to the train tracks whenever he left. Harry stooped and patted his head: "Go back to the house now, Halley. Take care of Ma."

This spring, he lived lavishly (compared to his depot-days) in the city. War-fever had stirred passions all across the state; the league's membership had jumped at the first of the year. Tenant farmers were dropping away, but new members came from the towns, from the industrial working class: people afraid of the draft. With the extra dues, league organizers put Harry up where they thought they could use him the most.

A week after Wilson's speech, the *Appeal to Reason* declared America's entry into the war an "international crime against the workers of the world." Harry's father wrote to say, "Be careful, son. An ugly mood is strangling the nation. Wherever you speak, make sure you've got a handy escape-route. More than ever, short-tempered men will want to argue with their fists.

"A somber note," the letter went on. "Your old schoolmate, Randy Olin, was killed last week at Fort Sill. He was one of the first volunteers from this area. His unit was practicing maneuvers when some kind of accident happened. The paper was vague about it. You knew him pretty well, I seem to recall. I'm sorry, son, to be the one to tell you."

Harry set the letter on his bedside dresser. His temples throbbed, his hands felt numb. He had never liked Randy Olin. He wouldn't miss him. But *dead?* Crouched in a cardboard box, maybe, squatting in the cotton fields, waiting to torment poor Jimmie Blaine, but surely not dead.

He splashed water on his face from a porcelain basin by the door, rolled down and buttoned his sleeves. He couldn't sit here with the letter. He was set to give a speech.

The league had scheduled a rally on South Central Avenue near Douglass School, an all-black institution. Lately, newspaper editorials had been targeting Negroes, suggesting that young black men could "rise in society" by "serving their country with pride."

Harry arrived at the site just after noon. He helped his comrades unfurl linen banners—"Drive War Off the Earth," "Remember: When the People Speak It Is the Voice of Command"—and make a speakers' platform out of packing boxes. Pupils from the school, on their lunch break, drifted across the street to watch them work. Harry hadn't been surrounded by so many dark faces since that summer near Taft. He hoped for a warmer welcome here.

He leaped onto the platform. "Friends, let me tell you who I am," he began, pacing, gazing directly into the eyes of his listeners. They all wore plain, but finely-pressed, dresses or suits. "I'm a Socialist and a child of God, first. An American, second. Now what does this mean?" He added a little spring to his step. "It means, friends, that I'll serve my class before I'll serve the industrial giants who own this misguided nation!"

The crowd began to whisper. A few heads nodded. They were all so young! *His* age. Randy Olin's age. He felt a tug in his throat, a sting in his eye. His fingers tingled.

He wasn't going to cry for Randy Olin, of all people. Not here. Not now.

"Friends!" His voice cracked. He coughed, turned away from the street to regain his composure. He spoke more softly now, for better control. "Never will I serve the bankers, the food speculators, the ammunition makers who, with the wealth they've stolen from us, *the people*, are leading us into the maws of violence and greed!" He glimpsed a puzzled girl near the platform. The uncertainty on her face, the darting eyes, reminded him of Eddie McGarrah, and now he *did* begin to cry. Poor, dumb Eddie. Always needing Randy to show him the way, never acting on his own. What would he do now?

"What do we do?" Harry said. He didn't stop to wipe the tears from his cheeks. He paced even faster than before. "Our country is the world. Workers, our countrymen. To them and them alone we owe our allegiance. White, Negro, Indian." Another catch in his throat. "If we're workers, we're brothers and sisters." His agitation seemed to have stunned the crowd. They watched him closely, fascinated, maybe even a little frightened. "The papers tell you if you march off to war, and survive it, maybe when you come back home you can start a better life here." He shook his head. "Neighbors, hasn't the Negro race heard 'maybe' one too many times?" he asked, recalling the long-ago words of Bobby Springs, Taft's Deputy Mayor. "Don't be tricked or persuaded this time by hollow promises. Follow your conscience. Follow—" He couldn't finish; sorrow choked his words. He looked to his colleagues for help. They didn't know what was happening to him, so he jumped off the platform and ran down the street, rubbing his eyes. He didn't stop until he reached a hash house he knew on Northwest Twenty-third.

For hours he sat in a corner booth, sipping coffee, smoking cigarettes. He couldn't believe what he'd done. His face burned with shame. He'd never failed to finish a speech. And all because of Randy Olin! Because Europe had come to Oklahoma.

Outside, he noticed, shiny Fords were beginning to park beside the curb. Across the street, a cinema house, the Centurion, had opened its doors: *The Adventurers* starring Charlie Chaplin. Harry had never seen a moving picture. He was curious, but he couldn't spend the league's money on silly entertainment.

From his seat inside the restaurant he saw men remove their hats, women adjust sleek stoles on their shoulders, as they entered the Centurion. A short while later they shuffled back out, laughing, blinking. Their faces seemed glazed, as if the watery light had left a sheen on their skin.

Harry paid for his coffee and walked to his room, chastened, still, by his afternoon performance. Up ahead, the quarter-moon appeared to be lying, tossed and forgotten, on the concrete roof of a shoe factory. It looked like a soft, wrinkled bag glowing from within.

He didn't sleep that night, or for many nights afterwards. He dreamed repeatedly of standing on a platform, before an audience of Randy Olins, bony and pale in a bloody cotton field, unable to move his tongue.

THE MORNING AFTER HIS birthday he filed his name in a busy Selective Service office. The clerk there was too overwhelmed by paperwork and people to answer questions; competing rumors had confused Harry about the age of conscription—was it twenty-one or younger? His father, also puzzled, had warned him not to break the law. "Probably the authorities are already watching you because of your political affiliations and your activities. Don't give them any more reason to follow you," Andrew had written. "Maybe you won't be called. If you are, we'll wrestle with it then."

Governor Williams had established a State Council of Defense, to educate civilians about their wartime responsibilities. After leaving the draft board, Harry found a street corner near a state agency and told the passersby, "This is a rich man's war and a poor man's fight. If forced to serve in the military, if ordered to murder my fellow workers, I will instead die fighting humanity's enemies in my *own* ranks!" No one stopped to listen to him, but he felt better about himself.

He'd spent his birthday alone. He didn't know his comrades here very well. They were all older than he was—grocers, factory workers, union organizers. He missed the old days with Kate O'Hare, Fred Warren, even J. T. Cumbie. Kate O'Hare was slated for an Oklahoma rally in early July, after a speaking tour in the West. Harry hoped she'd make it. His spirits needed boosting.

The night he turned nineteen, he debated with himself, then broke down and bought a ticket at the Centurion. This was a misuse of official money, he knew, but he'd worked hard, he was lonely. He owed himself a treat. "That'll be a dime," said the woman in the box office. In the booth's yellow light, her teased blond hair was a giant parfait. Harry blinked. "I thought it cost a nickel," he said.

"This ain't no nickelodeon, son. And this here's what they call a *big* picture."

He hesitated, scrabbling for coins in his pocket. A noisy line had formed behind him; he spilled ten pennies into the booth's silver slot and hurried inside. The place was opulent: red carpet, glass chandeliers. Boys bought candy and fizzy drinks for their girls. He was hungry but he'd already overspent, terribly.

He took a plush seat in the back row; it nearly swallowed him. A blue velvet curtain hung on the auditorium's front wall. The room smelled of chocolate and shoe leather, rose water, and a faint trace of mildew. Though the crowd laughed and whispered excitedly, the surroundings were almost solemn. They promised miracles, a Grand Experience. Except for the dancing women, carved into the walls on either side of the curtain, this could be a church, Harry thought.

The lights went out, the curtain rose slowly, seductively, the way certain ladies lifted the hems of their skirts to adjust their sheer stockings. He wished he had a girl to sit with.

He felt a cool draft of air. His heart beat rapidly. The Chaplin picture had closed last week. This one, *The Birth of a Nation*, he knew nothing about.

The glare on the screen, the many movements at once, dazzled and bewildered him. At first he couldn't follow the flow of events. He was looking at a room. Next, people on horses. A man's face. A woman. He didn't know what was happening. Eventually, though, he grew accustomed to the rhythm of the changes, lulled almost, and the story began to make sense to him. It was about the Civil War. Two families, North and South. He nearly laughed with shock and delight. He'd been delivered into a different era. He felt he could reach out, pluck the actors' sleeves, they looked so *present*, yet they moved with a simple grace missing from daily life. Near the end of Part One, Abraham Lincoln's assassination was performed with such clarity and detail, he felt he'd actually witnessed the crime. It unsettled him. He clutched the arms of his chair, helpless.

Part Two chronicled the rise of the Klan in the South. As images slipped by like shuffled cards on the screen, Harry watched with increasing anger. The story portrayed most Negroes as licentious, greedy, crazed with freedom. In one scene, they overtook South Carolina's House of Representatives, propped their bare feet on polished wooden desks, gobbled fried chicken, and sipped secretly from bottles of whiskey. Finally, the Klan restored order.

Bull! Harry thought, recalling the men who'd beat his father long ago. Murdering pond-rats is what they are!

(Days later, he read in a paper that Woodrow Wilson had praised the picture as "history written in lightning," but it was history that never happened, Harry thought, history as a twisted tool designed to sow fear.)

As he left the theater that night, he felt an awful dread. The city's streets almost *rippled* with tension, anticipation, over the coming war. People were afraid to look at each other, to stop and talk; no one knew how his family was going to be affected.

"On the avenues, my mind whirled with images from the film," he wrote his father later. "Clearly, motion pictures are going to be the century's most important form of communication—more influential than any single speaker could ever be. Their power is obvious—the power, among other things, to turn lies into truth. Hate into heroic action."

Eventually, after seeing the movie that evening, he wandered back to the hash house and ordered a cup of coffee. He huddled in a dark corner, feeling swept away in a flood of antic light from Hollywood.

He looked up from the table and saw a man watching him from across the restaurant. The face looked familiar—round and fair. He wondered if he was being followed, if he'd glimpsed this man at rallies, in the shifting crowds, without fully registering him until this moment. He paid for his coffee and hurried outside, glancing over his shoulder every two or three blocks.

THE ESPIONAGE ACT, PASSED by Congress in June, enabled the government to punish "whoever, when the United States is at war, shall willfully cause or attempt to cause insubordination, disloyalty, mutiny, or refusal of duty in the military or naval forces."

The *Appeal to Reason* was banned; Socialist speakers were rounded up and thrown in jail all across the country. In an auditorium called the Cozy Theater in Bowman, North Dakota, Kate O'Hare was arrested for allegedly saying, "The women of the United States are nothing more than brood sows, to raise children to get into the army and be made into fertilizer."

Harry knew, then, he'd never see her again. The day he read about her lock-up in the paper, he stayed in his room, crying.

Kate. We need you. Damn it damn it damn it. Dear, stubborn woman: she'd never learned to tone things down.

In the next few weeks, over nine hundred people were imprisoned under the Espionage Act. The *New York Times* ran an editorial pleading with "every good citizen" to report acts of sedition, like antiwar rallies; photos of soldiers and patriotic flag-wavers spiced the front pages. Meanwhile, people flocked to the cinema houses, grateful to be distracted, momentarily, from the world's deadly news.

"In this fearful atmosphere," Andrew wrote Harry, "perhaps it's best if you suspend all your speaking engagements. Sitting in a cell won't serve any cause."

He told Harry his mother was pregnant again, watching her health. "We miss you and pray for your safety." Harry missed them, too, and wondered if it was time to make Walters his home. He wasn't sleeping or eating. He trusted no one. His speeches were all impromptu now, never announced. This made for small, indifferent crowds, but insured him some protection from the law.

One rainy evening he staked out the Centurion, hoping to siphon off a few folks from the movie crowd. That week, Theda Bara was starring in *A Fool There Was*; posters called her a "lusty siren"— a much greater draw than a "good, loud speaker." Harry shivered; his shoes were soaked. "Your rights are being yanked from under your feet," he yelled. Rain spattered his face. "Today, the Postmaster General bans the Socialist press; tomorrow, who's to prevent him from silencing *you?* What protections do you have? Are we going to allow this censorship, this unwarranted persecution? Hear me, friends!"

No one stopped, except one old fellow who called him a "German." Men emerged from the theater, laughing about the actress's "vampy eyes," her "pouty mouth." They popped open umbrellas, shielded their dates. "Kiss me, you fool!" a woman called, and chuckles echoed down the block. Harry, discouraged, ran for the hash house. He was sneezing by the time he ordered his coffee. He found his favorite booth, collapsed in its seat. Water oozed from his shirt, the legs of his pants.

Stupid, he thought. What's wrong with me? Give it up. No one's listening. Grab yourself a pretty young lady and treat her to the pictures.

Stunning, the city's women, gorgeous. Bright skirts, tight blouses. He remembered the "hoity-toity" girls Carry Nation had chased down the alley years ago, and wondered where to find such women now. He shook his head.

Rest, he thought, imagining the pillow of a woman's arm, rest now . . .

The steam from his cup blinded him; he couldn't see the features of the man who suddenly joined him. "Well well well," the stranger said.

Startled, Harry blinked, alert again. The face settled into focus. It was the man he'd seen before, watching him here in the restaurant. He tensed. This is it, he thought. The clinker. I should have known better than to come back here.

"Still skittish after all these years. I guess I don't blame you. It's a tough time for you Commies. Harry, right? Isn't it Harry?"

His throat went dry. He knew this voice.

"You don't remember me, do you, kid? I've never forgotten *you*. You spoiled a good day's business for me once."

"The breathing mask man," Harry whispered.

"That's right." He held out his hand. "Bob Cochran."

They shook. Harry's sleeve dripped like a sieve. Bob Cochran's hair had thinned, his face had puffed out a little. He wore a nicer suit than he had in Anadarko, blue with gold buttons. "Still pitching a better life, I hear. Not many takers."

"No," Harry said, still nervous, still shocked to see this man after so much time. "I'm afraid the country's headed for disaster."

Bob Cochran laughed. "It's not as bad as all that. You Commies are your own worst enemies. Never developed a sense of humor."

"I'm not, and never have been, a 'Commie.'"

"All right, all right. I'm not the Attorney General."

"What are you, then?" Harry asked. "Still a salesman?"

"In a manner of speaking." He grinned. "State Representative. Greer County."

He ordered two slices of blueberry pie, one for himself and one for Harry. They ate in silence for a while then Bob Cochran waved his fork in Harry's face. "You were a great inspiration to me, you know that?" he said. "I watched you steal the crowd from me that day in Anadarko, and I realized there was much more profit in the affairs of men than in the whims of the gods." He sipped his coffee. "I drummed here and there for another six months or so. Everywhere I went, the preachers and the politicos were packing 'em in, and I thought, 'That's the way to go.' I didn't think I could live clean, exactly, like a man of the cloth, so I got myself elected. Took me four tries, but I finally made it."

Harry played with his pie. He wasn't really hungry.

"But you, kid—look at you. Still out in the rain, literally *and* figuratively," Bob Cochran said. "This radical message. It's not going to get you anywhere."

"It's what I believe," Harry said.

"Hell, what good are beliefs if you don't have the power to implement them? You want to know how it's done? Listen: speak softly, appeal to the mainstream, work your way into the system, *then* worry about your beliefs."

"Is that what you did?" Still hawking, Harry thought.

"Absolutely. First—I learned this early, kid, pay attention—you've got to turn to the right. That's where the money is. Then, once you've got the backing, retreat to the center."

"Why's that?" Harry said.

"Most folks vote middle of the road. Where *you're* standing—this spot on the left—it's nowhere, son."

Harry shook his head. He raised his cup, signaled the waiter for a warm-up.

"I've been listening to your soapboxing," Bob Cochran said.

"Am I under arrest?"

He laughed. "I don't have the authority to arrest you. But I'll give you a little friendly advice. Leave the city."

"That's *friendly?*"

"Tomorrow, if you can. Governor Williams is about to pull the plug."

"Do what?" Harry had never heard this phrase; it took him a moment to understand it. *Pull the plug.* Of course. He should have thought of this before: modern inventions—electricity and the movies—were adding whole new words to the stockpile of language. Amazing! On the streets, he'd have to listen harder to the con men and hawkers. He could invigorate his talk.

"Commies—sorry, Socialists—are going to be carted away. That's the word I get."

"Why are you warning me?"

Bob Cochran shrugged. Secure, with savvy and charm, he was hard for Harry to read. "Soon's I recognized you the other day, I remembered you'd got me started on this path. I'm . . . hell, I don't know . . . returning the favor, I guess. I'm serious, though. Time's running out. The governor's a Methodist, you know. Methodists are a little indecisive. They believe in forgiveness. If he was a Baptist, your ass'd be in the stir by now."

Harry nodded. "Thanks," he said, reaching into his pocket.

"No no, on me," Bob Cochran said. He looked at Harry. Then: "Have you been inside the new capitol building?"

"No."

"It belongs to you—to every concerned citizen."

"I don't think so," Harry said. "Not to me."

Bob Cochran smiled. "Things're drying off outside. Come on. Let me show you."

Before Harry could answer, the man started off. Harry followed him down a brightly lighted city block. They walked for twenty minutes, not talking. People nodded to Bob Cochran as he passed. He moved with dignity, importance. Harry felt jealous, and a little disgusted. This fellow was just running another scam—yet people respected him now. Harry wore his lungs out every day, but it didn't matter. Men spat at him, called him names. Just yesterday, he'd been chased down a wretched alley by a gang of newspaper boys: "Kaiser lover! Coward!"

American politics.

"Here we are," said Bob Cochran.

The capitol had only recently been completed, all except the dome: that would be added later, when extra funding was available. Harry stood gazing at the thick round columns in front of the door. All his angry feelings fell away. The walls were creamy white, almost weightless in appearance, but with a gravity of presence, an austerity grounded in the very plainness of their lines. Harry nearly wept at this glorious expression, this solid home, of political will.

"Session's over, but we're just now moving into our offices," Bob Cochran said. "This way." He opened the massive front door, led Harry inside. Their voices echoed in the vast, dark hall, in the rarefied air. Bob Cochran pushed another door and they stepped into the House chamber. He flicked a switch: a sudden, silent blaze.

My God! Harry was overwhelmed by the beauty of the lights on the walls, the dignity of the desks in their strict, even rows, the solemnity of the room's muted colors. Above the main floor, a gallery for spectators ringed the chamber, with wall paneling as green as a lake. On either side of the House Speaker's chair (a massive black slab made of leather), cream-colored columns of wood rose toward the shadows of the ceiling.

Bob Cochran smiled. "Impressive, isn't it?"

Harry swallowed. "It is."

"And you know what? No Commie will ever get to work here. Think about it."

Harry glanced at him furiously. But he *did* think about it.

He knew his father wouldn't approve of this place; Andrew remained convinced that "money men" had stolen the capital from Guthrie, that the state's business was wholly corrupt. But the podiums! Tall and polished, so new they smelled of their origins still: bottomland woods, thunderous skies over golden rods of grain. Gingerly, Harry sat at one of the desks. He looked ahead at the Speaker's seat. I'm an American, he thought. An Oklahoman. He cleared his throat, as if readying a motion. Goosebumps prickled his skin.

"Feel at home?" Bob Cochran said.

Harry felt his face flush.

"It's not all fun, you know. Last month the First Regiment of the National Guard arrived here from Mexico. Did a fine job—chased Pancho Villa all the way to Hell and back. The men have earned a rest, but we're sending them straight to Texas to train with the Thirty-Sixth Division. God knows where they'll end up. France, maybe." He stroked the wisp of beard on his chin. "Dead, some of them."

"And your beliefs?" Harry said, watching him carefully. "Where do they figure in all this?"

Bob Cochran shook his head. "I don't always know. But right or wrong—like it or not—*this* is where the real business of the people gets done." He waved a finger in the air. "Your street-talk . . . it's just noise. It doesn't mean a thing."

"So *you* say."

"So say the people."

Harry tapped his fingers on the desk. "Indians?"

"What about them?"

"Are they among the people you represent?"

"Sometimes. It depends."

"On what? Money? Influence?"

Bob Cochran smiled. "You're not as naive as I thought."

"What happened to Sue-Sue?" Harry said.

The man laughed. "Sue-Sue. You still remember. Amazing. You liked her, didn't you?"

"She was very pretty," Harry said.

"That she was. The color of her skin, eh? Her hair?"

"Yes."

He nodded. "I see. Fond of squaw sugar, are we, kid?"

"I just asked—"

"Something else we've got in common."

"No," Harry said. "I don't care."

Bob Cochran shrugged. "Pretty little Sue-Sue became a liability. It was a shame. I liked her too, but the first time I ran for office, my opponent made an issue of the fact that I kept company with a Kiowa woman. I lost by a landslide."

"Was it the 'keeping company' or the Kiowa part the voters didn't like?"

He shrugged again. "You can represent Indians. But you sure as hell can't sleep with them. Not if you want to serve in this chamber."

Harry's chest tightened.

"You're drawn to this place, aren't you?" Bob Cochran said. "I thought you'd be. Let me tell you something." He took a seat next to Harry. "A lot of men think they want to serve, but it's like the Puritans used to say: 'Few are chosen.' You've got a great raw talent, a full spirit. I saw that years ago and it hasn't changed. You've stuck with it—that, by itself, is impressive." He leaned close. "But the state's changing, kid. Modernizing. I told you it would. You need a better horse to ride. Socialism—and this is the best advice you're ever going to get—has reached the end of its trail."

"We'll see," Harry said glumly.

"Yes we will, we will." He laughed. "Well. Take a last look around."

Harry did.

Outside, on the capitol steps, Bob Cochran warned him, "Remember what I told you about the governor."

A fresh drizzle had started to fall. Harry, missing the chamber's warmth, raised the collar of his damp white shirt. "This isn't just your way of running the competition out of town, is it?" he asked.

Bob Cochran grinned. "That's what politics is all about, kid." He offered his hand. "Good luck to you. Maybe I'll see you again."

IN THE MORNING HARRY packed, then cleared his room bill. As usual, someone had left a *Times* on a couch in the lobby. This would be his last chance, at least for a while, to see a New York paper. He thumbed through it, looking for news of Kate O'Hare. Sure enough, her picture appeared on page three. The tone of the accompanying article convinced him she wouldn't stand a chance at her trial. She was described as an "active seditionist" interfering with the war effort. Bowman, North Dakota, she said, was a "little sordid, wind-blown, sun-blistered, frost-scarred town on the plains." Jurors would love that, Harry thought.

He read that the *Masses*, under pressure from the Postmaster General, had ceased publication; Art Young, an artist whose work Harry had admired, had been called on, in court, to justify his political cartoon in which a newspaper editor, a minister, a politician, and a capitalist whirled in a gleeful war dance, flinging handfuls of silver coins, while the devil led a cannon-playing orchestra behind them. Young explained, glibly, "I'm simply illustrating the fact that war is hell."

Harry left the city with a mighty sense of failure. The world seemed determined to bloody its own face; no amount of talk could save it from itself.

He hitched a ride with a traveling salesman: pots and pans, mostly, a few garden supplies. The man, about Andrew's age, Harry guessed, with startling blue eyes and a thick black beard, asked him what had brought him here.

Harry hesitated. The word "Socialist" could get a man killed these days. "Just looking for work," he said. "No luck, so I'm going home."

The wagon bumped over dusty, rutted roads. "There's a salesman where I'm from, man named Avram," Harry said. "Nice fellow, same goods as yours."

"Sure, I know Avram. Greenbaum, right? Jewish?"

"Yeah. Must be him."

"Tough bargainer. But he's fair. I hear he's off the road now."

"Really? Doing what?"

"Got hisself a store. Saved rent money for ages. Lord, how he used to dream about it, ever' time I saw him! Finally got hisself a stake."

This was the first pleasant news Harry had heard in months. "Good for him," he said. He began to relax a little. The beauty of the rivers and trees astonished him after so much time in the city. The sky was free of soot. He felt he was learning *blue* again. With no movies or rope tricks to distract them, men understood, right away, that life was tied to the soil, Harry thought. Cars and signs and eastern newspapers had nothing to do with it. They were all just entertainment. Real life was here. In the woods, on the farms.

Stop it, he told himself. What was he doing? Convincing himself he'd never take to town. But he *had* to give it a chance: that's where his family was now. That's where the future was.

The land was lovely, though, and he felt he'd lost it when his father gave up the farm. He watched a purple martin flit from the arm of a southern magnolia into the thick, protective canopy of a sugar maple. Wild orchids ringed its trunk. Pitcher plants trembled in the breeze, waving their long red skirts.

The pots-and-pans man dropped him just west of Ardmore—

"End of my line," he said. Harry thanked him, leaped from the wagon's seat with his bundle, washed his face in a thin, forceful stream. East of here lay the Osage mines. He thought of Sherrie, the dancer in the "Beaver Trap." He thought of the pregnant girl, always standing in line in front of the outhouse. What had become of them? The mines had been closed for two years now, after a series of violent strikes. The company had tried to hire Mexican labor; migrants from the south worked cheaper than Anglos, Negroes, even the Italians who'd come to stay. The veteran miners wouldn't work with them; their presence, they felt, would lower all their wages. Early one morning, when a hole boss discovered, stabbed to death in the bunkhouse, two young "pepper-bellies" (as the local papers put it), state investigators *pulled the plug* on the whole operation. Osage had plenty of other mines in northern Oklahoma, up into Kansas and Missouri. The company could afford a few idle holes here until trouble blew over—especially during wartime, when demand for its product was high.

Harry spent the night in the woods, stretched beside a fallen oak for support and shelter from the wind. He dreamed of the mines, of moist rocks and the smell of creosote, sulphur, paraffin torches. When he woke at dawn his skin was gritty and wet. Castor and Pollux, the twin stars in Gemini, were fading in streaks of yellow in the east; Cepheus rose into stringy morning mists and disappeared.

He bathed his arms and face in a stream. Down the road about a mile he saw the first of many oil rigs crisscrossing the sky, which was smoky and dim. Slender wooden derricks loomed over restaurants, barbershops, first aid stations. Harry noticed a sign that said "Healdton Oil Field—The Boom Is Here, The Time Is Now!" The air smelled like a thousand angry skunks.

Trucks and Model T's blared their horns at him. He half-stumbled off the road into a little coffee shop with red-checked curtains in its two grimy windows. Frying bacon, scrambled eggs routed the outside odors, which wafted through the door whenever someone entered. Harry set his bundle of clothes on the gouged wooden floor, took a seat at a table, and spent the last of the league's money on a lukewarm cup of coffee. He asked the woman who poured it if there was any action over at the Osage mines. She laughed. "Who'd work for them now?" With the pot of coffee she gestured out a window toward the rigs. "Oil's the future hereabouts."

"I guess so," Harry said. He looked around the room. The mineral, the means of production may have changed, but the men hadn't. Stooped, scarred, burned; weary and resigned, they ate their breakfasts listlessly, didn't speak. The other kind of men were here too, the kind like Dugan and Fawkes of the mines, who always appeared whenever desperation mingled with the possibility of fortune. Harry watched these men, in their dark suit coats, smile and slap each other's backs.

"If you're looking for work, kid," one said as Harry rose to leave, "see Ewing in Building Sixty-three, next door."

This remark offended Harry deeply; the man's assumption that everyone here was fuel for his fire. "No," Harry said quietly, suppressing his rage. "I don't need a job, thank you."

The land used to be sumac, snakeweed, chinquapin oak. Now it was gas flames, stagnant oily pools, level roads. Women in bright red dresses stood in the open doorways of wooden shacks, yelling and whistling at the men. Their strained good cheer reminded him of Sherrie. One winked at him. Her sloppy make-up covered yellow bruises on her cheeks. He fast-walked down the road, filled with sorrow for the waste of lives and land.

By the depot, on a side track, an old passenger car had been set up as a Red Cross canteen. Women his mother's age served hash and ham, coffee and tea to soldiers on their way to or from Fort Sill. The fresh recruits stood in line for candy, cigarettes, chewing gum. Most of them were just a little older than Harry, clearly scared and confused, but like the shack-women, laughing loudly, kidding around, making the best of what they had.

Harry didn't get another ride until midafternoon when a soldier in a Model T offered him a lift. The boy had gotten a day-pass to visit his father, who was laid up in Walters with a weak heart. "They're shippin' us out next week," he told Harry. "This may be the last time I'll ever see my old man."

"Where you going?" Harry asked.

"Dunno. We were just told to get ready. France, more'n likely."

"Were you training at Fort Sill?"

"Yep."

"Know a guy named Olin?"

"Olin . . . no, don't think so. Why?"

"No reason. He's just a friend."

The boy's father had been a farmer who couldn't pay his bills. Like Andrew, he'd sold all he owned and moved into town. "Purty soon, city streets and oil derricks gonna gobble up ever' bless-ed acre of corn and wheat."

"Looks that way," Harry said. When they arrived in town, just at dusk, he told the boy to drop him anywhere. "Good luck over there," he said.

The boy grinned. "Them Huns don't got a prayer with me on the prowl. I'll trim their whiskers for 'em."

Harry nodded and shook his hand.

He remembered the day, years ago, he'd come to town without his mother's permission. He recalled the young men stringing electric wires. Modernization. Bob Cochran was right. Beneath a dim, flickering streetlight, a small marquee read Wollam Theater, and below that "Now Playing—'Flirting With Fate.'"

He watched the soldier drive off, then strolled past dress shops, beauty parlors, pharmacies, Wallace's Grocery, the Wilhelm Hotel. He saw his father's livery stable, and down the block, across the street, a small store, the Emporium. In tiny letters on the plate glass window, "Avram Greenbaum, Prop." Harry smiled. So it *was* true. Avram had done all right for himself.

He peered in the window. Shoes, soaps, bottles of cremes. Tonics in containers of green and brown and clear cut glass. Harry would come by tomorrow for a nickel cup of lemonade.

He shouldered his bundle and shuffled down the walk toward his parents' house. The downtown buildings were dark, the streets deserted. Dinnertime. He began to whistle a tune—until he heard footsteps behind him, urgent whispers. He paused, looked around. Nothing. He walked a little farther, stopped and turned. From the corner of his eye he glimpsed a figure in an alley near the livery stable. He pressed against the wall of the nearest building, held his breath and watched. The figure emerged from the alley followed by four others. They ran into the middle of the street and raised their arms. Harry couldn't see what they held in their hands, but they all made swift throwing motions; the next thing he heard was the crash of shattering glass. Avram's store. The men yelled words Harry couldn't understand, then scattered into the shadows.

8

Annie Mae put a finger to her lips. "Oh my," she said, staring at the shards on the walk. "What happened, Mr. Greenbaum?"

Avram nodded at her, at Andrew and Harry, obviously grateful for their friendly concern. He explained to them, painfully, that he'd received a steady stream of threats ever since opening the store. Graffiti. Anonymous notes. "I don't know why people think the telephone is such a marvelous invention," he said. "It's just a faster way to spread hate." Callers told him they didn't want "someone like him" settling in their community. "I've lived in this area for nearly twenty years. As long as I moved about in the wagon, no one thought of me as part of the place. They were happy for me to serve them. But now that I've established a business in the center of town . . ." He shook his head. His appearance still had the power to surprise Harry, to put him off a little. Avram wore his flat black hat even inside the store. In the city, Harry had seen dozens of Jewish men and women—the Orthodox kind—but he never got used to them. Though it shamed him, he understood, somewhat, people's impulse to keep strangers out of their midst. Difference meant unpredictability. Chaos and fear.

Socialism still has a long way to go, Harry thought, even in the hearts of its bearers.

While Avram swept and threw away the glass, Harry looked around. Mops and brooms, dishwashing soaps, bubble baths, cleansers, and the dreaded chill tonic he'd swallowed so much of as a boy. A row of novels, some still with their pages uncut, filled a wooden shelf on a wall. *The Red Badge of Courage. Marching Men* by Sherwood Anderson. Frank Norris's *The Octopus*.

Harry recalled the summer encampments, a few years ago, where intelligent men and women talked art, literature, politics. Those nights around the supper fires seemed a miracle of sanity now; he feared they'd never return.

By his big black adding machine, Avram had framed a photo of an elderly couple. His parents? Their clothes, the formal pose, even the indistinct drapery in the background seemed European, somehow. Harry remembered wondering, once, if the man had a family, and he wondered again now. There were no recent pictures of a wife or kids. By all indications, Avram was solely devoted to his work.

Harry had learned, in the city, just how hard that could be.

"May I have a look at your piece goods, Mr. Greenbaum?" Annie Mae asked. "I've just about outgrown this old dress."

He led her to the rear of the store. She moved slowly. Her belly was big and she'd complained all morning that her back was killing her, her joints were terribly sore.

Make a good family, Harry thought. Loneliness jogged him, dizzying him, pinching his chest. His mother's swelling reminded him of Mollie, the day she'd told him she was pregnant. He hadn't seen or heard from her since; he'd been on the road almost constantly. Her child would be—what?—six or seven now? To steady himself, he grabbed the splintery edge of a plywood table, by a colorful stack of bath towels.

Andrew handed Annie Mae three dollars and she paid for some calico, spotted like a cat. "Broken windows notwithstanding, are you making a decent living here?" Andrew asked.

"Passable."

"Then, as capitalist traps go, you'd recommend retail?"

"It's not for everyone." Behind his counter, Avram raised the lid of a metal freezer and poured them all glasses of lemonade from a tall, pudgy bottle. "How's the speaking business?" he asked Harry.

"Most folks cover their ears."

"All the more reason to talk."

"I think we had this conversation once, didn't we?"

"So we did." Avram smiled.

Harry pointed at the broken window. He drained his glass. "Be careful."

Avram bowed and tipped his hat.

Back on the street, strolling with his parents, Harry noticed on nearly every building recruitment ads for the army. On one, a gorilla in a spiked German helmet grasped a helpless woman. "Destroy This Mad Brute," the copy read. "Enlist!"

Harry wondered, and worried, about his status with the draft board. Still no word.

Walters didn't please him any more now than it used to. He thought it ugly and flat. The buildings were too close together—he still missed the spaciousness of the farm—without the cozy charm of the big-city blocks he'd seen.

Andrew told Annie Mae he should run by the livery stable. She took a dollar from him for groceries, and asked Harry to wait for her by the butcher's shop. He gripped her paper-wrapped fabric, stared idly across the street at the barber's where he'd come to find Warren Stargell years ago, and saw, loping toward him, a long, familiar form. Doughy, more stooped than he used to be, but it was him, all right. Eddie McGarrah. Harry grinned. At first McGarrah didn't recognize him, then he didn't seem to know how to respond. He smiled, frowned, then simply stared.

"How you doing, Eddie?"

"Same old six and seven."

"You remember me?"

"Sure. The Boy Orator."

"That's right. Harry Shaughnessy. It's been a long time. Put 'er there. Where you keeping yourself these days?"

"Roughnecking mostly, out in the oil fields east of here." He looked at the sky as though something were in it. Nothing was. "Hard work, good money."

Harry shifted the package under his arm. "I heard about Randy," he said softly.

McGarrah nodded.

"Were you in touch with him, out at the fort?"

"Yeah. He was eager to ship out." He coughed into his hands. "Ready to serve his country."

"You know what happened, exactly?"

"Some kind of explosion's all we heard."

McGarrah seemed lost, unused to the daylight, out of practice talking. Why hadn't the army snatched him? Well, he didn't look healthy. In the past, Harry wouldn't have given him the time of day, but now he was grateful for the familiarity, however strained. Obviously, though, McGarrah wanted to be anywhere in the county but on this particular street corner. He didn't want to talk about Olin; Harry didn't press him. The encounter was turning gloomy. "Okay. Well. It's good to see you. Take care of yourself."

"Yep," McGarrah sighed, and shuffled away like a lucky rascal wriggling out of a scrape. Harry felt lonely watching him leave. He stood by himself, remembering his school days, craving a smoke (he'd promised his mother he'd try to quit), in this flat, ugly town that wasn't his home.

The house his parents lived in wasn't home, either, though Annie Mae had hung the old curtains. She had the latest Citizens National Bank calendar in her kitchen, and that recalled the farm. Best of all, though, she'd asked Mahalie to come live with her, to help out during her pregnancy. Mahalie couldn't turn back time, or ease Harry fully, but her presence seemed natural and soothing.

To insure a safe delivery, she insisted that Annie Mae wear a tight girdle just beneath her breasts; this would prevent the fetus from rising too high in her body, Mahalie said. She told Annie Mae to keep fresh willow leaves under her mattress. The leaves guaranteed fertility, health, robustness. Mahalie combed Annie Mae's hair each night before bed: plaits, even accidental tangles, might incline the umbilical cord to strangle the baby at birth. Annie Mae put no stock in these ancient Choctaw rituals, but they were harmless, she said; she was grateful for Mahalie's love, for her care and concern.

In his first few days in Walters, Harry didn't know what to do with himself. His mother was well tended to, his father had plenty of employees at the livery stable, he wasn't giving any speeches. To keep his mind off the draft board and the war, he accompanied Annie Mae and Mahalie whenever they took morning walks. Halley followed happily, fetching sticks. The old dog was sinewy, still a gasbag, twitchy with ticks and fleas and restless energy.

"Watch your step," Mahalie said one day. "If a pregnant woman trips on a rabbit hole, her child'll be a harelip." Harry laughed, then hushed when his mother frowned. He picked an Indian paintbrush and tossed it at her, playfully. This prompted another warning from Mahalie. "If the flower touches her face, her baby'll be born with a cherry-red stain on its forehead." Harry surrendered, shook his head, and walked away. Halley dropped a slobbery twig at his feet. He threw it again, glanced east, across the streets. A gray haze hung above the oil fields. Much as he hated to, maybe he should hire himself out, he thought. Make a little cash. Distract himself. He could speak to Eddie McGarrah about it. On second thought—poor, bashful Eddie—he'd learn the rigs on his own.

That night after supper, as he was standing on the porch, staring again at the smudgy glow in the east, wondering what to do with himself, his father suggested, "Let's take a little walk." Andrew lowered his voice so Annie Mae couldn't hear him. "Bring a smoke or two if you want." Harry smiled.

They strolled into town. Andrew's limp didn't slow him up anymore; it was just a part of who he was. Harry pulled a pouch of Bull Durham from his pocket, rolled a smoke for himself and his dad.

In a squatty barn behind the livery stable the Socialist League had gathered: Warren Stargell and a lot of men Harry didn't know. (A number of their brother-farmers had stopped attending meetings, Andrew explained; the new blood was mostly from the oil fields and the small petroleum towns near Walters.) Harry was shocked by Warren Stargell's thinning hair, the sagging yellow skin of his face. He was old and worn-out, though his lazy left eye still exuded light.

Cigarettes fogged the room. Everyone stood and talked—shouting and laughing—all at once. In the old days, the meetings were decorous and grave, well-organized. Tonight, a wild almost-violence peppered the haze.

Most of the new men were young, a little older than Harry—here, it seemed, for a high old time, for something to do. They were whiskery and rank-smelling, strong and nakedly bored.

Warren Stargell banged his hand on a tabletop, calling the meeting to order. "Is this a popular war?" he yawped.

"No!" the group—fifty or sixty men, Harry guessed—yelled back. Like a school game. He thought of Eddie McGarrah, of their scattered classmates.

"Who gave the United States government the right to ship our healthy bodies, and the bodies of our sons, to Europe?"

"No one!"

"That's right. The people don't want this fight. And the government serves the people!"

The men cheered, slapped each other's sweaty shoulders—more in the spirit of high jinks and play than with any true fellowship, Harry thought.

"Now, I've been talking to our brothers in the IWW—"

"The Wobblies? They're goddam cowards!" someone shouted. "They won't take a stand agin' the war!"

Warren Stargell raised his arms. "Wait, wait, now listen to me. Some of the men in the Local 230—up the road, in the city—they're starting to see things our way. They want to help us end conscription. But they're convinced the time for speeches and pamphlets has passed, and by God, I think they're right. Hear me now. We need a series of dramatic events—attention from the press—to make our point."

Harry's toes went cold. He didn't like the direction this was headed. He'd seen Warren Stargell excited in the past, passionate about planning, but the man had never been this raw, this close to losing physical control. His body jerked when he gestured. His voice cracked.

"You mean West Texas?" someone said.

Warren Stargell grinned. "But with better results."

Two months ago, a group of West Texas tenant farmers ("Red renters" according to the papers) had announced an "armed and forcible opposition to the oppressions of the capitalist class." They declared the draft a conspiracy to thin the ranks of workers, and began stockpiling weapons. Early one morning, federal agents and a band of Texas Rangers raided their compound near Mineral Wells. Most of the farmers were arrested; one was found with twenty-three gunshot wounds in his chest. Wobblies and Socialists around the nation were beginning to use the incident as a rallying point.

"We have to stand by our brothers," Warren Stargell said, "or the federal government'll swoop in here and stamp us all out! Now consider for a moment. Where is the government's weakness, eh? Think hard."

The crowd murmured. The room was close and hot; stirred-up straw-particles stitched the air.

"Communications. Roads," Warren Stargell answered himself. "How can they take our sons if the bridges are out? How can they call in the law if the telegraph lines have been cut?"

Harry glanced at his father. Andrew smiled eagerly, just like the men around him. Harry couldn't believe it. Warren Stargell wasn't a particularly effective speaker, but apparently the time was right for his message. The war had knocked people silly with fear. He worried about his father's opinion, but he couldn't sit still any longer. He rose and raised his right hand. "Stamped out?" he shouted. "You better believe that's what'll happen if we're damn-fool enough to fire at Washington."

Heads turned. A few whispers. "The Boy Orator?" "Yes. Remember? That's him." "You sure?" "Strike me dead."

Harry walked up a narrow space along the side of the barn, past yellow hissing lanterns, until he stood near the front. "I've pledged myself to class war, just like the rest of you, but guns and destruction of property, well, those are losing strategies. Warren, you and I have campaigned together many times in the past." This was the first occasion he'd ever called the man anything but "Mr. Stargell." "And you know as well as I do, we can't win the battle for a better America without broad public support. Capture the hearts and minds of the people, that was always our first aim. How are we going to do that if we're running around wrecking bridges and roads?"

Warren Stargell folded his arms. "Harry, you've always had a honeyed tongue, but we're in a national crisis, boy, and talk's no longer useful."

"On the contrary, Warren. We're talking now. And we damn well better hash it all out, right here, what we're going to do." He turned to the men in the room. "You oil workers. What do you earn?"

"Thirty-five cents an hour," someone said.

"For what? A ten-hour day?"

"Twelve."

Harry nodded. "Seven years ago, men just like you working the Osage coal mines made about that. A cotton farmer was lucky if he got thirteen cents a pound. Nothing's changed. *This* is the war we have to fight."

Muttering and shouting. "What about Europe?" a skinny man called from the rear.

Harry raised his hand again. "I'm coming to that. I suppose, because your wages are low, and because Standard Oil keeps raising the prices of housing, most of you can't afford to stay in any one place too long, is that right?"

Loud, angry assent.

"So you keep moving on, hoping to improve your situation."

"Yeah." "You got it."

"It's the same everywhere, isn't it?"

"You bet." "It damn shore is."

Harry started pacing, forcing their eyes—and minds—toward him, and away from Warren Stargell. He'd learned a trick or two, over the years, about competing with other speakers. "That's their power over you," he said. "Landless, migratory men don't vote. They're never anchored long enough in any one community to register. They can't organize—their population's unstable. Fellows, Standard Oil counts on the fact that you won't stick together. But what if you did?" He stabbed the air with each word. "What-if-you-did? What if you made a vow to each other, brother to brother? What if you sat right down in the oil field and refused to lift a finger until your working conditions improved? What would the company do? And—you wanted to know about Europe?—here's the kicker.

What would the government do without your oil to fuel its shameless war?"

"Land, land, land!" Warren Stargell yelled. "No no! It's not a question of land anymore. You're living in the past, Harry. The picture's changed."

"It hasn't changed a bit, Warren. That's the trouble."

"The stakes are much higher now. They're trying to kill the working class by sending our boys—boys like you—to spill their guts in the fields of France."

"This war is for the speculators, Warren, it's for the bankers and the lawyers who've found another way to line their pockets. What was it Wilson said? 'Financiers must be safeguarded by ministers of state, even if the sovereignty of unwilling nations be outraged in the process.' Yes, they'll use us, but the fighting will end one day, when they've stolen all they can, and we'll be faced with the same old dilemmas. Low wages. No land. They don't want to kill us off. They need us. But they *are* trying to wear us down. They're trying to provoke us to armed rebellion, so they'll have an excuse to break our spirit, just like they did in Mineral Wells. We can't let them do that to us. We have to hold steady."

"Right," someone sneered. "All we have to do is blubber and whine, and the next thing we know, Standard'll be planting posies under the derricks—"

"I didn't say it'd be easy," Harry said.

"That's Wobbly talk, boy. It won't work."

"Besides, time is running out," Warren Stargell called. "Selective Service is up and running—"

Amid the clamor of the crowd, the barn doors creaked. Seven or eight men, armed with rifles, alertly entered the room. Harry recognized one of them, a stiff, bowlegged man, as Sheriff Stephens, portlier now than when he'd jailed Annie Mae, and utterly bald.

Silence spread, soft as a rain of cotton, over all the hot bodies. Warren Stargell sputtered, "What, what's the problem, Sheriff?"

"This meeting is over, Warren."

"We've got a permit, we've—"

"I'm declaring a nine o'clock curfew every night, as of tonight."

"Why?"

"These are extraordinary times. The nation's at war."

"What does that have to do with us?"

"I won't stand for agitation, Warren. You're adjourned."

"We've been gathering like this for years."

"You heard me. Y'all get on home."

The crowd grumbled but no one moved. The sheriff and his deputies cocked their rifles, a deafening *clack*. The men hushed.

"I'm not going to tell you again."

The barn emptied quietly then in less than a minute, the lawmen watching impassively as the young oil workers sprinted down the streets. Harry watched Warren Stargell, muttering angrily, slip out the back. He knew his affiliation with the league was in danger. Kate O'Hare was sitting in jail for *speaking*; if Warren convinced his buddies to take up arms, that was the end of their movement. For good.

Crickets were thick in the weedy fields around town. A slice of moon stuck to the dark above Scorpio's flickering red heart. Harry glanced at his father. "I'm confused," he said.

"How's that?"

He remembered how much he'd wanted to please Andrew, those afternoons, years ago, practicing speeches in the barn. He remembered the ache of pride in his chest whenever Andrew had praised him. "You told me to register. Obey the law. But in the barn back there, while Warren was talking, you had a mighty fire in your eyes."

Andrew rubbed his stiff leg. "The truth is, Harry, my heart and my head are telling me two different things," he said. "My head tells me to protect you, no matter what. To keep you out of trouble." He sighed and rubbed his eyes. "My heart wants to smash the bastards."

Harry nodded. They walked past Avram's store with its shiny new glass. Gunpowder soured the air, riding a southerly breeze from Fort

Sill. Harry heard someone singing in a parlor, children's laughter through wide open windows, the sound of a bath being poured.

Halley ran to greet them as they turned into the yard. Annie Mae was sitting in a rocker on the porch, cradling her belly as if it were a mystery package she'd found on a table in the house. She sniffed. "You reek of smoke, both of you," she said, smiling ruefully. "You've been naughty boys, haven't you?"

"Not naughty enough," Andrew said wearily, and sat at her feet. "I think we're done."

"What do you mean?"

Cannon fire from the fort. Harry blinked. His eyes were tired; the moon seemed to wobble.

"That's what I mean," Andrew said, gesturing into the night, at fading echoes of the blasts.

Halley howled at something rustling in the grass: a possum, perhaps, a cat or a rabbit flashing past. Harry imagined Randy Olin, shattered, clattery-boned, rising from the dirt. Halley ran in circles, sniffing, whimpering. Thunder shook the dark, long after midnight.

EACH DAY HARRY ANXIOUSLY checked the mailbox. Still no notice from the draft board.

He wandered idly down to the creek south of Walters, where Mollie's father reputedly ran a shooting range and a gambling house. He saw no one among the blackberry brambles and patches of poison ivy.

He remembered one evening, before the podium heist, walking with Mollie in the woods. They were shy with each other, avoiding glances. They didn't talk: a quiet filled with import, a stillness bursting with force. Finally she said his name. He reached for her hand. Amazing peace; his life felt tinny without it.

But Mollie was gone.

Harry knew certain women dawdled near the oil fields, hoping to hook up with fellows who'd struck it rich. Even without much money in his pockets, he might find company for an evening or two, but easing the pressure in his body, he knew, wouldn't cool the cored-out ache in his spirit.

One morning, Harry had just finished his oatmeal when Mahalie called, "Bring me a towel, son, quick!" He grabbed a dishtowel from the kitchen cupboard and ran to his parents' room. Through the doorway he caught a glimpse of his mother, pale, sprawled on the floor, gasping for breath, before Mahalie blocked his path. "That's not heavy enough," she said. "We need a bath towel. Hurry!"

His mother's legs had been rivered with blood.

All morning he sat on a tattered hallway rug beside the bedroom while Mahalie and, eventually, a doctor from town ministered to Annie Mae. He heard his mother's muffled moans through the door. He wished his father were home from the livery stable, but he didn't want to leave to go get him. Finally, by early afternoon, Annie Mae was calm. The doctor left. Mahalie said Harry could see her.

He grasped her trembling hand. "What's the matter, Mama?"

"There could be a problem with my pregnancy, Harry, but the doctor thinks maybe the danger's over."

"Are you hurting?"

"Not much now."

"Is the baby?"

"We don't know for sure. Pray for me, okay?"

As if these words had summoned him, Father McCartney appeared on the porch. Mahalie let him in. He was thinner than he used to be, balding. "I just ran into Doc Harned downtown," he said softly to Annie Mae. "He told me you were feeling a mite poorly."

Annie Mae tried to sit up. Harry adjusted her pillow. "It's thoughtful of you to drop by, Father. I'm better, thanks."

She spoke to the priest for over an hour while Harry helped Mahalie shuck peas. "Mahalie?" he asked.

"What is it?"

Talking settled him some. "Where are your husband and children while you're staying here with us?"

"Back home, of course."

"They miss you, I guess."

She laughed. "They miss my suppers. My sister is taking care of them, and she can't bake a bean to save her life."

"When you had your babies, did it hurt?"

"The first time. My second child was easier. Your mother's had bad luck. Her back, and all. Maybe she's not built for giving birth. Some women are like that."

"What is she built for?"

Mahalie paused with a pea-pod in her thick, dark hands. "For kindness," she said. "Your mother is the nicest woman I've ever known."

"Yes," Harry said.

Father McCartney came out of the house. He reached down and patted Harry's back. "See you in church Sunday?"

"Sure, Father."

He nodded curtly at Mahalie. He hadn't said a word to her.

"He thinks I'm a pagan," Mahalie explained once the priest had gone.

"If you could get his picture into the paper, somehow, he'd cozy right up to you," Harry said.

Andrew returned at midday and spent a couple of hours with Annie Mae. Harry tried to listen to their whispers. Mahalie pulled him away from the bedroom door and put him to work in the kitchen, but not before he'd heard the words "virus," "clotting," "placenta."

That night, Annie Mae rested peacefully. Mahalie dished up peas and potatoes and a tender flank steak for Harry and his father. She downplayed Annie Mae's problems. "Doctor thinks she'll be all right, and the baby too. Don't worry."

"I'll try not to," Harry said. "I wish I could do more."

"Your mother knows that."

"I feel in the way." He glanced at his father. "I don't know. Maybe I'll walk over to the oil fields this week, see if they're hiring."

Andrew sliced his meat slowly. "They're not. I heard it in town."

"You sure? Wouldn't hurt to check. Seems they've got a new gusher over there every day, and I'm doing no one any good sitting here."

"Son, stay away from those fields."

Harry looked up, startled by his father's harsh tone. "Why?"

"It's rough over there."

"What do you mean?"

"It's going to get . . . I mean, there are stirrings—"

"What?"

"Just don't go near them, all right?"

Andrew wouldn't say any more. He finished his supper quickly then went to check on Annie Mae. Harry helped Mahalie with the dishes. Afterwards he went out and rolled a cigarette on the porch.

"Can I have one of those?" Mahalie asked, bumping open the screen door. She untied the apron around her waist.

Harry smiled and reached into his pocket for his papers.

"Smell the wisteria." Mahalie sniffed. "I think the purple flowers are sweeter than the white ones."

"Here you go," Harry said. He struck a match for her. She inhaled slowly as though she'd never known such pleasure. She placed her hands on her hips and bowed backwards just a little, stretching, rolling her head. "Lordy, what a day," she said. Harry nodded, watching the sunlight fade, exposing the Milky Way low in the southern sky. "Hard times," he sighed.

"It was that damned shooting star, remember?" Mahalie said, pointing up.

"Halley's Comet?"

"That's the one. I knew when I saw it, I said to myself, 'We're in for a decade of trouble. *At least* ten years.' God always sends a sign."

"I don't think—" He stopped, flicked tobacco flakes onto the grass. "Well, maybe," he said. He didn't want to get her started.

"Listen." She cocked her head to the east.

"I know. It's the Fort Sill cannons. They practice every night."

"No." Mahalie blew a stream of smoke from her nose. "It's closer than that."

Harry walked into the yard. She was right. These booms were much nearer than the fort, and in the opposite direction. Smaller, more intense.

Andrew appeared in the doorway, scored by the mesh of the screen, framed by lantern light from deep inside the living room.

"Dad?" Harry said. "You hear that?"

"Yes."

"Sounds like—"

Andrew cleared his throat, turned again inside the house. Harry's skin tingled. He didn't move until the cigarette singed his fingers.

The following morning, the *Herald*'s inky headlines smeared his palms with the news that three paved roads east of town had been dynamited, and that a series of explosions had "rocked" several pipelines in the oil fields. An editorial blamed "anti-war subversives for this insidious act of cowardice. What will the Reds do next? Poison our water supply? Plant incendiary bombs in our homes? These malcontents have menaced the state of Oklahoma long enough. We call upon Sheriff Stephens and his office to do whatever he deems necessary to rid Cotton County of this scourge."

On the same page, the editor announced that the Oklahoma Press Association had informed the state's congressional delegation that all their reporters would firmly support the war effort.

Harry carried the paper into the kitchen where his father was stirring sugar into a cup of coffee. "You knew about this, didn't you? That's why you didn't want me over there."

Andrew went on with his breakfast.

"Why didn't you tell me what they were planning?"

"Because I knew you'd try to stop them," Andrew said. "I didn't want you getting hurt."

"This is the end of us. You know that. We'll all wind up in jail."

"These younger men in the league now, they want—"

"I know. Action. Revolution now." He slammed the paper on the table. "Oscar Ameringer'll be horrified when he hears about this." He turned and left the room.

That afternoon, Mahalie sent him downtown for groceries while she looked after Annie Mae. He was still seething at the league, confused about the bad turn his father's mind had made. Distracted, he spilled coins in the butcher shop, fumbled his sacks on the walk.

The army posters upset him. Along with the local news, the morning paper had described a battle near St. Etienne, France, in which a German division had slaughtered most of the old First Oklahoma—renamed, for its duties in Europe, the 142nd Infantry. The regiment had been misinformed about the enemy's location, somewhere between the Rheims and Aisne Rivers, the paper said, and had met unexpected artillery fire.

He thought of the young soldier who'd given him a ride into town, just a few weeks ago now, and closed his eyes to squeeze back tears.

Downtown seemed almost deserted today, the merchants low on goods. He noticed Avram with a bucket of brown suds wiping a muddy scrawl off his window. *Die*, Harry read. He started across the street when he spotted Warren Stargell leaving the livery stable, and ran to catch him. "What are you doing?" Harry hissed. "You're crazy!"

Warren pulled his hat low, cocky. "Class war, Harry."

"This isn't the way!"

"War is war, son. There's only one way to fight it."

"Yes. By refusing to participate."

"Uh-huh, speaking of which, your daddy just told me you tried to register for the draft, though you're not even old enough yet. Doesn't sound like refusal to me."

Harry blushed.

"*I'm* not inconsistent," Warren Stargell said. "I'm not the one who's turned his back on his principles."

"Warren, don't you understand, every lawman in the state'll be after our hides—"

"So what's new?"

"They'll be relentless."

"Harry, listen now, I've watched you mature in the last few years, but you're still just a kid. Wait a minute. Let me finish. You don't know what's happening. Last week in Muskogee, son, a German-owned building was blown to bits, courtesy of some fine American patriots. Real true-blooded night-riders. You didn't read that in the paper, did you? No. Of course you didn't. There wasn't room after all the space devoted to tongue-lashing us sorry Reds." He lowered his voice. "We're in a fight for our lives here, Harry. You think there aren't 'patriots' in Walters?"

Harry rubbed his eyes. "Call another meeting. Please. Let me speak, let me try to talk some sense into—"

"Words've failed us, Harry. Words didn't do us any goddam good."

"Move on!" someone hollered. Harry turned to see the sheriff. "It's against the law to loiter and congregate in the streets."

"Congregate?" Warren Stargell said. "There's only two of us here, Sheriff. Having a friendly conversation."

"I'll tell you one more time, Warren. I won't stand for agitation in my town. And if I learn you had anything to do with that business last night, you'll never see the goddam sun. Now move along!"

Warren Stargell shrugged. Harry turned away, just in time to see Avram, who apparently couldn't scrub all the hateful words off his window, close his door and pull his brand new shades.

* * *

THE NIGHTLY RUMBLES FROM the fort and the sighs from his mother's room kept him jittery in bed. There were times when he wished Mahalie, who spent hours whispering sweetly to Annie Mae, would tip-toe in, sit beside him, and hum a tune to put him to sleep. *You're still just a kid,* Warren Stargell had said. But he wasn't. The fears he felt now weren't irrational or silly—like the nights he used to scare himself watching tree shadows leap across the walls.

Illness and war, destruction and death.

His father seemed to sleep through them all, snoring loudly, then ignore them in the morning blaze. Mahalie blamed the comet; when he thought about it, Harry was inclined to trace the family's troubles to that day in Anadarko when Andrew was beaten. His father seemed to lose some vital part of himself after that, and nothing had ever been the same. Sometimes Harry *longed* to be a boy again, to crawl into his father's arms and be consoled, but Andrew was a figure of disturbance now. Harry had only himself.

Late one night he heard nothing beneath his mother's heavy breaths and knew Andrew was not in the house. He got out of bed, pulled on his clothes, and ran into the yard. Andrew was just closing the gate.

"Dad, where you going?"

His father jumped. "Harry. You scared me. I'm . . . just going to walk into town. I couldn't sleep. Go back to bed now."

"Is there a meeting?"

"No."

"I think I'll walk with you. I can't sleep either."

"Harry, go back inside." Stern now.

He knew not to argue. He went in, peeked through the living room curtains until Andrew was several yards down the street, then slipped back out and followed quietly at a distance. Andrew wasn't heading downtown. Immediately, Harry knew they'd wind up, this night, in the oil fields.

New moon. Seamless clouds. Candles out all over town, and in the houses on the outskirts. Cornstalks rustled, papery, dry, in the fields; mint freshened the breeze. Crickets grew wary, hushed among pebbles and dust, when Harry approached.

For a man with a limp, his father moved at a pretty fair clip. Harry wheezed, trying to keep up. Damn smokes.

Dog-bark. A distant motor, chuffing.

Lanterns hung from crossbars on the derricks. Harry crouched behind a wooden tool shed (he guessed) with a big fat lock on its door. The lanterns hissed like snakes, sent hot air roiling down the back of his neck. His hair prickled. From somewhere near, a metal clanging, as constant as a child banging a table for attention. The dumb persistence raised a lonely pang in his throat. The night was heavy, rancid, rotten with grease and a faint, languorous odor of natural gas.

His father stood alone for several minutes, fidgeting. Then someone whispered his name. Once, twice. Andrew turned. Warren Stargell, accompanied by four or five young men Harry recognized from the meeting, but didn't know. "Glad you could make it tonight, Andrew."

He nodded. "Where's the bridge?"

" 'Bout a quarter of a mile west of here. You'll go with Al. He's got everything you'll need. The rest of us'll take care of the pipelines."

The men didn't waste any time. They split up. Harry didn't know what to do. Shout? Scream for them to stop? But that might get them arrested; surely, after the earlier blasts, this area was heavily patrolled. His spine stiffened. Why hadn't he noticed any cops? How could these fellows reach the rigs without being seen?

The conviction grew in him, then, that they'd walked into a trap. Warren Stargell's zealousness had made him careless—had softened his brain. Sure enough, as Harry followed his father to the bridge, he saw a dark car on a clay road looped between derricks. Its headlights were off. A long steel rod poked from an open window in the back. The sheriff's men wouldn't shoot without a warning, would they?

Andrew and Al, seeing the car, pressed themselves to the ground. Harry knelt at the base of a rig, his feet sinking into black, chewy mud which popped beneath his weight, releasing wretched little stink bombs of gas.

The car took a curve by a steep, grassy culvert, and disappeared. "Come on," Al whispered to Andrew, but just as they stood, a blue and yellow flame shot from the earth several yards to their left. Apparently, Warren Stargell and his boys had blown a pipeline. A billowing stench, dense and hot as cowhide, enveloped Harry as he shivered and shielded his eyes. The fire broke, orange then gold, as it ate its way up the sky. Another burst, then another, a rhomboid of fire as big as a gas balloon, and the night was a tattered furnace. The oil derricks loomed like skinless ribs against the light. Harry heard screams—shrill and high, like his mother—and watched in terror the shapes of shadows on the leaky clay ground. Randy Olin rose from the dark, clutching his bloody head; the ghosts of the First Oklahoma, a dolorous mist, rushed from the flames, waving bayonets. The man from the veterans' home—Hole—stuck his tongue through the dirt, right where Harry was sitting.

A plume of fire shattered just below Lyra: a giant yellow bird ripped at the belly.

One of Warren Stargell's boys rolled in the mud, trying to douse the blaze on his arm. He screamed and screamed. Harry saw the car slide to a stop in murky ruts. His father and Al took off. He started to follow, tripped, then scurried behind the base of the nearest rig. He couldn't see Andrew anymore. Spirits had emerged from the car—tall and white and plentiful. Swiftly, they surrounded Warren Stargell and the others. The boy who'd been on fire lay with his charred and smoking arm in the muck of the grass. He swore beneath his breath.

The men from the car, in hoods, in long, loose sheets, all held dull black rifles; one had a spidery hemp rope. It was curled into a noose. "Well, lookee here," said Warren Stargell with a tremor in his voice. "It's the Chamber of Commerce, come to greet us."

"You're a dead man, Red."

"We're the Distinguished Knights of Liberty," said the tallest ghostly figure. His voice was vast, but muffled by the cloth on his face. "And you." He cocked his gun. "You're about to pay for your sins."

The burned boy whimpered. The man with the rope walked over to him and fitted it around his neck, pulling the knot tight. "How 'bout it?" he said. "On that rig over there."

"This is quicker." The tall man shoved the barrel of his rifle against the kid's temple.

"Please," said the boy. "Sweet Jesus, don't, please—"

"Fucking Bolshevik."

Harry looked away. He heard a blunt roar, and almost simultaneously, a softer sound, like a watermelon crushed beneath the gait of an angry horse.

"Goddam bloodthirsty capitalists!" Warren Stargell screamed.

When Harry raised his eyes he saw the boy's fingers twitching in the mud. The rope that had curled around his neck lay in a dark red lump collapsing into thick yellow clay. Harry's stomach clenched. He crawled on his hands and knees beneath the derrick, heaving into the grass.

Another rifle-cock, then: needles of flame in the distance—a delayed reaction, perhaps, from the first blasts, or a slow-burning fuse. A wall of fire as wide as a house rose and shimmied in the sky, painting orange all the bumpy bottoms of the clouds.

Warren Stargell broke for the woods, followed by his comrades.

The Knights of Liberty, momentarily dazed, were slow to raise their guns. They got off a couple of shots then piled into their car. Harry bolted, back the way he'd come. Bile rose in his throat. He didn't see Andrew—maybe he'd gotten away. He heard a car motor, ducked between brambles but never slowed down. He had no breath. By the time he reached town, his lungs were ponderous stones, pulling him down. He fell to his knees in a dusty lot behind the livery stable. The dead boy came swimming, spasming into his mind. With each try for breath his stomach made a fist. Someone shouted in the street. He inched, crouching, along a birch fence to get a better view. The Knights again—only these were different men. Most of them were shorter, dumpier than the figures he'd seen in the field. Their hoods were large and misshapen. They raised their arms; a second later Avram's window flew apart.

The men began to scatter but this time Avram was waiting for them. He scrambled out of the Emporium, firing a pistol.

Grabbing a birch slat, Harry raised himself. One of the Knights lumbered past the stable like a big frightened steer; Harry pulled himself over the fence and fell on his legs, ripping his sheet, wrestling him into the dirt. He pounded the man's wide head until his flapping hood tore away.

"Thtop it, thtop it, pleathe!"

Harry's fists faltered, high in the air. "Oh my god," he huffed.

"Thtop it, I thurrender!"

"Jimmie? Jimmie Blaine?"

"Yeth? Who—?"

"Damn it."

"Harry? Ith that you?" Blood swirled on Jimmie's lip where Harry had hit him.

"Jimmie, what the hell are you doing?"

His old pal grinned. "Thit, boy, it'th good to thee you."

Harry's head ached. "Why are you here? Answer me!"

238

"Thcaring the Jew, Harry. We're thcaring the Jew."

"Jimmie, Jimmie, oh Jimmie." He wheezed. "You can't possibly—" He sat back, limp, on the ground. "Who told you to do this, huh?"

"Rick and Eddie and Thteve—"

"Eddie? Eddie who? Eddie McGarrah?"

"Yeah. Remember him? It'th tho thad, Harry. Hith friend died, the one we uthed to pick cotton with—you remember him, don't you?"

"I know."

"Eddie'th been tho thad." Voices faded down the block. "He thayth the only thing that helpth ith to root out the evil—"

"Jesus, Jimmie. Do you even know what a Jew is?"

"Yeth, Harry. They're witches. They live in caveth with big fat thnaketh—"

"No. No. Eddie's a liar, just like Randy was."

"I know the *cave* part ithn't true—"

"Damn it, Jimmie, none of it's true."

Avram rounded the fence. When he saw Jimmie's sheet, he raised a hand and aimed the pistol at his large, benevolent face.

"No, Mr. Greenbaum. Please. This one . . . this one doesn't know what he's doing," Harry said. "He was tricked by the others."

Jimmie just smiled at this, as agreeable as ever.

Avram looked confused. His arm wavered. "Bastard," he croaked.

"Yes." Harry stood. "But this one can help us. He can identify the others. He didn't mean any harm, really. He's just misguided. Trust me, sir. Please, please put the pistol away."

"Harry?" Jimmie asked.

"What?" Harry snapped, still focused on Avram's hand, on the big ruby ring near the trigger.

"Tell him to keep hith big fat thnaketh away from me, all right?"

"There aren't any snakes, Jimmie," Harry said. Carefully, he patted Avram's arm. "Don't worry," he said. "I'll take care of everything. We'll put a stop to this, I promise."

* * *

HE FOUND HIS FATHER at home, on the porch, spattered with mud and clay, rubbing his hobbled leg. Andrew said nothing when he saw Harry, also filthy and worn, open the gate.

"There's a man dead out there," Harry said. "One of your buddies from the league."

Andrew stared at his shoes. Crickets whirred in the grass. The eastern horizon pulsed with strident flames.

"They shot him right in the head. The others . . . Warren . . . maybe they got away. I don't know."

Halley, long-nailed, came clicking down the dusty gravel path, nuzzled Harry's hand. His mother's roses and poppies, dry, curling, browned at the ends, sweetened the air.

"What were you doing?" Harry whispered harshly.

"Fighting for my country," Andrew answered, equally softly, and just as fierce. But his face had turned pale.

"You've thrown away everything you've ever believed in."

"No." Andrew stamped his right foot on the porch's bottom step. "Changing tactics is not a defeat."

"So *I* have to obey the law. *I* have to be careful. But you, you can do any damn-fool, reckless thing you please—"

"You're still just a boy—"

"I am *not* a boy! I watched a man die tonight for no good reason." He wiped his eyes. "I'm not a boy anymore. Not anymore. No, sir."

"We're in a struggle for the working class, Harry. People . . . well, people die in struggles. If you can't accept that, maybe you should run off, then, and join the Democrats. You can sit on your keester in the city, moan and do nothing, right along with them."

"You sound like Warren," Harry said. "He's lost his judgment. You're smart enough to know that."

A Model T came ratcheting up the street. Harry's shoulders tensed, Andrew paled even further, but the car just shuttled past.

"You're smarter than this, Dad," Harry said again, glancing once more in the direction of the oil field fires.

Mahalie filled the doorway and shushed them with a finger to her lips. "Your wife's trying to sleep," she said. "It's been a hard night for her."

For all of us, Harry thought. And then he thought, It's over.

MAHALIE RAN THROUGH THE house unlatching the doors, prying open all the windows. "Got to unbind this place," she said.

Harry followed her. "Why? What do you mean?"

"If we loosen up all the locks, the spirit of release will blow through these rooms and relax your mama's body. It's time for her to drop that baby she's carrying. If she don't, I fear it's bad trouble."

"Can I see her?" He'd been kept from her bed all morning.

"She's in pain, child. You can see her after a while."

Flies and bees flew through the open windows. They lighted on the sugar tin in the kitchen; Harry smashed them with yesterday's paper. The survivors of the old First Oklahoma had been shipped home from Europe, he read, and were recovering in a military infirmary in Oklahoma City.

At midmorning, just as the shadows of the house's front eaves were starting to swallow Annie Mae's withered white roses, Father McCartney walked through the open gate, up the gravel path and onto the porch. Halley stirred and growled but didn't bother to bark. Tiny sparks of sweat wobbled on the priest's pale neck—the day was broiling already—and slid beneath his collar. "Howdy, Harry. Is your daddy inside with your ma?"

"Yes."

"Do you think I could see them?"

Harry shrugged. Father McCartney slipped past him, into the house. Harry sat on the porch scratching Halley's ears. A strong smoke-smell drifted through town, more powerful, even, than the dog's impressive odor.

At noon came the visit from the sheriff. Harry had been expecting it; he determined to keep his mouth shut as much as possible.

The sheriff got right down to business. "I want Andrew."

"My ma's real sick," Harry said. "He's inside with her. I'm sorry, but they can't be disturbed now."

This news unsettled Stephens. He twisted his hat in his hands. He sniffed the dusky air. "Trouble last night in the oil fields. Don't suppose you know anything about that?"

"No, sir."

"No, of course not. Seen Warren Stargell today?"

"I presume he's at home." He kept his hand on Halley's head.

The sheriff nodded grimly. "You tell Andrew I'm going to want to talk to him."

"I think you should speak to Jimmie Blaine," Harry said. "He might help you put a stop to all this violence in town. I know for a fact he can identify—"

Sheriff Stephens leaned forward on the first porch step and shoved his hat in Harry's face. "Jimmie Blaine is a simple-minded son of a bitch," he said. "That boy's got *nothing* to tell me." He turned to leave. "Besides, what violence are you referring to? There's no violence in town. The only problem here is Red agitators." He punched at the tincture of smoke. "But we're going to put a stop to that mighty quick, I guarantee it. I'll be back real soon to see your daddy, hear?"

Shortly after he left, Andrew emerged from the bedroom and went to the kitchen to spoon himself some onion soup. Mahalie had made it the day before. Harry told him about the sheriff.

"Yeah, I heard him through the window."

"What are you going to do?"

He didn't answer. He was haggard and his face was tight, like a man who'd slept in a blizzard.

"How's Ma?" Harry said.

Andrew shook his head and carried his bowl into the bedroom. Mahalie barred Harry's way. "She's resting now," she said.

"How come everybody else can see her but I can't?"

"You will, you will. Later. I promise."

The tone of her voice, his father's wasted look, the sheriff's angry warning . . . his shoulders and hands began to shake. He felt both chilled and slightly scorched. He paced the front porch. Halley watched him, half-heartedly thumping his tail. In the past several years, Harry had talked farmers into resisting their landlords. He'd talked miners into a joyful state of hope. He'd talked working men and women into believing they could better the nation. Now, with his mama gravely ill, with the memory of death in the field, he needed to talk himself into calming down. It would have to be the greatest speech of his life.

He cleared his throat, pointed at the flowers in the yard. "Listen to me," he muttered under his breath. "You roses, you poppies! Perk up! The rain is coming soon to ease your thirst. A cloudburst of recovery and redemption. I feel it! Raise your heads! Sniff the breeze! That freshness you smell," though in fact the air was even more full of smoke than before, wrapping the trees like brood mare's tails, "it'll wash the sorrow from this parched and bitter land!"

Halley got lazily to his feet, roused by Harry's rhythmic pacing. He seemed to feel the promise. The speech was working.

"Son? Harry, excuse me?" Father McCartney.

Startled, Harry nearly slipped off the edge of the porch. Halley rushed over and licked his hand. "Yes?" he said, embarrassed.

"Your mother would like to see you now."

Harry brushed his hair.

"You know, it's a great comfort at times like this to realize a greater world lies beyond this one," said the priest.

Harry felt annoyed. What was he talking about?

"We're all here for a short time, under God's watchful care—"

"Last night? Last night I saw something I don't think God noticed," Harry told him. "If He was watching, I'm pretty sure He wouldn't have let it happen. I'm pretty sure He'd stop the war. He wouldn't let my mother be sick." He scuffed at a splinter sticking out of the porch. "In fact, Father, I'm beginning to believe He isn't there at all."

"You mustn't talk that way, Harry."

"If God's watching, then why doesn't He—what's it called?— *smite* the capitalists who're sending boys to Europe? He does a lot of smiting in the Bible, doesn't He? Where is He now, when we *really* need a good smite? Huh?"

"Harry. Please. Your mother." Father McCartney held out his hand but Harry wouldn't take it. He pushed by him into the house.

In the bedroom, the creamy lace curtains were drawn. Annie Mae lay still in quivering shadows, under a thick pile of covers. Andrew sat on the bed, holding her hand. Mahalie stood in a corner over a basket of bloody sheets. Tears brightened her eyes.

Harry had always thought of his parents' room as his mother's place, mainly; a part of the world of women. Today it was no one's room. A presence he could feel but not see crouched here in the dark, a presence neither female nor male, exhaling a foul, earthen smell. It filled each corner. Harry shivered.

Annie Mae's arm rose, brittle. Her lips were dry; they crackled like blistered paint when she smiled. Andrew filled a glass from a pitcher on the night table, but she waved him away.

"Hi, Ma," Harry whispered.

"Son." She closed her eyes. "I want you to know . . ." Each word was like a stone, it seemed, passing brutally through her skin. "I'm proud of your speeches."

"Thank you."

"You're going to be . . . a fine leader someday. I know it."

Harry could hardly talk. She was too pale. "Is the baby coming soon?"

She shook her head briefly; her matted hair scratched the moist folds in her pillow. "Give me a kiss," she sighed.

Harry leaned over and pressed his lips to her forehead. The salt of her sweat . . . ever afterwards, it was the taste, to him, of pain.

Mahalie walked up behind him and pulled him from the bed. He squatted by the door, on a red throw rug, stroking Halley's ears.

The priest dabbed holy oil on Annie Mae's skin, blessing, with signs of the cross, her hands and feet, her eyes and ears, finally her lips—all the sinful senses. "Through this holy anointing and His most loving mercy, may the Lord assist you by the grace of the Holy Spirit," he said, "so that, when you have been freed from your sins, He may save you and in His goodness raise you up."

Andrew crumpled forward, sobbing, onto Annie Mae's chest. Her final gesture was to wrap her arms around him. "Shhh, shhh," Harry heard her whisper—her final breaths—as though her husband was the one who was dying.

Harry turned from the bed, patted Halley once on the head, and walked from the house, down the porch and through the little gate, out into the fields east of his street. He heard the grinding of car motors, the wheezing of trucks, from the center of town. Smoke sailed through the tops of maples and elms at the edges of the fields. He recalled the days, in years past, when his face had appeared on posters nailed to trees like these: "Come Hear the Boy Orator! Come Find Your Hope for the Future!" Bitterness rose in his throat.

For almost an hour Harry walked, thinking of his mother, with nothing to say to himself. Finally, when he'd cried himself to exhaustion, and he noticed that the sun had burnt off all the smoke, he paused, wiped his eyes, caught his breath, then headed back home.

Cotton County, Oklahoma, November 1918

Soon after the oil field uprisings, and all the shattered glass, Avram decided he'd had enough. He sold his store to Andrew, who'd done well with the livery stable and hankered to give retail a try ("Man wants to feed his family, he's got no *choice* but to throw his lot in with the capitalists, though he don't have to like it. I'm still a Socialist at heart, by God").

"They've won?" Harry asked Avram the day he placed his bags in the back of his dusty pine wagon.

"I'm too old to be a fighter. It's up to you young fellows now."

"Most of the other young fellows here . . . well, they're wearing white sheets," Harry said.

Avram shook his head. "All I wanted was to settle. A simple thing."

"Do you have family close by?"

"No."

"There are a lot of opportunities in the city, I think."

Avram looked at him. "Oklahoma," he said, "is not the Promised Land. For anyone." He snapped the reins; his mule took off.

Sheriff Stephens questioned Andrew, as he'd threatened (the very morning of Annie Mae's funeral), but got no satisfaction. He couldn't produce witnesses who'd place Andrew, or Harry, in the oil fields the night of the blasts. "You're lucky, the both of you," he told them. They stood in the hot sun in their suits and ties, ready to ride with Father McCartney and Mahalie to the gravesite. " 'Cause I know damn well you're mixed up in this. I swear to you, if I ever hear of you attending meetings—any meetings whatsoever, outside of church—I'll haul you in for sedition. It's finished, you hear me?"

And it *was*—throughout the state, across the nation. Warren Stargell was eventually traced to Anadarko, and sentenced to ten years in the pen. Stanley Clark was indicted in Chicago. J. T. Cumbie was handed a stiff sentence at Leavenworth for—as "Alfalfa Bill" Murray said in the papers—"misleading ignorant farmers" into rejecting the "loving bosom of their country."

On August 3, 1917, a band of sharecroppers and Indians, led by a relative of the Creek renegade Crazy Snake, gathered on the banks of the Canadian River, near the Chisholm Trail in central-western Oklahoma, to begin a march on Washington in defiance of the draft. They planned to survive on beef and ripe corn (hence their name in the press, the "Green Corn Rebels"), linking up along the way with others who hated federal "revernooers."

Before they could even cross the river, they were routed by a posse of seventy men. The newspapers branded the rebels "cowards," but one of them said, "It was our neighbors in that posse. We didn't want to shoot them in cold blood, any more than we wanted to go to Europe and shoot at Germans."

In the next week, 450 men were arrested for participating in the rebellion (far more than were actually involved); about half of them wound up serving time in the state pen at McAlester. The "Reds" had been crushed in Oklahoma.

Meanwhile, the Knights of Liberty prospered. No one was ever convicted of killing the young Socialist in the oil field. Jimmie Blaine told Harry the names of all his comrades—most of them came from prominent families in the county (though there were a few working class miscreants like Eddie McGarrah). Harry made a list and sent it anonymously to the sheriff's office, but Stephens never touched the county's leaders. Four months later, in Tulsa, a Knights of Liberty chapter lashed seventeen Wobblies to elm trees, stripped them all to the waist, and beat them nearly to death with wet hemp ropes. A carload of cops watched without interfering. The following morning, an editorial in the *Tulsa World* said the Knights were made of that "sterling element of citizenship, that class of taxpaying and orderly people who are most of all committed to the observance of the law."

JIMMIE BLAINE WENT TO work for Andrew in the Emporium. In his off hours, he sold rabbits in a lot behind the store.

Eddie McGarrah wasn't seen again in town.

Harry waited out the war with the MK & T as a station clerk. In November, 1918, he read that Eugene Debs had been arrested for violating the Espionage Act. "They tell us that we live in a great free republic," Debs had said, in the speech that finally hurled him into trouble he couldn't escape, "that our institutions are democratic; that we are a free and self-governing people. That is too much, even for a joke."

At his trial, he refused to take the stand or to call any witnesses on his behalf. In his own closing argument he told the jury, "I have been accused of obstructing the war. I admit it. Gentlemen, I abhor war. I would oppose war if I stood alone . . . I have sympathy with the suffering, struggling people everywhere. It does not make any difference under what flag they were born, or where they live." He castigated the national press for flooding the public with patriotic slogans, images of the flag; harassing citizens with constant, stupefying ads into spending their hard-earned money on war bonds.

He was locked away in the West Virginia state pen, and later in a federal penitentiary in Atlanta.

Kate O'Hare was incarcerated at the Missouri State Penitentiary in Jefferson City, where she befriended the anarchist Emma Goldman. Goldman said O'Hare had been imprisoned for trying to feed her fellow citizens, the way a child throws bread to needy birds.

One day, O'Hare refused her weekly bath; the woman who'd preceded her into the communal tub suffered open syphilitic sores. O'Hare demanded a sanitary cell block, better care. Her fellow prisoners began to rely on her for reforms; soon, she was beloved even by the prison guards.

Harry kept a newspaper picture of her and Oscar Ameringer tacked to an oak pole near a woodstove in the back of his father's store, when he came to work at the Emporium after the war. Andrew put him in charge of the outdoor equipment: fishing poles, catfish bait, waders, and lanterns. He watched over each of these items as though it were a bar of gold. Occasionally, he gave a kid lemonade from Avram's old cooler.

Sometimes an Indian couple would pass on the street in front of the clear, sturdy windows; copper-colored kids would scurry up the walk, laughing and chasing each other, and Harry thought of Mollie. Once or twice, he considered strolling over toward the river, trying to find her just to say hello, but he never did. Like his mother, like the movement, his first love was gone. He concentrated on the tasks at hand.

According to the papers, Bob Cochran turned out to be a pretty fair representative of his county, paving several roads and lowering taxes for the elderly: his record was the only political news Harry bothered to note.

Now and then, though, a customer would follow him to the back of the store while he searched for a particular fishing lure, or a new cork handle for a pole, and ask him who were the people in the pictures. In those moments, Harry felt his face flush with pride. "Oscar Ameringer," he'd say. "A saint." And the woman? "The woman." He'd reach up to straighten the curled edges of the slowly yellowing photo, crusty, rough: a farmer's calloused hand, stretching high above a crowd, yearning for salvation; a ragged meeting hall table, poorly hewn at the corners; a splintery patch on a makeshift stage; a papery cornstalk sheath, peeling back like the pages of the *Southern Mercury*, or a call for justice in an old *Appeal to Reason*, or a story by Upton Sinclair, or the edge of a tattered fan waved, with lagging energy, by a malnourished woman or man straining to hear. "A good, loud speaker," he'd say.

Emily Sandor

TRACY DAUGHERTY, a native Texan, was shaping stories even as a boy, creating fanciful scenarios featuring world leaders as Little League baseball coaches in his own illustrated comic books and distributing them to his Midland neighborhood. When Daugherty was ten, his allergy specialist submitted his poem about a child's fears of asthma to a national medical journal. His illustrated report on a meteor shower—stemming from his love of the big West Texas sky—was published when he was fourteen in *Sky and Telescope* magazine. By the time he'd reached junior high school, he knew he wanted to be a writer (or a drummer), and he has continued making sketches and reports wherever he has traveled, in Europe, the Middle East, and Latin America. To date, he has published three novels, *Desire Provoked, What Falls Away,* and *The Boy Orator,* and a short story collection, *The Woman in the Oil Field* (SMU 1996). His work has been honored with a Fellowship from the National Endowment for the Arts, an Associated Writing Programs Award in the Novel, an A. B. Guthrie Jr. Short Fiction Award, an Oregon Book Award, and a Southwestern Booksellers' Award. An associate professor of English at Oregon State University, he still plays drums in a band with a singing doctor and a bass-playing art teacher, doing gigs for friends and for late-night parties and dances in old, barnlike gymnasiums.